D1682099

Cloud Diary

A NOVEL

Steve Mitchell

C&R Press
Conscious & Responsible

All Rights Reserved

Printed in the United States of America

First Edition
1 2 3 4 5 6 7 8 9

This book is a work of fiction. Any references to historical events, real people, or real places are used fictitiously. Other names, characters, places, and events are products of the author's imagination, and any resemblance to actual events or places or persons, living or dead, is entirely coincidental.

Selections of up to one page may be reproduced without permission. To reproduce more than one page of any one portion of this book, write to C&R Press publishers John Gosslee and Andrew Sullivan.

Cover art: by Eugenia Loli
Cover design by Larua Brown
Interior design by Ali Chica

Copyright ©2018 Steve Mitchell

Library of Congress Cataloging-in-Publication Data

ISBN: 978-1-936196-85-2
Library of Congress Control Number: 2018932468

C&R Press
Conscious & Responsible
crpress.org
Winston-Salem, North Carolina

For special discounted bulk purchases, please contact:
C&R Press sales@crpress.org
Contact editors@cpress.org to book events, readings and author signings.

Table of Contents

ONE

Chapter 1	4
Chapter 2	17
Chapter 3	29
Chapter 4	45
Chapter 5	56

TWO

Chapter 6	69
Chapter 7	90
Chapter 8	99
Chapter 9	106
Chapter 10	112

THREE

Chapter 11	127
Chapter 12	142
Chapter 13	156
Chapter 14	175
Chapter 15	197

ONE

1

In Sophie's version, I was muttering to myself (which I was) when we met, muttering like some sort of professorial street-corner vagrant declaiming Milton between gulps of Mad Dog. We were standing in the produce section of a Harris Teeter and she was trying to get to the spaghetti squash while I muttered, gaze trailing to my feet, finger at my chin, until I finally looked up to her with a thin tremor of shock. She'd tell friends I appeared displaced, an alien struggling for his bearings in a strange, new world.

She liked to talk about it. She enjoyed telling the story, her body taking a new posture, a bit more erect, as she haltingly extended a hand toward the now-invisible squash and withdrew it, extended and withdrew, around my described movements. She might have worked that gesture into a hundred paintings, but in those moments, she simply enjoyed enacting it.

Our friends would laugh, every time; more at her joy in performance than the mysteries of the story itself, and I would half-heartedly attempt to explain myself, falling back finally on the easy but true excuse that, well, I was already in love. Josh would stump into the kitchen for another round and Sasha would nestle herself even deeper into the lumpy frame of the couch. Others would jostle their chips, or tidy the abandoned playing cards and Sophie would position herself before me, whether I was perched on a chair or deep in a couch. She would turn, throw out her arms, and fall backward into me as if into a pool.

Our friends knew the particulars, having heard multiple versions over the years. At times their responses resembled the audience-participation elements of a cult movie. Ellen or John might shout or mutter, for dramatic effect, "and then he turned toward me and..." or announce loudly and definitively, "I like Spaghetti Squash!" They knew the particulars, at least of her version:

The first words spoken, me to her, the following interjected questions usually stepping on the toes of her answers: "Uh, what do you do?"

"I'm a painter, what about you?"

"I'm a security guard, what do you paint?"

"Oils, acrylic, mixed media."

"Mixed media, what's that?"

"It means I can glue a bug to the canvas if I want. I painted a tree once. I mean I put paint on the tree and painted it. Once. What do you guard?"

"Space. I guard space." In response to her blank look, I elaborate: "Right now I'm guarding an empty building."

"Well...it's quiet, I imagine."

"Yeah, quiet. It's alright, I guess. It's just, you know...space."

In her telling of the story, the conversation might shift or stall, but some things remained constant. I continued to stand directly in front of the spaghetti squash and she, having already set her mind to the delicate threads of the fore-mentioned vegetable, determined to wait me out or shift me in my orbit. So, she continued to talk to me, despite my unredeemed social awkwardness, my late-onset Asperger's, hoping to negotiate a position from which to snatch her prize until, as she would tell it, something relaxed in her, the squash loosened its hold in her awareness, and she began to listen to me... she actually looked at me...and she began to enjoy our conversation.

So there we were, she liked to say: I look like I don't know what, coming from the studio covered in paint and glue and he's wearing a shirt with a frayed collar and some jacket his mother probably bought him ten years before (here, I would nod) and he would pivot to face me every time I moved, like a goalie protecting an invisible net. Oblivious, completely oblivious.

"Do you like it?" she asks, with an air of impatience I wouldn't have noticed.

"What?"

"Guarding space."

"I like the space. Not so much the guarding." She wrestles with this answer while I prod the conversation forward, "Painting. I guess you like that," grinning at my own awkwardness. "I mean, you wouldn't do it if you didn't like it."

"Yeah." She smiles. "I like colors." She fondles a stain on her grimy sweatshirt. "Red. Today was a red day."

"How do you do it?"

"What? Paint?"

"Just like that, he asked me how I did it. And there was something about the innocence of the question that compelled me to answer. I mean," and here her hands would rise before her in a semblance of mock abandon, "if a five-year-old asks what happened to Fluffy after she died, you can't just say, 'Well, she's rotting in the ground.' You have to make up some kind of answer.

"'Sometimes,' I told him, '…sometimes I put the brush on the canvas and wait for the first stroke…'"

He nodded, she would say, nodding blankly herself, he nodded as if he knew exactly what I meant but I knew, she would say, that he had no clue. It was only later I'd discover he understood completely.

She becomes exasperated somehow, impatient somehow, shifting one foot to the other in the produce aisle of the Harris Teeter. She rushes the next words in order to have the question and the exchange over for good: "…and sometimes I paint and paint and wait for the image to appear."

And I stand there, staring at her as if it takes a very long time for her words to fall within earshot. As if they are traveling over a vast abyss and I have to parse their meaning from fragments of echo.

Here, Sophie would pause quite a long time for dramatic effect, a gaping, puzzled, innocent look on her face, turning within the room to each member of the audience, attempting to impart a small measure of her confusion at my open expression and the stuttering pause in our conversation.

And finally, she would shrug, returning to the role of herself, but not before the gift of a glance to me, wherever I was in the room, a glance which held the tiniest nested caress.

She shrugs, shaking off the whole idea of a conversation, "But right now I'm thinking about dinner. Some sort of dinner."

She edges toward the obstacle that is me, a pantomime of shouldering to a crowded bar, muttering now to herself, "Squash maybe, but what kind?"

At which point the gathered crowd, taking my role, would intone in unison, "I like Spaghetti Squash!"

She laughs. And I laugh. She extends her hand to me, wherever I am, swallowed by the sofa or gangly on a ladder-back chair: "My name's Sophie."

Taking her hand, "Hi, I'm Doug."

She accomplishes a graceful half-turn and falls back into me.

We told the beautiful and variegated versions of that story, branching and returning as water strained through smaller tributaries and finally meeting again at a cardinal point, told and re-told it until we didn't any longer, until we were no longer together, until the once we were had faded, and each version of the story quietly folded itself into memory.

On our first date, I follow her up and down the streams of the street on one of those Friday night crawls in the bohemian arts district, two square blocks slightly off center from downtown proper, two blocks that, in the '50's, comprised a maze of thrift stores and barber shops and locksmiths that couldn't afford to be exactly downtown.

The streets are blocked off. It's a warm, humid June evening. When I'd asked her three days prior what she wanted to do, she'd replied:

"Take you to the neighborhood. Introduce you to the family."

She paused then, on the other end of the phone, and I had the impression she was looking me up and down the way a mother inspects her child before sending him off on the first day of school.

"Don't worry," she assured me after a moment, "you'll be fine."

So, I follow along behind her, something like a reluctant terrier on a leash, my legs whirring to keep up as she negotiates the unseen currents of the street.

She knows everyone. Everyone. I bounce in the wake of her constant hellos, how are yous, what's going on, the people she acknowledges breaking past me in a divergent wake. We make our way from a parking lot three blocks away to enter the main drag. We pass a tall, reedy woman in flowing earth tones who Sophie addresses as Marsha, hovering over a gaggle of children kneeling or sprawled in the center of the street around cairns of chalk and a swirling mandala scraped onto the asphalt.

We pass a guy on the sidewalk picking out tunes; he has a banjo, a beard, and what is either a dog or a small pig at his feet. A collective shout erupts further down the block, near the intersection of the main streets and the chunky rhythm of African drums churn the summer air, resembling the slap of large wooden machines stirring to life. Sophie stops before me and I nearly bump into her, then right myself, bobbing at her side.

The sky above is bluish, shifting to pink. The light in the windows and on the brick storefronts a dim golden wash, a kind of gilded smear. The street before us is littered with small galleries and shops, people spilling in and out in all directions. Some of the galleries double as studio space while others appear very upscale, staffed by dry women with pinched smiles. The real crowds, Sophie tells me, won't arrive until near dark.

"Let's start here," Sophie declares decisively, as if announcing the first step of a grand campaign, sidling gently to the right. She provides commentary, with a general wave of the hand, on the shops we pass:

"That's Mary's place. She paints irises. That's the Sacred Stone store. That gallery's all doctors' and accountants' wives. That's Megan's place. She sculpts placentas."

There are some things I have no real desire to investigate further.

We enter a stuffy, glass-fronted box of a room. The walls are ringed with twenty or so frames clutching at their centers, like insects under glass, tiny architectural lithographs in bright colors. A couple of folks drift along one wall while three or four are clustered in the center of the room. We make our way to them.

"Maggie," Sophie slides her palm along the woman's forearm as she comes to rest beside her, "how's the crowd this evening?"

Maggie is about forty-five, a little heavyset, wearing black tights with sparkly red sandals and an orange dress that comes to her knees. Her hair is approximately the same shade as her dress, her eyes an amazing deep-set and clear blue. She angles her shoulder into Sophie's.

"Still pretty light. Probly the heat. College kids came early, drank two half-gallons of my wine before I knew it. Had to hide the rest in the back until the real people show up."

Sophie turns Maggie on her heel toward me. "Maggie, this is Doug. We met in the squash aisle."

We shake hands. "Good to see you, Doug. Sophie givin' you the tour?"

"Yeah, we've just started, though. Best thing I've seen so far is the pig-dog."

"It's a dog," Maggie chuckles. "At least, I think it's a dog."

"Are these yours?" I ask, motioning toward the walls.

"Yep." She holds up a hand to forestall comment. "Don't worry. You don't have to like them. I don't even like them that much. But they sell." Maggie chuckles again, squeezing my arm.

"You gonna open tonight?" she asks Sophie.

"I don't think so," her eyes cant toward me. "I think we're going to paddle and drift."

Maggie nods, her smile resting somewhere between Sophie and me. "Well, come back by later in the evening, if you have a mind to. I may have some Gallo Apple Merlot and Animal Crackers left. We can debauch ourselves."

"You have your own gallery?" I ask Sophie as we make for the door.

"Not a gallery, a studio."

"Are you going to show me?"

"Thinking about it."

Three doors down I meet Bill, who crafts stunning furniture from single slabs of knotted wood. His shop is clean, well-lit and freshly painted. Each table or chair rests singly atop its own platform. There is no more than a dozen. A framed price list hangs discretely near the door, tens of thousands of dollars. Bill has large and strong hands; one of them reaches out from another time to close around mine. I imagine he'd arrived at the gallery on horseback, defying phantom highwaymen.

Across the street, near the drummers, we find Ellen, rail-thin with mousy hair and a red, chapped nose. Her pastels of oceans and sunsets seem nice enough. They are pretty and calming and bland. Her husband Nigel is some kind of actor or semi-actor or might be writing a screenplay or trying to get a film together. He talks nonstop, pumping my hand while patting my shoulder at the same time as if it's a secret initiatory rite.

I'm introduced to photographers and dancers, musicians and sculptors. We run across others, whose names I instantly forget. I meet more people in one night with Sophie than I have in the three years previous.

We wander into the street from a coffee shop, she with a raspberry gelato, me with coffee, and hover there for a moment like mayflies.

"What do you write?" Sophie asks obliquely, spooning gelato.

"What?" I delay, already embarrassed.

"You told Bill you were a writer back there, when you guys drifted off toward the end table,"---and I had, God knows why---"so, what do you write?"

"Unfinished stories."

She turns to me, studying my awkward expression. I shrug and a smile curls to one side of her mouth, lingering there. Then, she releases me, her eyes sliding to the street.

"One day, maybe you'll show me."

In the street, a man and a woman are stacking dark wooden boxes, each about six feet long and two feet wide. They interlock one box with another until they've assembled a graduated platform about eight feet high.

The man, dressed in a black leotard-ish thing, mounts the structure and immediately balances into a handstand, then lifts one hand from the platform. He returns his hand to the platform, settling into a crouch, his hands wide. He raises his body perpendicular to the ground, holding it there for a minute or two. The crowd applauds. He lowers himself and stands slowly, offering his hand down to the woman, waiting at the base. She takes it and climbs up.

She wears white to his black, blonde hair pulled away from her face with a black bow. She climbs along his body and onto his shoulders, his strong hands lacing around her ankles. Her knees at his shoulders, she lowers herself along his front as he grips her tightly.

We watch them silently, their bodies sliding one along the other. He is supporting her as she extends upward or outward, and she supports him with his feet in her knees as he arches backward. The crowd applauds with each new position. The couple continue to entwine for our pleasure, changing shape, black to white like a playful yin and yang. I'm exhausted just watching them.

"Okay," Sophie confides, motioning me toward the edge of the crowd, "time to throw you into the deep end."

We make our way to a short alley close by. She unlocks a wrought iron gate and we pass into a small courtyard with what might once have been a fountain; a wall about two feet high, six feet square, inlaid with alternating white and indigo tiles. It's filled with dirt, flowers interspersed with herbs in raised beds. A single door is lodged into each of the three walls of the courtyard, the scene resembling a test of fate from an ancient Arabic tale.

She unlocks the door on the left and disappears, leaving me at the threshold to peer in like a street urchin studying expensive toys. Lights click on in the back, making their way toward me. There are whirring sounds, as if tiny helicopters are leaving the ground, and a slight breeze rustles the loose sheets scattered over a trestle table against the wall. The fans make everything tremble just a bit. I hear a trill, this strange exclamation of hers soon to become familiar, a vocal thrill of anticipation.

"Don't just stand there like a Mormon missionary," I hear her before I see her, "come on in."

I have the impression of entering a coral reef, like the ones I've seen on TV: tall forests of color shimmering with the sway of tides, gradations of light and dark thriving as living things.

Easels stand in irregular lines, some holding two or three paintings, other work on paper hangs on clothespins from heavy wire crisscrossing the room. The walls are covered with sketches, paintings or photographs. A high bank of windows opposite the door run the length of the room, revealing the deep blue sky.

She sweeps me into her current. First to the shelf by the window, littered with odd figurines and small rocks, a bit of bark here, something hard and electrical, disgorging wires.

"I don't know what this is. I found it near the bus station," her hand tousles the wires gently, "but it looks so much like a bug from another world, I had to rescue it. And I love the pink and green wires. And the burn mark here. You see?"

She holds it before me like an upturned turtle, legs falling back over her hand, so I can study the scorched underside and the broken tab where it once connected to a larger mechanism.

"Maybe it's a turtle," I offer.

"Could be," she replies, but she's already moved on. On, to an ancient roll-top desk, open to a surface stacked with envelopes, pictures and papers, and cubbyholes housing an assortment of small ceramic cats, some that appear Russian, Indian, Chinese, some she might have made, each with a different inscrutable expression.

"My grandfather's desk. I refinished it myself. It's cherry."

"How old is it?" I ask.

"Old!"

A small framed picture of a young girl clutching a baby goat. She points, "That's Christina. She's my..." pausing for a second to puzzle it out, "...my niece, my cousin's daughter."

"And the goat?" Another awkward question from my limitless supply.

"It's a goat," she smiles, "not one of the family."

She takes me to the trestle table where the riot of color resembles seedlings of transparent aquatic plants sprouting in wisps and lines from rippling paper. She maneuvers me around the spiky promontories to the more beautiful shades. Huge swathes of pink and magenta and deep blue, all wafting around us, all alive. We enter pockets of cool air and linger there, then ease away, finding a warm pool near a corner, coming up to surface, penetrating the skin of the water and discovering a wall pitched in horizons, the meeting of earth and sky, or sea and sky, the colors of the reef draining upward into the air.

"Eight months I painted only horizons," she tells me, "don't know what it was about them." She shrugs, "And then I was done with it, or it was done with me."

She never asks me what I think of her work. For her, the important transaction is this promenade together through color and motion. I'm clueless anyway, hardly knowing what I think or feel, more overwhelmed by the sheer energy and volume and the vibrant pulse of the room.

She brings us to a stop before a large canvas resting on a metal easel held together with fraying duct tape. The blue background nearly matches the visible sky overhead. Bands of red embrace the blue from all sides, as jagged as torn ribbons billowing the breeze. Her hand glances the side of my leg as we stand before the painting and she hums, first one note then another, then the first again. It isn't a song she's singing; it's more that she's articulating in sound the two colors on the canvas.

For years I'd call her studio to mind with a kind of idiot reverence, relishing its distinct atmosphere. The room had its own weather, a climate that settled around me once inside the door. It was composed of color; the sound one color makes sliding along another or flowing over it; the lilt of reds along blues, the deep angle of an earth tone into green, the rumble of blacks and greys, sometimes nearly hidden beneath the rustle of the helicopter breeze.

Later, I'd watch her as she worked. The fluid way she moved between the tables, gathering brushes and paints and foul-smelling chemicals. The way she brushed her hands on her thighs leaving behind layers of accreted paint and glaucous substances just below the pockets. The way the room fell away from her once she began.

I sit in the kitchenette, on a stool by the sink and the ancient gurgling coffee pot, and glimpse her through the shutters of the easels, standing before the blank white, turning this way and that, brush first at shoulder height then gradually falling to her waist, rising slightly then sinking away again while she sways before the canvas as if finding a breeze.

Then, with a single stroke, something lightens in her body, one foot lifts from the floor for an instant, the fingers of her left hand curl, and she stands absolutely still in the posture of an exotic bird.

I glance up from my work to find her poised there, brush arrested an inch from the canvas, and I watch until she finds the next stroke, settling gently back to earth, one foot touching down then the other, and I stare at the open page before me and pray for a grace that seems impossible.

The ringing phone wakes me from a nap or a daze. It's Sunday afternoon. Later, I want to believe I'd been dreaming of Sophie's studio, of her foot gently lifting, before the first ring but perhaps that's just a story I invent to defer coincidence and chaos.

"Hey Doug is that you? God it's been so long. Too long! I don't even know how long but I had to call you 'cause she'd never call you herself and, I don't know, I just think you ought to know and I would never have known but I ran into Roger at Target and he told me. It's Sophie, how long's it been since you've seen her?"

"Six years, seven," I reply with the candor of surprise. Betty had been three sentences in before I recognized her voice.

"Well, me too. It's been a few years since I've talked to her. Me too. She's not that far away now you know, got a small house in Barwick, that's what Roger said, been there a few years, with a studio out back, but the thing is…"

I wait patiently to hear what the thing actually is, my gaze tracking from the desk to the muted blue window. My hands fiddle with objects on the desk, betraying an air of uncertainty I'm catching up to.

"The thing is…" she repeats, "it's Sophie…"

Betty takes her first breath of the conversation. "It's cancer. Leukemia. Something like that. She's done the radiation, she did the chemo for a while but now she's stopped. I thought you should know, I thought about you when Roger told me. She stopped the chemo because there's no point."

I stare at the window for a long time, long after Betty has delivered the number and the few additional details in her possession, long after the obligatory and half-hearted catching-up questions that must be asked and answered. I tell Betty I appreciate her call and, really, I do. Sophie might have called eventually, but maybe not.

We haven't really talked since I took her to the airport. Once or twice in the first few years, we might bump into each other on a sidewalk or in a store. We'd stammer through pleasantries, smiling, quickly remembering we had to be somewhere else soon. I assumed she'd moved out of town when I stopped seeing her at all.

She might have called, but maybe not.

I stare at the window until the muted blue drains from it in the failing dusk and a thin web of condensation forms at the corner. Then, I draw myself from the desk chair, peel the loose pages from my arms, and stand on creaking limbs. I stand with great intention, as if there are a number of things I must do immediately but there is, of course, only one thing to do.

I dial the number before me. It's important to accomplish it before I think too much, before I consider possibilities. Sophie answers at the other end, her voice quieter than I remember and a bit far away.

"Hello?'

"Hey Sophie, it's Doug."

A fractional pause. "Hi Doug." A slow and barely audible exhalation.

"Okay if I come and visit?"

No pause. "Sure. When would you like to come?"

"How's Friday?"

"Friday's fine." A low chuckle. "I'm not going anywhere. Lunch?"

"Sounds great. I just need the address, I can figure it out from there."

She tells me and there's another pause, a space blooming there, threatening to become something I'm not quite ready for. The thought of seeing her terrifies me, of sitting across a table and attempting to maintain a conversation. The thought of what the illness or the intervening years might have done to her, the knowledge of what those years have done to me. Remembering her burning eyes that knew me, her slender paint-spattered fingers, the shape of her mouth that knew me.

"See you then."

"I'll be here."

2

I've always been slow to approach the first kiss, unable to see it as a casual exchange, awaiting a sign or omen to make the act definitive. For me, a kiss is declarative and direct; it's the beginning of a sentence I've committed to complete. Even in the intervening years I haven't been able to approach it much differently.

It's late on a June night, Sophie and I have gone out four or five times already, and still I haven't kissed her. We've been downtown for another of those endless studio crawls, drinking cuplets of cheap wine and staring at incoherent art, smiling and praising with wide eyes in the gallery, falling against each other and muttering our critiques once on the sidewalk.

When we arrive back at her apartment, the night is muggy and quiet with a feathery breeze high in the trees. I walk her to her door, stopping beneath the glow of the porch light. I grab her hand with my usual awkwardness, quickly squeezing it tight. "I'll call you tomorrow." I turn and walk away.

I'm halfway down the walk when she stamps her foot, sighing in frustration. I turn back for a look and she stamps again, "Come back here!"

She faces me. Her hands are on her hips and her eyes are sparking. I can feel them in the darkness bearing down the walk toward me. When I reach the step, she moves back to allow me up and I face her, awkward and chastised. Her eyes a mixture of playfulness and hurt, her hands still on her hips. She sways just slightly in the drift of some kind of private joke about to become public.

I know what's required. I lean in to brush her lips with mine, eyes canting away from her.

Her hand comes to my shoulder. Her fingers close slightly and something about the gesture, the weight of her hand and the loose suggestion of her grip, makes her real in a new and ridiculously sensual way; in a way I've surely been avoiding by limiting proximity.

A heat rises into my face, I feel myself spinning into her, and then we're pressed into the brick corner by the door, her arms around my neck, my hands at her waist, we're breathing into each other.

I remember her smell (cinnamon and lemons and something exotic and unnamable) and the assurance of her body like a thing just born into the world already with a sense of history and a momentum, a thing hurtling along its own rail. She places her hand on my chest, pushing me gently away, catching her breath. A moth skitters along the ridge of her hair, drawn by the glow of the porch light.

"It is accomplished," she says, with a short, quiet exhalation and a wry smile, tugging at the hem of her blouse.

Two weeks later, she's onstage at the Naked Scrawl, one band dismantling behind her, a large guy handing up equipment on the left. It's around midnight and the club is full. She takes the center microphone and swings one arm wide to sweep the room:

"Hey everyone!" she shouts, waiting a moment for their attention then shouting again. She straightens her arm to point toward the far back of the room, in my direction: "I want everyone to meet my boyfriend!" The entire room turns toward me and I find that I cannot vanish into the wall.

"His name's Biff!" she shouts, smiling loudly. "He's a writer!" The room bursts into cheers and whistles, less for me or my assumed profession than in collusion with Sophie's joy and excitement.

For the rest of the night there are friendly claps on the back, offers of free drinks, questions about what I write to which I stammer nonsensical answers, to which they smile, squeeze my arm, and reply, "That's great."

The Naked Scrawl is a ratty club on the fringe of the downtown arts district. A cinderblock box with a plywood bar; a place that had once actually been a small two-bay garage. It provides cheap beer, and day-old cupcakes for a dollar baked by one of the barmaids. Live music five nights a week, one night for trivia, one night you're-on-your-own-so-shut-the-hell-up-about-it.

While I trudge up and down the empty hallways of a cavernous building, enjoying my hermetic silence, Sophie pushes brimming plastic cups through three layers of bodies, manhandles the rowdies toward the door, and argues with the band about where they can park their van.

She's the manager there, inasmuch as the operation has any oversight exerted in its direction at all. It supports her painting however, or it supports her and allows her the time and the light in which to paint.

She always closes up about 3 while I hand over my vast responsibilities at 6. Sometimes I discover her sprawled on my couch when I open my door. I tug on her shoulder, she blinks up at me, and we totter out the door together to find breakfast at one of those dim, grey restaurants that never really close, but never seem completely open.

She tells me about the band that night, The Ice Cream Revengers, or Dead Hole Head, or Smirch Engine, critiquing their music and performance ("Great band, but the poor things can't write a song to save their lives," and, "Find a new drummer and they might be alright"), or the petty controversies of the regulars, or the story of that one guy who gets himself completely blasted every Thursday night. I, of course, don't have much to talk about. Space is simply space and that's exactly how I like it.

When our working nights don't overlap, I visit her at the Scrawl, hanging at first in one damp corner, shoes glued to the floor by strata of unknown substances. I mutter a response if anyone attempts conversation but fortunately the club is loud, the bands are loud, loud even when setting up their equipment, the air itself is loud, and there isn't a lot of room for conversation.

I learn to pick Sophie's laugh from the general din, learn the spectrum of color sent out when the bracelet I bought her catches the light, learn the tenor of her bartender-shout which could bring even the most comatose patron into momentary awareness.

After a couple of weeks, Sophie appears in my corner with a stool.

"No use in you standing up over here," she shouts over the din of Headbangers and Mash, a heavy-metal Irish folk band. She pecks me on the cheek. "Make yourself comfortable." After that, you could find me hunched over my notebook in the corner, working in my own quiet bubble within the noise and shuffle, cultivating my small circle, nested within hers.

"Come on up to the stage, Biff!" Sophie shouts over the repetitions of the crowd chanting Biff-Biff-Biff in an orgiastic fervor. Her hand turns and curls to beckon me with the confidence of an elder Greek siren. "Come on!"

I have no idea why she dubbed me Biff that night. She always answered the question with a shrug and a wink, but the name stuck and ever after I was Biff at the Naked Scrawl.

I push my way through the crowd blushing, probably trembling, more backslaps and shouts bubbling up around me. I climb to the stage and come awkwardly to rest beside her.

She swings to the crowd, arms up, then swings back in my direction, her arms closing around me. She's damp and her clothes are limp with the night and her mouth tastes just slightly of beer as it takes mine and we kiss.

The crowd goes wild.

We fall away from each other. Her arm thrown over my bare chest. Her arm is damp, sticking to my skin. I'm aware of the line of heat it casts, the tide of my chest rising and falling beneath it. She rolls onto her side along the length of my body and her warmth and nearness is almost too much. I want to sit up as if gasping from a vivid dream, but I don't.

She's limp beside me. The sheets are spun around my ankles, arresting my legs. We're lying on a raft of blankets in my living room floor. My spartan single bed instantly proving itself too small, we'd migrated here dragging sheets behind us like breathless refugees.

Sophie raises herself at my side. I brush the slope of her breast and her stomach, allowing my hand to fall into her lap. She peers down to me, head tilted to one side, her glance flitting over my body and the tangle of the sheets; she's somehow aware of the entire room at once.

She is casting lines into memory. The trace of an arm, the blue light at a cleft of skin, the sway and fold of the sheets as we move. Her attention is teasing out detail I would not have noticed. I enjoy watching these disconnected, almost random observations bank up behind her eyes, filling some space of joy.

She compels me into a kind of heightened awareness. I notice the strands of hair matted with sweat near her left ear, the tiny beads of damp above her breasts, the deep earthy scent of our sex, hers crouching near me, mine where her hand returns again, fingers coming back to her mouth, mouth lowering to mine and the taste of her, the taste of us, tasted reluctantly at first, somewhat askance, but then falling into it, into her, pulling her back over me like a net.

It's a Saturday morning and there's nowhere to go and nothing to do until late afternoon. We lie together on the makeshift bed, basking in some invisible light like turtles on a log, the pond around us a misty and vague horizon not quite real.

We talk about our first loves. That first glaring sun-bright burst of desire, hers when she was 11, mine at 13. Joel Comstock. Tessa Mills. We describe them to each other in detail, then imagine that the sardonic wit of the universe has thrust them together, married them and given them three children, all loud and rheumy.

"He was two, maybe three, years older. He had that kinda sandy blonde hair boys rake to the side. He rode my bus and he never noticed me, the nerdy girl, peering over her book for a glimpse as he talked to five girls at once, all of them giggling. He wore dark

Metallica t-shirts and jeans with slits halfway down so I could see his tanned knees."

She's staring at the ceiling, her open hand on my stomach, fingers slightly curled. It's an essential image of Sophie, her hand lying loose somewhere, upturned, her long and elegant fingers cupped so slightly as if cradling a thing treasured and delicate.

She's silent for a moment, completing some kind of picture in her head, then turning to me with a sudden commentary, "You know, the problem with reading literature at too early an age is that you come to believe all true love is tragic or unrequited."

I nod solemnly as if this were a perfectly obvious truth.

"I thought about him constantly. Backlit like a Hollywood Norse God. Thought of him especially when I did not touch myself, because I never touched myself, not nearly every night in the glow of my panda night light, not in my bedroom, the door only four feet down the hall from the living room where my parents were watching God knows what, no I never touched myself and I never thought about Joel Comstock when I didn't do it."

"Glad you cleared that up," I replied, once she paused for a gasp of breath, "'cause I was gonna…"

"Nope, never. You?"

"Every chance I got."

She leans in closer, squirming with interest. I can smell last night and this morning and the loose-limbed release of her sleep. When I don't confess immediately, she arches an eyebrow, prodding my stomach gently with the heel of her hand.

"Tessa was my age, but girls seemed so far away then, they might as well have inhabited another planet. She was in my Latin class, two rows up on the right."

"You took Latin?'

"Yeah. I wanted to be a Roman senator when I grew up."

Sophie nods.

"I can't really remember what she wore. She had long, dark hair and she'd curl it behind her ear whenever she bent down to write.

And when she was listening, her hand would flatten along the top of the desk, all except for her forefinger, which would tap out some light, personal rhythm. She was always writing in this small notebook with a drawing of a cat on it and I always wanted to know what was in that notebook, harboring the belief, of course, that there were long passages about me."

"And the other? You know..." Another gentle poke.

"Sometimes I'd be thinking of Tessa. But I harbored carnal thoughts for a teacher or two. And one bus driver. It wasn't long before I moved on to musicians, singers. Bjork. PJ Harvey. I had a passing obsession with Stevie Nicks, twirling and slurring her words in old videos."

"How old were you," I turned to ask," when you started not doing that?"

Sophie squints, as if studying a dusty calendar in the dim distance. "Twelve, I think. You?"

"About that."

Sophie's hand lolls on my stomach, then turns over and strokes me lightly. "It was the most amazing thing. It was a mystery it seemed no-one knew about, 'cause, I mean, if they knew about it, why weren't they talking about it? Why had no one ever told me, you know, that I had a body and it did nice things for me."

Before this, our first tentative month or two had been all shapeless groping and formless conversation, vague gesture becoming inarticulate word becoming new vague gesture. Finally, inexplicably, we settled into an acceptance of each other. It was an incidental yet definitive occurrence.

In that prelude, we were hard edges and nerves that might dissolve in an instant, then re-form. We talked endlessly, struggling toward a shared language. We touched with an awkward persistence, bumping each other, teeth clacking when we kissed too hard. We were like children, children who had never accomplished a kiss, a hug, a declaration of intimacy, afraid to laugh at ourselves, afraid the other might take offense somehow, shrouded in a seriousness that only made everything more comical.

Then, one day, the awkwardness simply vanished, from both of us at once. I remember the moment. I picture it now standing in the middle of my office, unsure of what to do with my hands after hanging up the phone, already anxious about our upcoming reunion.

The sunlight streams through the window, throwing wide angles along the floor and up the bare white wall and perhaps it's this band of light that reminds me, placing me again near Sophie in the booth.

I walked into the restaurant to find her waiting, a bright band from the window cutting the table in two and falling onto her quiet hands. She looked up as I came around the corner, the door hissing closed behind me. I met her eyes and we settled into each other once and for all. We smiled different smiles than we might have managed in the previous weeks.

Because I am plagued by a dismembering desire to understand things, I often wondered what level of faith was needed for us to navigate those awkward months and why we did it. What kept us from simply ignoring the phone when the other called, or not answering the door?

"Stop worrying about it," Sophie chides me, stretching naked at my side. "Sometimes you just know something and even if it doesn't happen tomorrow or the next day, you believe in it. It's not a thinking thing."

"But why you? Why did I have the patience or the conviction with you? Why not the girl in the checkout line the day before?"

"What girl in the checkout line?"

"What happened that kept me in it? 'Cause it was awkward and uncomfortable."

"What girl in the checkout line?"

"Forget the checkout line," I tell her, grabbing her hand and pulling her toward me on the floor, "I'm telling you you're important to me and I don't know why."

Sophie resists, leaning away from me. I release her hand and she takes the opportunity to gather the loose sheet and draw it around her shoulders, concealing her body. My hand drops slowly to my hip.

"If you ask me," she says, her gaze shifting from my eyes to the room and back again, "perhaps we shouldn't see each other until you've fully worked that out. I mean, I can't expect you to participate in something you don't fully understand. It just wouldn't be fair."

I pull myself into a sitting position with a start, working to defend myself, but she pushes me down again with the flat of her hand.

"The answer to your question is simple," she tells me, the sheet falling away from her. "You already loved me---before we ever met."

I feel her synapses threading into my brain. She throws the sheet over my head and the world goes black.

The drive to the airport usually took a little over an hour but we leave with enough time to stop at our favorite park, a trail through the woods which winds toward and away from a slow river. It's summer and the ground is damp from the previous night's rain, the river swollen and a bit faster than usual. We hear it through the trees as a kind of insect hiss.

I park the car by the entrance to the longest path and we get out, shuffling indecisively by the car door as I arrange her luggage in the back seat, just to delay for a moment the beginning of this last walk, leading us to the airport and some other kind of life.

I don't want her to go. I don't think she wants to go. We don't know what else to do. The six-month residency in Denver comes at just the time when we've exhausted our options and ourselves.

She'd been crying again but not enough that I'd realized it until she stepped into the room, her eyes red-rimmed and puffy, her body exuding an oily heat. She stood before me for a moment, shoulders slumped, hands at her sides. She raised one to offer me the letter.

"I got the residency," she told me, "They liked the Horizon Series."

In an alternate history, the kind that supposedly exists for everyone somewhere in the universe, this would be a cause for joy and celebration, the first real recognition of her work. We'd be excited, leaping around the apartment in celebration. I might even have talked about going with her.

But too much had happened.

I took the letter from her and she remained before me, head down, sniffing discretely, while I read it. I read it slowly, line by line. I looked up at her, "You leave in a month?"

Sophie nods. "I've been holding onto the letter. I wanted to tell you. I didn't tell you. I didn't know what to do. Except to tell them yes."

In that moment, I think we were both relieved. It wasn't a relief we would have given voice to. A month. We could get through a month. A month and then something would change, for better or worse, at least something would change.

And our mood did lighten in the following weeks. Sophie cried less. She'd already returned to her studio, tentatively stepping between the rows of canvases as if traversing a stream on small stones. Now she spent more time there.

I was able to find a small corner of quiet where I could begin to think again, a tiny open space not claimed by the last months. We watched television together side by side on the couch; we fried vegetables and rice and she ate across from me at my wobbly table.

But the weight returned with a vengeance on the way to the airport. We entered a different gravity and it pressed firmly on our bodies, pushing us deep into the seats of the car, making us anxious to leave the seats for the woods.

We walk the path together. It's an obligatory gesture, possibly a shadow of the walk we would take in our alternate history where we might be rife with plans and enthusiasm. We walk because we have time before the airport. It's early summer and the trees are dense and lush around us, small creatures dashing across the path. We see a cardinal and, later, a lone deer, and we meet and re-meet the river pulsing past, an occasional branch swept up by the storm drifting slowly by.

I think, at some point, my hand slips into hers and she holds it, or perhaps it happens the other way around. So, for a time, we walk by the river hand in hand. Then, she releases my hand or I release hers.

We have no words left. We've exhausted the vocabulary of our relationship. We walk side by side quietly. When one of us stops to study a leaf or bird, the other stops too, but we have nothing left to say to each other.

The pressure of speech is still there. We're plagued by the hope something could be said that might make a difference. We feel the weight of emotion that has no outlet, a heaviness in our chests, pressing in upon our bodies. Now and then, there's the sharp intake of breath as if one of us is about to begin, but we can't find the initiating note and often that breath becomes a sigh.

We watch the water for a long time, facing the other bank, side by side. I can't look at her. I know she's crying softly and I know I'll cry if I see her tears. I glance at my watch.

"Time to head back, Soph."

She turns up the path and I allow my hand to rest on her shoulder for a moment then slide down her arm as we enter the shade of the trees. By the time we reach the car our atmosphere has changed a little and on the drive we speak slowly, quietly, about the practicalities of the trip, tickets and layovers and baggage claim.

"They're giving me half a duplex only a few blocks from campus so hopefully I can walk back and forth. And studio space in the Art Building. It'll take a couple of days to get everything set up but I'll take some pictures and send them to you so you can see what everything looks like."

"That'd be great. Take some pictures of Denver too, if you can," I draw a slow breath. "You always take great pictures."

I wait with her as she checks in, then follow her to the security gate. Thankfully, there isn't much of a line. Sophie turns back toward me, her eyes at my chest. "Well, this is it."

"I guess so."

She raises her eyes to mine and we're able to look at each other for a last time.

"I'm going to miss you, Doug." She smiles her curling, crooked smile, her head tilting slightly. "A lot."

"I'm going to miss you."

My hand rests on her bare forearm. She kisses me on the lips, a salty, swollen kiss which chooses not to say more than a simple goodbye. She turns away toward the security line.

I watch her until she makes it through security, watch her as she shuffles in her purse, as she takes off her bracelet, smiling at the Security Guard. I watch as others form a line behind her, inching her forward and through the counters and metal detector. Once on the other side, she turns back to me, throwing up a hand and a smile, and then she is gone.

I wade back to my car, picking my way past kiosks and doorways, my body handling all negotiations on its own. I find my keys and start the car, manage the parking attendant and the on-ramps, but two miles outside of Burnsville I pull off the road and cry.

I know she's settling into the seat she'd chosen by the window, staring out at the convection waves rising from the tarmac, shivering into the green of the trapped grass and the blue horizon. I know her smell and the way she fingers the bracelet of small shells I gave her months ago. I know she's crying the same tears.

I never love her more than when she leaves.

3

Sophie backs through the front door of the apartment, soaked to the skin. Water drips from the hem of her hoodie and her tennis shoes make gurgling, squishy sounds on the hardwood floor. I'm up from the chair toward her, thinking something might be wrong in the way she holds her hands at her waist, but when she turns I can see she's cradling a lump that soon pushes its head over the line of the zipper, revealing itself to be a drenched, rat-faced kitten, all big eyes and mew.

"Poor thing," she tells the kitten, hugging it to her breast. "Poor thing," she tells me, standing before me a dripping mess, a puddle forming at her feet.

"Where did you find him? Her?" I'm sure I'm shaking my head. "It?"

"In the middle of the road, two blocks down," she says, eyes wide with disbelief at the vagaries of the world, "poor thing was just squatting there by the double yellow, squalling, cars whizzing past like nobody's business. You'd think they couldn't tell the difference between an animal and a rock."

The chorus of squeals inside her hoodie is ceaseless and tuned to a very specific, abrasive frequency. The tiny thing peers out again from the fold of her jacket, blinking. I can see its tiny pearl teeth and pink tongue. It squawks at me like a rabid seagull.

"So, I pull over…" she extends the lump, still coddled in the hoodie, "here, take him," ignoring my hesitation, "take him so I can change clothes."

I reach into the heat of her jacket and fish for the animal. He has almost no form, tiny and weightless, his hair soaked and matted. His thin claws catch on her shirt as I pull him away and his squawking becomes louder when I lift him. Once against my chest, he quietens a bit.

Sophie pulls the hoodie and shirt over her head, dropping them to the floor with a wet slap. "So, I pull over and all this traffic's whizzing by and I'm afraid if I just come up on him he'll dart under a car. So, there I am in the pouring rain, stopping cars in both lanes so I can get to him and when I finally do, he's motionless, crouching low, and he just looks up at me with those big eyes, that big mouth."

She's in the hallway now, pushing off one shoe with the opposite foot, then kicking herself out of her jeans.

"Sophie, what are you going to do with this thing?"

"Raise it from a cub and train it for the circus!" she shouts from the other room.

"We don't really need something else to take care of, you know," I shout back, tiny claws digging into my chest through my shirt. "It's not like we're the most responsible people in the world."

"We manage…" she re-enters the room, wrapped in her puffy blue bathrobe, arms encircling me, the kitten between us. She looks at me until our eyes catch. "We manage."

She takes the kitten from me, its squall rising an octave as she pulls it away. "C'mon," she pitches her shoulder into mine, "let's give this thing a bath."

"That appears to be the last thing it needs."

"You'll see."

We kneel by the tub and drop him in an inch of warm water. Sophie soaps him until he resembles a used dishrag, then scrubs at him head to toe. The kitten stands still, legs splayed to steady himself with nothing to grip in the tub, squealing. Sophie soothes him, doctor to patient, explaining the next operation before she begins.

"Okay, now we're gonna wash your belly," flipping him onto his back in her hand and rubbing briskly. "Now we've got to get behind your ears."

I pull a towel from the rack behind us and she places the rinsed kitten in its center. I fold the towel over him rubbing his back and head as she drains the dirty water speckled with drowned fleas. She turns from the tub toward me. I'm watching the creature between us, its hair in unruly tufts, shivering, its mouth moving but its voice exhausted.

"Beaker. He looks like that Muppet, the way only the bottom of his mouth moves. You know, the scientist's assistant who always gets blown up. He's Beaker."

The kitten stares up at us, legs braced wide, claws dug into the towel. He's all eyes and mouth, the mouth opening and closing rhythmically, now emitting an insistent high-pitched squall each time.

A year later, she's watching the cat. Slung across the sofa, her arms at odds with her legs, she stares at Beaker, who is extending his furred self to his utmost length atop a pile of clothes in a patch of sun with that specific feline abandon that seems a denial of physical form, a looseness implying he might have suddenly become a rug.

Sophie's head is cocked to one side, her eyes half-open, her lips likewise barely parted. There's a deep gentleness in her watching, as if she's dissolved into the bright space around the cat and the textured nap of its fur. She's forgotten her own body and her awareness delicately overlies the animal in the heat from the window, the glow of the demarcated floor, the spin and swirl of dust hanging just above.

The dirty clothes are heaped in the living room and Sophie's banging in the kitchen. It's easy to bang in Sophie's kitchen since you can barely manage to turn around; a tiny narrow stove on one side, refrigerator on the other, three feet of walkway between and a single sink at the end, linked by tiny counters hardly wide enough for an open book. It's dark and damp, resembling the interrogation chamber in a particularly bad dream.

The entire apartment had been hewn from the attic of a two story brick building. The downstairs had been a hardware store in a past life but now houses a shop trying desperately to be overpriced and trendy, yet only ever managing the former. It sells an inexplicable collection of clothes and polished stones and dragon sculptures and magic potions. Its strange smells seep through the planked floor into Sophie's apartment.

Sophie's banging around in the kitchen while I toss damp towels onto the pile in the living room floor. She peeks around the corner to advise me, "You need to take those clothes off and wash them, baby. You've been wearing them for three days."

"I don't have anything clean to put on," I whine. "We should've done laundry last week."

"I know," she sighs, disappearing back into the kitchen, "it's gonna take us hours to get all of this done."

"Should we take a movie or something?" I call back, picking through the pile, withdrawing something now and then to sniff it and judge its relative foulness.

"Maggie and Jim aren't gonna like any of our movies. They like those English costume dramas with Queens and carriages."

I stand in the doorway. Sophie's opening cabinets, withdrawing and studying cans, manhandling a pot from the cabinet beneath.

"This is the best I can do," I tell her, leaning against the door jamb. "Anyway, you're one to talk. Look at your jeans, they're supporting hundreds of life forms."

"Yes, darling, but they're studio jeans. Everyone knows that's how studio jeans are."

We lived on box wine, crackers, peanut butter, and ramen, splitting our time between her cramped apartment and my own, gathering change every Friday for a night out. Our cars were held together with wire and hope, our clothes harvested from yard sales and Goodwill. We attended any gallery opening or reception where there might be free drinks and shrimp. Our married friends occasionally took pity and invited us over for a real dinner.

"We need to pull the sheets from your bed," I remind her, "they're rank. They smell like, you know, sin and debauchery."

She turns to me, a saucepan loose in the hand at her hip: "What kind of smell is that?"

"It's a nice smell," I backtrack, "as long as it's your own sin. Other people's sin is always disgusting. But your own, it's comforting in its way."

"We should be proud of ourselves," she winks.

"Agreed." I peer into her closet of a kitchen. "Finding anything?"

We tried to do laundry every Thursday but sometimes it didn't happen. It had been three weeks and we were out of clothes, our towels limp and swampy. The entire apartment smelled like a damp compost heap covered in wet sheets.

Once a week we'd pile our smelly clothes into the trunk and drive out to the heart of the suburbs where Maggie and Jim lived in a relatively new split level house nestled in raised beds amongst other split level houses. Jim had some indeterminate job with a local corporation that allowed Maggie, since the children were off to college and their own lives, to paint and photograph and weave and sketch and run her small gallery downtown.

Maggie and Jim made dinner for us as we piled our clothes into their stainless steel washer. We always brought a dish to share but it was really only a token, since they cooked lavishly, enjoying their joint project and the sharing of it, with wine in bottles instead of jugs or boxes.

I liked Maggie. She was effusive and witty with a loose, bright energy constantly radiating in five directions at once. Their house overflowed with paintings she'd painted, quilts she'd sewn, vases she'd thrown, random objects she'd arranged in eclectic combinations. I sometimes thought she might have raised the house itself in a single afternoon by sheer force of will. The woman created more in a day than I had in my entire lifetime.

Jim was quieter, with a wit so dry you had to listen closely to find a trace of it. One evening, with a wink and a gentle tap on the shoulder, he ushered me into his Fortress of Solitude, leading me down the hall from the kitchen to his workshop in the garage. He opened the door to the crisp scent of cut pine, damp and fresh. Every tool hung in perfect alignment upon pegboard walls. The room was so clean it seemed to defy use. But I knew he used it; I'd seen his refinished end tables, his restored antique telephone stand. Sophie had told me about their massive headboard he'd made by hand.

"Check the fridge for me, wouldja?" Sophie asks, struggling to come up with a palatable dish from what she can find in the kitchen, both of us drifting at the far border of our paychecks. "Have anything at your place?"

"I don't know, I might have a can of tomato sauce." I open the refrigerator and stare into its bleak landscape. "I've got a dollar or two," I call back to her, "I could run to the store."

"We really don't have time now. What's that back there? Is it rice?"

"I think so. It's got hairy things in it." I gingerly draw the container toward me.

"That's cilantro, goof," Sophie assures me with a laugh, taking a step to peer into the refrigerator beside me, resting her warm palm upon my back. "Hand it over. And the Tabasco too."

"What are you going to make?"

"Egg and tofu jambalaya."

"Here's part of an onion," I call out, quite pleased with myself. "D'ya want that?"

"Sure," her fingers linger an instant in my palm as she takes it. "Will you handle the sheets while I throw this together?"

"Deal."

We're nestled in the womb of the den, downstairs after dinner, the low hum of the washer and dryer far away on the other side of the wall. Sophie and I have drawn pillows up to one side of the coffee table, slouching into them and each other, eyes lazily focused on the board in the center. Jim sits at the edge of the sofa, as he always does, while Maggie has pulled her feet beneath her, leaning into the armrest. We each have our wine, and those thin chocolate cookies

Maggie always buys. The room is brown and warm and we've settled into a slow moving current.

We're playing Shelton Scrabble, Maggie and Jim's proprietary version in which couples could share tiles and any word was valid as long as you could convince the majority (Sophie once scoring 124 points for 'oints' which, she explained, was the sound I made whenever I stubbed my toe. And I, for one, had to agree).

The board is spread on the table, my tiles lined on the sloping rack beside Sophie's. I'm staring at the chaotic line of letters, trying to come up with at least a decent nonsense word; Sophie is picking at a glob of paint on her bare ankle, trying to get a nail under so she can peel it away.

"You never told me you had a grandson, Mag," she says, engrossed in her ankle, "I saw the picture on your bedside table when I went to the bathroom. He's so tiny."

Maggie smiles, but it's a smile that won't hold, fading to a blank stare before she pulls herself from the armrest, unfolding her legs.

It's the kind of immediate shift of atmosphere that makes me want to withdraw. I'd rather leave the room, but I'm too embarrassed to be party to this stumble into a dark and unnamed area. I've suddenly found myself in some dense and barbed thicket and all I know to do is back out. Sophie doesn't notice the temperature change until she looks up. Her hands drop into her lap and she turns toward Maggie.

Maggie smiles again, a different smile this time, recognizing her previous reaction and the innocence of Sophie's question, sharing their complicity. "A son. He was born premature. Seven weeks. And back then, there wasn't much they could do," she says, her voice low and soft. "So he died. Four days after he was born."

Sophie is about to speak, but Maggie stops her with a raised hand. Her feet flatten on the floor. Her body shifts gently as if she's settling into something. "It's alright. Funny how it can still sneak up on me, even after more than twenty five years, it can catch me by surprise."

She pauses and the room is still for an instant. She seems to be holding an image, or a thought, for a moment, and the rest of us wait patiently for her to let it go. Jim slips back from the edge of the sofa, into the cushions, his arms at his sides.

"He was our first. Bobby. God, we were so young," Maggie's eyes are bright and wet, trained mostly on Sophie, occasionally sliding toward mine but never lingering, sensing my unease. She reaches over to pat Jim's hand before continuing. "He was so tiny, and we knew something was wrong of course, with him coming so early and all, and in those days, they just took the babies away from you, the nurses, away to the nursery and everything.

"Jim had to cause a stink, make a scene in the hallway with the doctors," here she pulls herself erect, tucks her chin into her chest, adopting a deep and over-articulated voice. "No one's going to tell me I can't hold my own son. After that, they'd bring him to us and we'd keep him for as long as we could. We'd talk to him, touch his fingers, his hair. But they knew he wasn't going to make it. Maybe we did too. We were just trying to get to know him a little before he went away."

I'm staring at the floor, embarrassed by the intimacy of the moment, avoiding eye contact with Maggie or Jim, feeling prickly and uncomfortable with a strange sensation, hot and needling, in my hands. I study Sophie's ankle, glancing up to Maggie just long enough to manage the demand of the room, which has grown warmer, smaller.

"It was the worst thing that ever happened to us. We walked around in a daze for months. Both of us. I cried, just all the time. I'd come downstairs at night, two in the morning, and Jim would just be staring out the window. For hours on end.

"I thought I would die. I honestly thought my body would simply curl into itself, tighter and tighter, squeezing like a fist until there was nothing left. I wanted to die. I wanted Jim to leave me alone. To let me die. But he wouldn't."

Jim reaches out to her, allowing his fingertips to rest on her bare arm. She doesn't turn to him right away, but her features soften almost imperceptibly, something slight but deep releasing in her body. She continues to stare across the room for a few seconds longer, then turns to him, placing her free hand over his.

"I don't know how he had the patience."

Jim clears his throat quietly before speaking, and when he speaks it isn't to Maggie but, strangely, to Sophie and I: "It was desperation. I couldn't lose both of them."

There are tears in Sophie's eyes. While I'd been retreating, she was moving in closer. I hadn't meant to look but her hand rising to wipe them away caught my gaze, drawing it toward her. Maggie's sadness floods into me. I feel a lump rising in my throat, through Sophie and into me. I stare at her ankle again but it's already entered, this awareness of suffering which I struggle to keep at bay, and I don't know what to do with it.

I hadn't noticed Maggie's scars when I met her in the gallery, or any time in the safe and well-lit conversations at her house. I'd never wanted to see them. And I'd never had to, until this accidental conversation revealed them. Now, I knew they would always be visible, in every conversation and chance meeting, giving her a depth and texture, a reality I'd never wished for.

Later Sophie will tell me: "She didn't have to talk about it. She could have just blown it off. She wanted to tell us. Because we're friends. Because she trusts us. It's a good thing." This was probably true but it didn't make it any easier for me, now that I was left to carry a small part of her pain.

I look up again and Sophie is watching Maggie, her head tilted slightly to the side, with a soft smile: "What was his name?"

"Robert," Maggie replies. "Robert Allen Shelton. His grave's just a couple of miles from here. I still go and talk to him now and then."

"Could I go with you sometime?" And Sophie, immediate and sincere, opens up the room again with the question, in a completely natural and spontaneous way I could never accomplish, the tightness in my chest easing with the question and Maggie's immediate response.

"Of course."

It was the kind of magical thing Sophie could always seem to manage, a thing that seemed impossible to me. While I still can't really look at Maggie, I watch Sophie as she sniffs quietly, wiping her eyes with the heel of her hand then laughing, with Maggie, at the awkward intimacy of the moment.

"Thanks," Maggie tells Sophie softly, "It was nice to have him with us for a minute."

It's late when we finally get back to Sophie's apartment with our mountains of bright, folded clothes. They give the place a certain shine by their presence, making it seem cleaner and more inviting. We're tired, both from the hour and the pleasant demands of being sociable, but we help each other stay upright, padding room to room, putting away clothes.

I separate mine into my ramshackle basket, broken rattan spikes poking my hands as I stuff the clothes in. I leave them by the door. I'll eventually take them home; or, I'll work through the basket piece by piece, never managing to get back to my own apartment at the right time. Leaving the clothes by the door is a tacit agreement between Sophie and me, as if never putting my clothes in her closet might maintain the slightest thread of denial that we might be living together.

We stay busy, passing each other at the baskets. The sounds of drawers sliding open and shut, closet doors swinging wide, then creaking closed. We're quiet and she doesn't put on any music. It's stuffy and hot in the apartment so I open the street-side window for a little air and noise, dreading all the time that we might have to talk about Maggie and Jim's tragedy and I'll have to awkwardly demonstrate I care; and it isn't that I don't care, it's just that I don't know how to talk about it. But Sophie merely smiles, humming absently to herself in a sort of domestic reverie.

The last job is to make the bed, me on one side of her lumpy futon and she on the other, one tossing the sheet to the other then pulling it taut between us and lowering it slowly to the mattress. Sophie slides off to the bathroom and I settle into the surprisingly cool and crisp sheets. The only light in the room is the dim streetlight outside the open window. There's a flare when she opens the bathroom door but she extinguishes it and I lose her for an instant as my eyes adjust to the room. By then she's climbing in beside me, sitting up to arrange the sheet and pillows.

"I feel so bad for Maggie and Jim," I tell her in the darkness. "But I never know what to say, what to do, what am I supposed to do?"

I can see her profile in the backwash of the window, the soft cast of her skin as she curls her hair around her ear, the way the light catches the edges of her teeth as she licks her lips.

"Oh, baby," she shakes her head slowly, drawing a breath. "Baby..."

Her eyes sweep the bed deliberately and come to rest on my face: "Love's a feeling, not a plan."

I let it go at that. Later, as I drift off to sleep, in that weird place where the edges of the world become fluid, I turn toward her. She's lying on her back, completely still, staring at the vague shifts of light on the ceiling. There's a tear running down the side of her face toward her pillow and I know she's crying for Maggie and Jim.

Beaker lies stretched to his full length in the window sill, front legs against the glass before him, his tail spilling over, tip twitching into one comma after another as he dozes. Now and then he positions himself anew for full advantage of the sun, one leg rising, claws splaying the glass. Now and then, he opens a wary eye to me, then slowly closes it again in complete disinterest.

It's early spring and the afternoon is still cool. Even though the sun is bright and warm, the glass gives off a slight chill. The trees are budding, with random leaves here and there, throwing irregular shadows along the floor as I work.

The morning after the phone call, I busy myself with errands in order to be outside the house most of the day. I pick up some stamps, I get the oil changed. I buy grapefruit. I concentrate away from Sophie, away from our memory, all the time feeling it working on me like voices heard in the far distance. Back home, I return emails, waste time on Facebook, and half-heartedly attempt research for a new project.

I know I don't have the concentration for anything more than menial tasks. A door has been closed and there is now nowhere to work. Though the room is no different, suddenly there is no space within it. All has been crowded out by the past.

Recollections return, collecting themselves into a simple image. The image condenses and holds, opening outward into some spectrum of feeling and association, random and shocking. A single symbol with a deep history.

It's the image of Sophie's tears in bed that night, of her crying for someone else's pain. It's a feeling so alien to me, yet so real, in a reality I can only imagine. I busy myself while Sophie takes possession of me, one cell after another, not as a developing story of the past because memory is not a linear, unbroken line, but as a series of associations slipping in and out of focus, calling forth new ones.

It's an image so iconic and so personal it has the mysterious density of dream. As if it never actually happened, as if a deeper part of me conjured it as a symbol for something else. A marker holding the place of a question.

All day it is there, in every breath and blink. Churning up other pictures, snatches of conversation from long ago, fluttering trickles in my chest both cold and warm. An anxious, tentative excitement.

It's 6 p.m. before I finish everything, pushing my chair away from the desk, taking off my glasses and absently rubbing my eyes. The light is already beginning to fade in the window. Beaker is restless but languishes nonetheless. I sit back, extending my legs, allowing my eyes to lose focus at the darkening window.

I haven't finished anything; I haven't brought any task to a close; I've simply surrendered all pretense.

In my mind, on the page, I try to capture our history. But it's a cloud diary composed of shifting shapes, new dimensions, set off by broad expanses of vast blue space.

I remember her face, that night, framed in profile by the open window, the slowness of her breath and the slight occasional sigh. I'm not sure she was aware she was crying, not sure she noticed her own tears.

I remember the heat of her body beside me in those times when I climbed into bed after she'd fallen asleep, her low, shallow breathing, and the occasional single snore nearly awakening her but not quite; the way she settled back into her pillow beside me, her bare leg sliding along mine beneath the sheet.

I know what's important, all these years away, by how often it returns. Not in the way I cling to it, calling up pictures and plans, but in the way it clings to me, rising full and unbidden, in the way it presents itself before me. Complete again, for an instant.

After so many years, I still remember the day after our first date, the scent of her hair lingering in my car. Noticing it made me smile, and I smile again in the memory, this trace of another person having tumbled into my life and come to rest.

I would walk the long, empty hallways of the warehouse I guarded, aware all at once of that scent on my skin, or a phrase entering our joint vocabulary; or I'd smile at the remembrance of a glance, almost inconsequential, because it's the inconsequential that always sticks, identifying us like a fingerprint.

I'd curl myself into her battered sofa with my tattered, abused notebook and the knowledge that she slept in the next room, feeling that she was holding an open place for me in the world. I'd struggle to find a way to get that on paper, filling page after page with a restless script that could only circle at a safe distance, stumbling back over its own tracks time and again.

Knowing completely that words might describe this mix of feeling and sensation; knowing also that I could not articulate it, might never articulate it, no matter how many tight lines I might fill in my notebook.

It's late when I realize I'm hungry. Beaker has abandoned the dimming room long ago. There are few passing cars on the road and the street is nearly as dark as the house which holds the anticipatory stillness of spring, slowly releasing, a little more every day, the chill it has held all winter. I think about dinner, but just for a moment.

Everything begins before it begins. Long before I stand in her studio that first night. I'm remembering the day Sophie became beautiful. The moment I understood something had happened inside me already that I was just now discovering.

I think, it's at a ratty coffee shop two blocks from her apartment. I think it's a late morning in June and we're sitting at a wobbling table near the curb. She's wearing a floppy straw sunhat with fake plastic flowers she found at a yard sale, and a bright yellow sundress exposing her shoulders and the warm slope of her neck.

I look across the table to her and she's blindingly right in a complete and deeply satisfying way. Not because of anything she's done, or anything she's said; she hasn't changed. I've finally found the right perspective, caught the perfect light, my eyes opening wide from the best angle. I've stumbled upon the way to see her.

And it becomes an article of faith. My vision on the road to Damascus. It's insanely simple: the possibility, the beauty, of another person. It's thrilling and overpowering. It's terrifying.

The thing about a vision is this: it never leaves and it cannot be undone. It insinuates itself into every experience, changing me completely in an instant and all the past stretching behind and around me alters tone within its frame. I haven't moved and the world spins exactly as it did seconds before. Only not quite. Some fundamental yet transparent shift has occurred just out of sight.

All my articles of faith are stained with cynicism and an assurance of the depths of human delusion. Even when my faith is strong, doubt constantly nags at its heels, worrying it like a neurotic Chihuahua. Once faith appeared, it took years of dogged determination not only to grasp but to accept it.

"You gotta use the apocalypse you're given," Maggie told me once and maybe that's true. Or maybe the apocalypse uses you, inching its way into each cell like a virus from a science fiction novel.

I didn't have the words then. I couldn't really talk about it.

Later, at Nigel's party when we were alone in a hallway, Sophie leaned in to me, close, her lips almost touching my ear: "You know, all your fake sarcasm doesn't fool me. I've seen a sunrise take your breath; seen you stop what you're doing, close your eyes, to listen to a piece of music..."

I cocked my head toward her, my eyes coming up to meet hers, our lips nearly touching. I could feel her breath on my face.

She whispers: "I've seen tears in your eyes during movies, not because they're sad but because they're beautiful."

"Just don't tell anyone, okay?" I whisper in return. "I'm sort of undercover."

"Don't mess with me then." Her arms come up to my shoulders, her fingers lacing at my neck. She holds her lips just beyond mine. "This whole cynical awkward dolt routine. You need to know that I know. Your tricks don't work on me, Buster."

We float before each other in a moment that lasts a century or two before her lips touch mine.

At the wobbly table, on what might have been a June morning, I find a home with Sophie and it's not something I inherit or adopt, but a shelter we will into place around us.

I could never say then what I can allow myself to say now, in a darkened room, to only myself and a hungry, sulking cat:

Sophie was the first faith I ever had that was truly my own, long before writing took a shape and became a force. It was borne outside my field of vision, from moments occurring between us, from experience, not from need. Though there was certainly quite a bit of that. Faith comes, it seems, as the things we care most about bump up against one another inside of us.

That faith brought me into definition, helped me to wrestle myself to earth. We became a sacrament of my new religion but not the whole of it. It spread from her, from us, slowly out into the world like that virus, subtly infecting everything in its path. As if all the distance I'd steadfastly maintained toward every other person had melted for an instant and I'd joined, all at once and forever, a joyous fringe of the human race.

It's a thing I've struggled not to define too clearly over the years. Like any religious experience, it demands a kind of quiet and distracted nurturance. It flattens out or vanishes altogether when I try to look at it directly.

It comes to mind now, this conversion experience, as if some answer might arise where none ever has before, as if these maps of belief might lead any other place but to the home that is Sophie and me. But the images are mute. They've seeped so far into my body that now they no longer have words. I can press for answers but it's like begging secrets from a dreamer.

4

Sheaves of paper tremble on my desk like delicate creatures shuddering toward life. I watch them, pouting. Sophie is near the window, edging a glance in my direction. She'd appeared at the door after a tense exchange on the phone. So, here we are, Sophie and I, and my desk, locked into a kind of inter-animate staring match.

"You need to get out of here. You need to talk to other actual human beings. I'll be right there," she reassures me. "I know you can do it---have a conversation, be charming and all---I've seen it happen."

I'd told her I needed to write but, even before she arrived, that desire had lost much of its glamour and reduced itself to the possibility of pacing my apartment and staring at my cluttered desk in the hope that the glorious muse I didn't believe in might suddenly appear and issue its demands, removing all doubt.

Writing was this thing I was supposed to be doing while instead I was doing something else. It was the thing always hovering just outside my frame of vision. I wanted to feel something come into being at my fingertips. I wanted tiny intimacies to unfurl into graceful scenes and stories. I wanted to make something solid, tangible, something that moved of its own in the world.

All I could manage were random thoughts and run-on sentences. I doubted I had, or would ever have, anything remotely interesting to say. Nevertheless, I continued to carry my notebook as if it were some sort of flag or flotation device, the naïve airline passenger dutifully clutching his seat cushion as the plane goes down.

Sophie's voice lowers into a register of resignation. "But, if you say you need to work, then I'll understand," she sighs, in a tone that assures me there will be no understanding involved at all.

"No, no..." I reply, pulling myself up from the tattered sofa, "I see your point. Nothing's going to happen here tonight anyway." I glance around the apartment. "I'm just a hoarder, you know. I collect all this stuff in my head. If I could just clear enough space to move around in there, maybe I could manage something worthwhile. As it is I just move piles of crap from one side of the room to another."

"Baby, you make everything so difficult."

"I know," I laugh, but not happily. "I know. It might be the only thing I'm good at."

I join her at the window. We turn to watch a squirrel scrabble up one tree then leap from its branches into another. It's late afternoon and the sun has angled low and quiet, leaving a strange light hanging in the trees at the edges between leaves. I haven't been out of the apartment all day.

"I can't be like you. I want to, God knows, I want to. But I can't just throw stuff up there and somehow will it to work. It's amazing how you do that. How do you do that?"

Sophie shrugs. "I do it first, think about it later. You just need to be a little more Buddhist..." she chuckles, "or drop acid and tour with the Dead, or unlock your inner child..."

"Or join a twelve step program."

"Or accept Jesus Christ as your personal savior."

"Or, maybe, I could spend a year living in the wild with bears and ferrets."

"Yep, everything's better with ferrets."

"Thank you for your hope and understanding."

"Anything for you, Doug."

I walk away from the window, unsure of where I'm going, but turning back into the apartment, I find it's still the same place I've just turned away from.

She bursts into a laugh at my blank look, stepping forward to take both my hands: "Do you want to go to Ellen's or Alex's?"

"Might as well do both," I mutter, rousing myself from my funk now that her skin is on mine, finding my voice and raising my arms in declamation: "Let the Wild Rumpus start!"

An hour later we stand arm in arm at Nigel and Ellen's doorway, box of wine and bag of blue corn chips in hand. Sophie tugs on my arm, tilting her head into my shoulder, daring me to kiss her before the door opens. It's a dare I take.

We arrive at Alex's duplex much later, around 1 a.m. We've been drinking for hours by then, but stop off for a red eye on the way. We're met at the door by a tall, pale guy I don't know whose straight black hair blots much of his face. He immediately attaches himself to me, his hand closing around my arm:

"Hey, man, gimme a cigarette..."

"Sorry, I don't smoke."

He jerks a thumb toward one corner of the room. "Well, could you bum one offa Joe over there, 'cause he won't give *me* another one."

Alex's apartment smells like dirty clothes mildewing in a damp cardboard box. It has the ambience of a grotto. I expect to see water trickling down the walls and moss blooming near the ceiling. But the features of every room are a little uncertain for me now, nestled as I am between an alcohol mellow and an attenuated caffeine jangle.

The place is hot and stuffy, either from lack of money or some principled protest against air conditioning. There seem to be hundreds of people crawling through the house and yard and I know many of them. They often drop by the Naked Scrawl at, or just after, closing time. They hang out and have a beer once the doors have closed, sometimes inviting us to parties or jams after. Most of them have the complexion of those pale, eyeless fish swimming in caves far underground.

In the living room, there are clusters immersed in discussions of politics, religion and reality show etiquette. One couple makes out hard on the couch. In the corner, a group of gamers are hunkered before the TV muttering, their voices rising now in excitement, then falling in disappointment.

Sophie and I drift, room to room, until we find Alex in the back of the house. He's sitting cross-legged on the floor, back against the wall, with about twenty others as Josh, seated on the bed, picks out Neutral Milk Hotel songs on his guitar.

Alex pulls himself upright when he sees us, picking his way through the congregation to give Sophie a kiss and clap me on the back. He leads us to his spot and the rest of the group makes room. Josh starts in on *Oh, Comely* and we all sing along softly, making the song sound like a choral piece broadcast from a distant universe that has gathered other-worldly static and asteroid debris in its travels.

Goldaline, my dear, we will fold and freeze together.

Alex is a waiter and artist, in that way most of us at 20 or 22 are artists, unsure of our medium or what we want to say, knowing only that no other place in life quite fits us. He and his girlfriend Sasha write five minute plays for themselves which they perform on crowded city busses around town.

"The new piece is seven minutes long," he tells us later as we lean against the kitchen counter, beer in hand, "It's my response to a Yeats poem. But the thing is, there are only four places in the whole city where the bus is moving for more than seven minutes at a time, so Sasha and I have to take the same two routes over and over."

Alex combs the room and the deck outside for Sasha. Finding her near the back steps, he calls her inside. She's loose limbed and stocky with a high shock of bright red hair. They slide into each other as he explains: "I was telling them about the new piece."

Sasha grins broadly: "I love it! I get to play Mary Shelley."

"Yeah, one day I hope we can get costumes," Alex adds, "I think some of the references are lost when we're just in street clothes."

'What about you guys?" Sasha asks Sophie, a mischievous and inexplicable twinkle in her eye.

Sophie's fingers snake up my arm to the back of my neck and thrumb there: "We just had our nine month anniversary." I hang my arm at her waist.

"I gave him a beautiful ceramic cat. He gave me a purple crayon." She rolls her eyes, as if I'm the embodiment of a specific cosmic inscrutability. Alex and Sasha patiently await an explanation.

"It's a pretty little ceramic cat..."

"It's really cool. About this high, black with whiskers and everything," I explain. "She called it The Waiting Cat. He sits there, eyes wide, looking very attentive. He hangs out at the Scrawl now, in my place, watching over Sophie's desk."

"...and I got a crayon."

"It's a special crayon," I turn to Alex, in a futile search for common understanding. "You know, *Harold and the Purple Crayon*."

Alex and Sasha stare back blankly.

I sigh: "It's a children's book about this hydrocephalic child who goes wherever he wants, does whatever he wants, by drawing it on the wall with his purple crayon. So he draws an ocean, then a boat, and he's sailing. I thought it was a sweet present..."

Sophie leans into me, "It was a sweet present..."

Alex and Sasha continue to stare as if we're speaking Bantu. After a moment, they give us the kind of smile I imagine missionaries practice in the mirror to demonstrate their acceptance of the vagaries of foreign culture.

The conversation is interrupted by loud and savage whooping from the gamers in the corner, celebrating the death of the Alien Queen or the fall of a civilization.

Alex's parties were like weddings at a bus station, filled with concurrent conversations, music struggling for dominance over shouts and games and arguments.

The get together at Ellen and Nigel's, on the other hand, had been more akin to the meeting of focus groups prior to a marketing deployment. It was an obviously civilized crowd with better liquor and smooth jazz playing discretely in the background; mostly gallery owners and artists from the downtown district, nearly all of them at least a few years older than Sophie and me. Our box of wine was immediately hidden in the kitchen pantry, far from the frosty bottles resting in the stainless sink with chunked ice. We weren't offended in the least.

They had a small house on the shifting border between the ghetto and gentrification, a boxy two-bedroom starter home. Ellen was a nurse, and Nigel called himself a consultant, which as far as I could see meant he stayed home farting around on the internet. For some reason, it amused me that the second bedroom had been turned into Nigel's office.

On his front porch, Nigel poked a finger in my direction. "Sophie says you're a writer," he said, his tone vaguely accusatory. I'd stepped out for a little air; Nigel was returning from the store with more ice.

I shrugged, always uncomfortable with the way she announced these things to anyone who would listen, while leaving me to explain the lack of details as best I could. I tolerated it though, assuming that, like a bitter medicine, it was good for me.

I could almost feel like a writer in the barren, empty corridors at work, when my mind wandered its own labyrinth, backing its way out of dead end after dead end. I felt less like a writer when I was actually trying to write, staring at the scraps of paper I'd collected on my desk like curls of dead skin.

Whenever Sophie mentioned my writing to others, I just felt like an imposter, even while being proud she thought enough of me to proclaim it to the universe, a thing I could never bring myself to do.

"We should talk sometime, you know," Nigel continued, moving closer. "Not here, you know. Somewhere we can think. See, I've got this idea for a feature but it's all locked up in here."

He points a single finger at his temple. "I need a writer, you know, someone who can write, someone who can help me get it down on paper." Here his hands open up before him in what he believes to be a posture of surrender: "Full credit, of course. I mean, you never know where these things can go."

I could think of nothing closer to my vision of hell than being entangled in some sort of project with Nigel. At least I had scraps of paper and a worn keyboard to show for unrequited efforts. Nigel, as far as I knew, had never actually begun a single thing.

Thankfully, I was saved from further conversation by Ellen, who had seen his car draw into the driveway and called him inside.

"Later, man," Nigel grinned conspiratorially, as he made his way toward the kitchen.

Fifteen minutes after, Sophie found me wandering the hallway like a stunned sheep.

"Hello, darlingness," Sophie said, taking my hand, "What in the world are you doing?"

"I think I'm lost. But I know my trail of breadcrumbs is around here somewhere," I remember saying, only half joking.

"Damn birds..." she began.

"...always eating my breadcrumbs." I completed the thought.

"Well, come with me," Sophie shifted direction toward the den with me in her wake. "I want to show you Ellen's new landscape."

The hall and the den seemed to be empty, everyone having gravitated into the living room where Maggie would be holding court and the talk would be of juried shows and corporate commissions. Others had moved to the backyard for extreme badminton, complete with grunts, screams and arguments about the best wide receiver in the league.

Sophie glanced back at me. "You've crawled up into your head to hide."

"Nigel cornered me. I had to go somewhere."

We were before the painting by then, a muddy wash of happy colors I assumed should resemble a seaside, hanging in a room trying too hard to be cheery.

"My God, he's my worst nightmare."

She attempted to soothe me: "Nigel? Nigel's harmless."

"He's not even that. I wake up in a sweat some nights terrified I'll become one of those people who never actually does anything, but talks endlessly about what they're going to do."

Sophie patted my hand in the way she did when she thought I was being overwrought and silly. She had a great patience for me that allowed her to listen to the longest, most incoherent tirades and extract a single intelligent thought to comment on. But I wasn't really in the mood for a tirade; I simply wanted to complain a little. I knew I was being overwrought and silly but I was enjoying it.

"I think Ellen's really getting so much better," she told me.

I leaned into her ear and whispered: "These guys, they're all holding on to the things I want to get rid of. They're solid in all the wrong ways."

I leaned out, working to turn my attention to the painting, but feeling the need to add: "Except Maggie and Jim. Maggie and Jim are cool."

"I like the way the clouds fade in and out of the blue here," she said, her fingers sweeping a high edge of the frame.

I realized the room was out of focus, the house was out of focus, the wall shuddering, the floor blurry. I stood before the painting, squinting until I could bring it to clarity, Sophie's finger providing a point of reference, a known object amidst so much unfamiliarity.

I decided it wasn't such a bad painting after all. Particularly the blue.

At Alex's, later, time changes shape. Slows or stops. We might have been at his party for days. The hard logic of the conversations at Ellen's earlier in the night has given way to a gentle chaos, the purposeful conversations surrendering to a kind of formless vitality at Alex's that could just as easily be wordless.

Sophie and I can break apart and reunite, then rediscover each other again in the living room or den.

We can fade into the sofa together for minutes at a time, kissing, petting, cooing to each other. It's safe and thrilling and I have a chance to live some high school vision of romance I could never achieve in high school. Our kisses are loose and wet by now, both of us tasting of stale coffee and beer. She slips her hand under my damp shirt and I cup her breast as she curls into me.

"I'll eat you up I love you so," she growls softly in my ear.

Josh falls into the sofa beside us and Sophie unfurls herself, curling her legs by my knees. She tells him: "Doug wants to start his own religion."

"Ah," he says with mock certainty, "now I understand. You were practicing the sacraments just now. You know, 'this is my body'..."

"I like to think of it as religious molestation," I reply. Sophie gives me a look.

"We're sitting at a restaurant the other day," she continues, "and he gets this idea. Wants us to buy a small figurine, like one of those Hummels, and put it on the table between us, so we can pray to it."

"We'll be Anthracites," I explain, afraid she won't get all of the details right. "We'll put the figure in a blue velvet bag, maybe a Chivas bag, pull it out and say some gibberish prayer. I'll hold a hand out to the waiter as he approaches, so he won't interrupt our ritual. Why not, the Christians do it."

Josh nods, considering the possibilities. "You know, there's a store on Fourth, Hamlet's or something. They sell those Hummels."

Sophie turns to me, her eyes wide. "We should make him a bishop!"

"We could give him a franchise."

"Even better!" Josh replies.

Josh wanders away, perhaps to consider nailing his own *Ninety-Five Theses* to a door somewhere. Sophie abandons me to retrieve new beers from the kitchen, then slides over the armrest of the sofa into my lap as if she were dropping into the leather seat of an expensive sports car.

It's like we're part of an extremely slow and gentle form of crowd-surfing, cresting on the warm generosity of the group. Everyone holds us up, passing us back and forth. We balance and float for a long time.

Some silent signal awakens us from our personal dream. Alex and Josh are handing out instruments from a box near the doorway, Alex passing them to Josh who walks them to the rest of us. There are drums of various sizes, tambourines and maracas and other rattly bangy things, a couple of guitars and a few wind instruments. There's even a toy piano and a Fisher Price xylophone.

It's a tradition with Alex and Sasha to have an impromptu jam at every party. The only condition: everyone must play an instrument they don't know how to play. Those of us who can't play anything are easy enough, but it's a challenge finding an instrument for someone like Josh.

People meander in from the porch and backyard, everyone sitting shoulder to shoulder wherever they can find a space; it's some bohemian version of a sweat lodge. We're ranged around the living room, some in chairs or leaning against the wall. Sophie and I are on the floor near the television, which has been turned off in profound deference to the ritual. I have a large skin-covered drum someone had dropped into my hands while Sophie has a small white ceramic drum in her lap. By now, Josh is leaning in the doorway, struggling to force sound from a flute while Alex plucks Josh's guitar like a harp.

Someone starts the first song with a simple rhythm and everyone else clamors in one at a time, Josh finally managing short chirping sounds on the downbeat. Sophie is pretty good at rhythms that sound complicated to me. I have no talent whatsoever, struggling to maintain a simple four-four beat in time with everyone else.

The songs gather a gradual momentum, each player struggling to find a way to enter and then a way to keep up. The music swells suddenly, unexpectedly, with great force, then dies to nearly a mutter just as unpredictably. In the quiet bits I can discern Angela, far in the corner with only a tiny bell or Bill, so much beard and bushy hair I can only really see his eyes and make out the fierce concentration he brings to a tiny toy guitar. It's a great lumbering din, reminding me of a heavy rusted truck bouncing down a rutted road, losing things out the back at each bump.

Sasha bangs on a pot in time from the kitchen where she's concocting some sort of vegetarian stew she'll serve us later for breakfast with great tufts of fresh bread heaped in stoneware bowls.

Now and then, between songs, we trade instruments. At one point, I'm playing a wonderful talking drum. It fits between my arm and my body and, by squeezing it I can change the pitch. It doesn't make me a better drummer, but it makes me feel like a better drummer.

We play on and on; some leaving the room, replaced by others, handing off their instruments in the doorway. Songs don't so much end as shrug and shuttle quietly out the back, allowing a moment or two of ringing silence before the next rhythm erupts.

The room smells like a single, damp and exhausted body by now, the body of a five-year-old wavering stubbornly at the edge of sleep. It's after 4 and the remaining guests are playing just to stay awake for Sasha's meal. The scents of stew and baking bread waft through the rooms, carried by the night breeze from the open windows. Some doze against the wall, others have collapsed into chairs or on the sofa. The gamers are all outside on the deck sharing a joint.

The music has become a slow, groaning drone punctuated by the two-note combinations Josh has managed to teach himself. Sophie is asleep at my shoulder, one hand in her lap, the other upturned on the skin of her drum. Now and then, I notice my hands scruffing out their own rhythm. Only a few of us are still playing out of stubbornness or persistence, or because we like the tender, primitive wail we've managed to bring into the room. Alex glances up from the guitar he's plucking. There's a faraway look in his eye and when our gaze meets I know I probably have the same expression.

I imagine the scraps of paper on my desk back home folding gently into themselves for the night like morning glories closing in the cool, dark air. I fall asleep leaning into Sophie, knowing they'll wake us for breakfast.

5

Sophie glances up from where she kneels on the sidewalk. Her features have shifted, become fluid; there's a flickering glow in her eyes. She's searching my face for a response. A softness and a question, dark and mysterious and terrifying. She's inviting me, something in her body inviting me.

And something turns in my chest to meet her, a new and undiscovered organ locking into place, matching her frequency, bringing with it a feeling that doesn't have a name, a new and intimate communication between us.

I want to turn away. I want to smile and shrug off the exchange. She doesn't say a word, her eyes returning to the little boy before her.

She'd seen him coming half a block away, toddling along beside his mother, his attention completely focused on the ice cream cone in his hand. He turned it, working his tongue diligently around the low edge. His mother, a tall slender woman with dry straw hair, occasionally dropped her palm to the top of his head, steering him ahead of her.

Sophie squatted in his path, bringing herself to his height as he approached. "How's the ice cream?"

He came to a halt directly before her, stopping completely with a bump, then turning his body in her direction as if each movement must be distinct, as much as he could manage while holding ice cream. He registered her question, eyes flashing, his attention reluctantly deflected.

"It's great!" he told her, words high and clipped, body rocking slightly on his heels.

Lately, Sophie had begun to notice children. For me, babies and toddlers were like the homeless; they never really came into focus; they simply faded into the blur of my world. I never noticed them unless Sophie made a point of it.

And she'd begun to make a point of it; sometimes with cooing sounds and sighs, sometimes with a quick snuggle and rub. She'd stop to comment on their pretty dress or their soccer ball. She'd play silent games with kids in grocery stores, making faces they would match across aisles in the checkout line.

I'm struggling to bring the kid into focus. The mother has come to a stop beside him with much the same restless annoyance I'd seen in dog owners when their charges pause to mark a post. He's probably about three, wearing a Yankee jersey and ball cap with khaki shorts. I'm struck by his tiny sneakers and the way his socks are folded over. It's something his mother had done, obviously, but it doesn't occur to me then; I simply think he's an extraordinarily meticulous child.

The ice cream overruns his cone, dripping into his fingers. He watches Sophie patiently, still rocking, licking the chocolate absently from his lips.

"What flavor did you get?" Sophie asks, easing to her knees.

And she looks up at me, something in her entire body changing shape almost imperceptibly, becoming more round and full for an instant, drawing me toward her. There's something frightening and bottomless blooming in her eyes when I look down at her.

And we have seen each other.

"Chocolate Chip." He cocks his head toward her, extending his goopy hand. "Want some?" His arm is locked forward, his eyes on her face and her tongue.

"Tyler," his mother drops her hand to the boy's head. He glances back and up toward her, his arm still extended.

Sophie cocks her head, winking at Tyler. "No thanks. I just had lunch." She refuses to look up to the mother: "Nice of you to offer, though."

Tyler shrugs softly. "Okay." He takes a bite from the closest side, smearing it along his cheek and the tip of his nose in the process. Then he turns away, bumping off, further down the sidewalk.

"Bu-bye," he calls back over his shoulder.

His mother manages the smallest constipated smile and nothing else. She follows him.

It's late Saturday afternoon and we're a block from Sophie's studio. She's dropping by before her night at the Scrawl to pick up a couple of brushes for Natalie, who'd found cans of purple and white house paint abandoned on a street corner and wants to paint her bicycle to resemble a zebra. Sophie will open up in about an hour but I have a rare Saturday night off and I've rented movies to fill the time until she's free again.

She rises up to me, her arm interlacing mine, her body resting against mine, eyes following the boy as he disappears around the corner. I take a few steps forward while she leans into me. We weave across the sidewalk, a drunken boat attempting to tack.

There's an open door between us now, a door we watch together. Sophie sighs. It's nearly inaudible bubbling up from somewhere deep, a place even she doesn't recognize. She can't resist a surreptitious glance, her face tilting toward my shoulder. I pretend not to notice.

It's not just this liminal, voiceless question between us, articulated by the cast of her eyes from her meeting with the boy. I'm terrified by the way her look touches something in me which shifts to respond. I watch myself melt into her wish, responding without thought, in complete agreement.

It's not just the idea of a child, but the line extending into a future where there has been no space before, just a set of daydreams and vague wishes. A future opening up that feels, in its vastness, oppressive and suffocating.

We're crisscrossing the sidewalk like talentless participants in a three-legged race. Sophie's arm curled around mine, our fingers laced. She is all I could ever want.

"I don't know about kids; they're awfully small and smug." I shrug, attempting a self-mocking sarcasm. "They're like parasites...or property. People acquire them the same way they get dogs or IKEA furniture. Most people who want children should just buy an end table instead."

I feel her draw away then catch herself, intention overriding instinct, settling back closer though not as close as before. She snorts at my misanthropic nature, pinching my bare arm hard with her free hand. It hurts. Her expression twists into a kind of mock-demonic glare. She pinches me again. I nod, accepting my punishment, watching as something bright and delicate recedes within her.

We make it to the Scrawl, presenting an enthusiastic Natalie with her brushes. We're holding hands and Sophie is close. I can feel her heat, but I have mapped a stance just to the right of us, as if I'm walking one step behind.

Years have passed now. And years don't help. Years turn events into a story I haven't chosen. No more or less true than anything else. One more version. As if I needed another.

It's only now and then that I can catch some thread of a truth not muddied by the weight of narrative. A thing that isn't part of a journey or a process. A thing that simply is. Like the moment Sophie knelt before the boy with the ice cream.

I did my best to apologize for the rest of the night. While she was working and I was sitting at home watching old French movies. After *The 400 Blows*, I dropped by the Scrawl with ice cream, Cherry Vanilla, knowing she'd need a snack around 10. After *Breathless*, I brought coffee (good coffee, because the coffee at the Scrawl was an embarrassment) and two peanut butter cookies from the shop a block away.

She turned her back to the chaos of the room, to the dim clatter of the band and the bounce of a hundred loud conversations.

She leaned against the counter, legs angling out, feet resting on a low shelf opposite.

I enjoyed a moment of her body, its lanky diagonal sleek before me. The noise and jumble of the room faded while I appreciated the full length of her legs from the cut-off jeans all the way to the tops of her Chuck Taylors. She never wore shorts when she painted. She was too messy, she said, it was too hard getting everything off her skin. I didn't often see her legs in public, so it was a treat to suddenly come upon them, brown and muscular, slanted before me.

She twisted the lid from her cup and took a tentative sip, glancing down the length of the bar behind me, then catching me in her glance.

"You've got to let me..." she began, as if the afternoon's conversation was continuing without interval, the distance from the sidewalk to the bar an illusion.

"I know..." I put my finger to her lips, still warm from the coffee. "You're right. I know..." I slid my hand into the small of her back, just to feel her warmth and the delicious press of her body. "I'm sorry, I really am a dick sometimes."

After Chloe from 9 to 5, I returned, watching the last customer stumble toward the door and into the amber streetlight glow of the night. I'd manhandled a keg to the bar for Sophie, sliding it under the counter after she'd attached the hoses. She stood upright, leaning against the bar, throwing her head back, stretching, staring at the ceiling, exhaling a deep breath.

The band had stopped playing a half hour earlier and the customers had slowly drained away; all the sheep wandering from the pen to find a new place to be lost. Two skeletal, bearded guys are tugging equipment through the side door and into the parking lot.

When the band finally leaves, Sophie clicks on the overhead lights; they throw hard shadows to the floor. The place is damp with stale beer, stale perfume and stale pheromones. The overheads always make the Scrawl look even more like the Dive at the Edge of the Universe. I can see every nick in the mismatched chairs, every chip in the Formica. The tattered band posters papering the far wall.

A sofa in the corner is missing a leg, which has been replaced by a brick. For some reason, the limp appendage of a bra trails beneath it, white and curling, abandoned, forlorn.

We're alone save Alex and Sasha, who'd turned up for a beer an hour before. Sasha perches on a stool at the bar, legs crossed at the knees swinging her sandaled foot, one hand resting on her half empty bottle. Alex meanders around the small raised stage thirty feet away, scuffing his soles on the floor.

We're at that point in the night when we have to decide whether to go home for bed or re-start in a new direction. Alex and Sasha are obviously as unsure as Sophie and I, lounging restlessly, awaiting inspiration or direction. Each of us are hoping one of the others might rouse us from our lethargy.

Sophie's turned the music off, so the room is unusually quiet. I can hear her breathing next to me as she takes a moment before closing out the cash register. I point to the purpling bruise on my arm, nudging Sophie with my shoulder. "You hurt me."

"You deserved it," she assured me, not the least bit penitent.

I nodded. "I deserved it."

She rubs the bruise with the flat of her hand then pushes away gently toward the register. I watch her punch it open and begin to stack cash on the wooden counter.

I'm trying to decide whether I want another beer. Something about the decision is the hinge upon which the rest of the night might turn. So I ponder it, absently watching Sophie's hand smooth the bills.

"Now, what's all this?" Alex calls from the stage in his usual mocking tone. I turn toward him and he's smiling but the smile goes wrong. It sags, and doesn't so much fade as the rest of him evaporates behind it.

There's a rush from the door and a dark wave of motion. Instinctively I step forward to the end of the bar, in front of Sophie. A hard hand on my chest stops me.

Two men in dark ski masks. The smaller one lagging behind. The large one stands tall and broad before me, arm extended.

Hand on my chest. Hanging limp at his side in the other hand is a shotgun. The smaller guy, shorter, thinner, motions Alex toward the bar with a pistol.

The hand drops from my chest. The blood that had been churning in my ears, drains away. I'm terribly cold. The sound returns to the room and I feel Sophie behind me, motionless by the register. The skinny guy herds Alex beside Sasha.

"What do you want?" Alex asks, incredulous. No one bothers to answer him.

The big guy motions Sophie toward me, directing us to the other side of the counter. We shuffle awkwardly near Alex and Sasha, the big guy moving up the other side of the counter behind us, the skinny one waving his gun in our direction.

"Phones on the counter," he says. His voice is tight and clipped with a slight tremulous shudder. We dig into our pockets and drop them to the bar. He slides the pile down the counter toward the end.

It's the first chance I have to look at Sophie. She's pale, her face taut, eyes darting around the room. I take her hand and her arm is stiff, her palm cold. When I touch her, her eyes come to my face; she's blank and very far away.

"Look," I say, hearing the tremor in my voice, "we don't want any trouble. Just take what you want."

"We will," the man behind me says, snapping the bills from the counter. His voice is hard like a heavy stone dropped to the floor.

I turn toward him as he punches open the register. His hands are broad, his fingers thick. He lifts the drawer, fishing out a couple of larger bills from beneath. As he withdraws them, I see his hand tremble and this terrifies me even more. We are six frightened people, two with guns.

Sasha is motionless on the stool beside me. She's drawn up her legs and turned into Alex's chest. The small guy before us shifts from one foot to the other, one arm extended with the gun, the other hand hooked into his jeans pocket by a thumb. His ski mask is a dark polyester knit with a royal blue stripe circling it. His eyes are blinking quickly. His eyes are brown and small.

I look to Alex. His hand cradles the back of Sasha's head, his fingers opening a little to me in a question I can't answer. Sophie's nails are digging into the palm of my hand. I hear the man behind me breathing, it's hoarse and ragged. He's a smoker, I can smell it now, on his clothes. I turn back toward him but he's moving to the end of the counter, stuffing bills into a small zippered bag.

There's an instant of hesitation as he comes around the bar. I believe I can see this. Or, later I think I had seen it. My mind inventing the possibility of breath, or a different place to stand. An instant in which he almost calls his partner and they almost move toward the door.

The moment opens up, then it closes down hard. He looks at us. His eyes are dark and empty.

"Now we just need the cashbox. Then, we'll be on our way."

I put my hand on Sophie's arm, pulling the other hand free from her grasp, taking a step forward. "I can get it for you. It's back in the office." I motion toward the door along the back wall, curling my free arm back and around her body as if I might make her disappear.

"I want her." He raises the end of the shotgun slightly in Sophie's direction.

She takes a sharp inhalation and, in an instant, steps around and is past me. "This way."

He follows her to the door. They go in. He closes the door behind them.

I'm standing, away from the bar, hands at my sides. Sasha sobs quietly into Alex's chest. The skinny guy hasn't said a word. He's watching me, shifting foot to foot. I stare at the barrel of his gun. He blinks at me.

My vision breaks into loose images, and my eyes skitter over the room. I realize my hands are clenching, unclenching, in a ragged breathlessness. The skinny guy's dark jeans are dirty, with dust at the knees and smears near one pocket. His t-shirt is faded, shapeless. He keeps sagging then raising himself erect, as if he can't decide whether to collapse or explode. He lowers his arm for an instant, moving the gun to the other hand and extending it. His palms are sweaty.

There's no sound behind the closed door. It would only take a moment to go to the chipped grey metal desk in the corner by the empty kegs, open the locked drawer and take out the box. It would only take a moment to stuff the bills into the bag.

I look at the empty stage. There are wet smears on the floor reflecting light, spilled beer or sweat, collections of grime at the edges. Abandoned plastic cups on the floor. Scraps of torn paper.

The light is hot. The room is hot. The brick beneath the sofa. The band posters blanketing the far wall, eyes peering out. I'm trying hard to breathe. I'm trying hard not to be stupid. I look back to Alex. He makes a point of not looking at me. There's no sound behind the closed door.

The skinny guy's getting restless. Tired, bored. He's watching the door. I'm trying not to watch the door. I'm listening. All I can hear are the sounds outside the building, the rest of the night going on with its business. Cars pass in the street with a hiss. There are birds in some distant tree, noisily anticipating dawn. Not too far away, a siren.

His gun looks heavy and old. It's the color of worn tires. His fingers are clenched around it as if he's afraid he might drop it. The stock is grey between his fingers. He looks at me, his eyes traveling across my face then down to my shoes. He looks at Alex and Sasha. There's a slit of moisture on the mask where his mouth must be.

I stand away from the bar, arms at my sides. Alex rubs Sasha's hair. I can smell her shampoo. A distant airplane overhead. A car horn. The slight squeak of the skinny guy's soles on the floor. His hand comes up from his pocket to adjust the mask, pulling it down toward his neck. The neon beer sign. The band members staring out from the wall. My lungs are wrenching, my muscles contracting. The world is slowing to a stop. The skinny guy watches the door, turning his body in its direction. I try not to watch the door. Listening.

We wait in place. We wait a long time. The skinny guy and I. Waiting together. Alex and Sasha have faded, vanished. The room is very large, heat baking from the floor, and the space between us is vast.

The door clicks and I am moving. I don't really see where I'm going, I'm not paying attention. I shoulder past the big guy in the threshold, his body hard and immobile, tilting slightly in its skin as I push by. He stops in the doorway, turning to look at me.

The room is still. Sophie slumps in the office chair, head down, her face curtained by her hair, arms loose at her sides, palms upturned in the chair. I come up in front of her, both of my hands on her shoulders. She doesn't look up.

I glance back to the threshold. The large man is there, half turned toward me. The shotgun dangles at his leg. In his other hand, he's absently fingering Sophie's ceramic cat. I look in the direction of his eyes but I can't see them, only the darkness of his face, his mask. The large fingers turning the figure. He shifts toward me but then loses interest. Slowly his hand comes down to his side and the cat slips from his fingers, shattering at his feet. And then he is gone.

Sophie stares at the floor. Her bare legs are dirty. Her t-shirt is pulled to the side. Her face is wet, her eyes red. She has a small bruise purpling at her left temple. I touch her shoulder gently.

"Sophie, are you okay?" Something in her stirs, something rousing in her shallow breath. I kneel at her feet, my hands resting on her knees. She doesn't see me.

"Sophie?"

She raises her head imperceptibly, her eyes make a flickering contact with mine, and she tips forward with a sob. The full weight of her body takes me to the floor and we fall together, her head at my chest. I pull myself upright, my legs to the side, drawing her into me. She's limp at first, arms and legs scattered, sprawled on the floor, her sobs shallow and clipped between quick breaths. I try to gather her in.

I feel the wail rising in her, feel it jut out like a rolling darkness, her entire body unspooling into it as it leaves her and fills the room, tearing the air around me. The floor falls away and great sobs wrench up from her waist, her body curling around mine, clutching and releasing like a fist, tighter each time.

My breath catches and my limbs will not move, I will not breathe, clinging to her and her terror as the room spins. And I am crying too, without noticing until tears fall into her hair. My shoulders are shaking, pulling her toward me, a deep cold opening within me, an emptiness.

She cries and I hold her. Her arms move up from my waist along my back to clutch at my shoulders, and I hold her as her body clenches with sobs, her heat dense and hard along my chest, in my face. I hold her as tightly as I can, the ridges of her ribs between my fingers, the top of her head at my chin.

Sasha appears in the doorway, stopping short, terrified to enter the room. Her head bobs back to Alex, who takes a step toward me, saying something about going for help, then turns to leave. Sasha lingers at the threshold, unsure, tears running down her cheeks now, arms rising and falling at her side. Then she slowly recedes, backing from the doorway, out of sight.

I'm angry at her, both for being in the doorway and for leaving, because she is a witness to our terror and because she abandons us. I want to shout for her to come back, to do something. I don't know what I want.

I want to have convinced Sophie to call in sick today. To stay home with me and lie in bed and watch old movies. I want to have kissed her and said, "Don't go. Call Natalie. She'll work for you, she needs the hours."

I want to have thought to lock the Scrawl doors once the band left.

I want to have found something heavy in my hand the instant the big man appeared before me, to have smashed his head before he ever said a word.

Someone has hurt her. I've done nothing.

I want to have done something.

My face burns hot. I try to be still for Sophie; I try to be calm for her.

Her body contracts around mine, her hands clutching at my shoulders. I kiss the top of her head, making promises.

The world is very small, gnarled and airless. The world pushes in at us. I hold her as tightly as I can, her legs curled around me, her fingers digging into my skin.

"I'm sorry," I say. "I'm so sorry."

I say it over and over.

TWO

6

We never fully lose the people we once were. The world changes, we change. We are no longer 8 or 12 or 21, but those selves never leave us.

Sometimes I want to believe my life is a seamless whole. I try to imagine that transformation from caterpillar to butterfly as a gradual karmic flowering, but I can't hold the picture without recognizing its absurdity. My experience won't line up with the images; there's a gap between the two, some unbridgeable magnetism pushing them apart.

All these people I've been, I am still. They're dolls nested inside me, uncovered or cracked open by a scent, a song, a glimpsed gesture or face; whatever illuminates a memory for an instant. My selves are constantly sparking in different directions like heat lightning in a distant bank of cloud. The eight-year-old exists simultaneously with my current self, especially if ice cream is involved. When I meet a woman for the first time I'm always fifteen, always the twitchy teenager with the averted eyes.

I try to carve out some sense of who I am between my selves. I want to believe I'm more than simply an accumulation of years eventually accruing a hardening core through a steady drip of experience like a stalactite in the deep underground. I believe in a self, but I only see it when it chooses to be seen, never when I search for it. It comes as a sudden break of cloud and banner of blue sky, or as singular pockets of clarity, small and shifting.

Or, perhaps, the separating selves matter less, in the way the whole of the performance is more important than the individual characters in a play. Each character's orbit defines an aspect which is only truly clear when the curtain drops and I'm left with the sensation of the full performance, an experience I struggle to bring to coherence, often condensed in the end to a simple gesture or a single exchange.

Now and then, a glimpse of a self in which I recognize something.

I'm never just one person, but to accept this is to give up a certain illusion of control with the artifice of unity. It's to understand that I rationalize my past every moment of every day, shifting my thoughts and memories around to accommodate themselves to the things I've already done, as if they were accomplished by a singular person; to present myself with reasons for my actions and a narrative for my life.

In writing, I keep some of the control, in life not so much. I prefer writing.

Eight years ago, Sophie seduced me into humanity with her and somehow made it easy. She lured me from my Cro-Magnon, teen-aged past. I think it was all her sheer force of will. I was pretty happy in my Cro-Magnon past. I'm not sure I would ever have left it on my own. I was the ape in *2001* waking one day to find the monolith. She made me happy and grateful, she allowed me the belief in a beautiful and opening world. She changed my life.

That's what our first real love does. It makes us a different person, more a person than we thought we could be. It draws us from the muck of our past, establishing us on new ground. We feel we have discovered ourselves. We feel we have been seen, for the first time, truly seen. We feel whole, yet unexplored. We feel whole if only because we are seen for ourselves freed somehow, for a moment, from who we were just a moment before.

I'd had teachers before impressed with my intelligence and curiosity, high school girlfriends impressed with my smug arrogance, friends impressed with my bottomless scorn, but Sophie saw something else and she wouldn't allow me to turn away from it and she wouldn't allow my moron nature and she loved me. I'll always be who I was with Sophie but, perhaps, I can also be someone else.

So, it's wasn't the past that weighed on me as I drove to her house but the obvious obstacle of a future, a future not simply an extension of that past. We'd both changed in eight years, I knew. I wanted us to be more than relics for each other. To be new seemed the only way of justifying the past. It also seemed impossible.

I'm nervous and itchy. It's one part excitement, one part dread, my mind spinning in a hundred competing scenarios and, much as I try, I cannot seem to return to the mythical pure state: the state of simply being happy to see Sophie again. One moment I imagine us in bed together, the next I see myself bringing her coffee every morning; one moment we're devising a multi-media project, the next all the old resentments return, all the boiling pain bubbles up and we're powerless before it. One moment I'm falling in love again, the next moment I'm not. Both are equally terrifying.

I buy a box of flowery stationery and a small goofy doll at the Family Dollar in Barwick but on the way to the car I know I can never give them to Sophie. I open the door and toss them into the back seat.

I fold my hands on the wheel, staring through the windshield at the desolate parking lot wriggling in the convection waves of early autumn. The lot is flat and square, its lines newly painted. The entire strip mall looks as if it's patiently awaiting the moment it becomes a ghost town. I get out of the car again.

Sophie's house, when I find it, is small, about thirty yards off the road in the center of a large, flat lot. It had probably been an old farmhouse but now it's hard to tell since it's wrapped in blue siding and topped with a fresh roof. There's a low deck facing the road and wide circles of stacked stone in the front and side yards which were once flower beds. The dried skeletons of tall plants lean against one another in the beds fronting the porch.

A small red car with a crumpled front quarter panel waits at the edge of the driveway as I slow to turn. The man inside is in his twenties, stocky, with a bushy red beard. He looks puzzled when I stop, crooking a finger on the steering wheel to motion him forward. He studies me curiously then smiles, small white teeth breaking through the chop of his beard. He waves and recedes toward town.

Sophie hadn't said anything about a boyfriend or a husband and I, of course, hadn't asked. I never think to ask those kinds of things in the moment, I only later wish I had.

My car comes to rest in the loose gravel beside a battered green Subaru Outlander that must be Sophie's. It's dusty and dinged, bumper stickers plastered over the back hatch. A floppy straw hat and large white sunglasses on the passenger seat. The back seat folded down, an easel resting diagonally along the length of the interior.

The car makes me smile. I stand beside it in the still noon air for a moment. It's possible I stroke the hard shell of the hood, clouding my fingers with dust and a glaze of autumn pollen, before moving toward the porch.

There's a swish of the weather stripping sliding over the floor like a rush of released air when Sophie opens the door. Reflexively, my eyes fall to the sound then jerk themselves upward. My breath stops for an instant; I'm gazing into her pale hazel eyes, which are limitless, and struggling to take in her frail image. She's thinner, slightly stooped, her skin a gauzy white revealing bluish veins in her neck and hands. Her face remains striking, a starker impression of her previous features; the ridges of her cheekbones are more defined, her eyes a little further back, her lips thinner and paler.

A bright red kerchief is tied around her head and wispy clouds of fine hair curl irregularly over its border. She wears a plain silver chain at her throat and the skin around her powder blue blouse seems nearly transparent.

There's an instant like a sigh, a release for me, the kind of smiling acceptance I feel when I've spent twenty minutes searching for my car keys only to find them in exactly the right place and I think to myself, "Of course that's where they were. They could never be anywhere else." The things I'd thought were out of place were in place all along.

We're standing at her doorstep. I'm on one side and she's on the other and we simply stare at each other for an instant. She's watching the feelings crawl along my face, tilts her head to one side and smiles. It's a broad, hopeful smile; it's Sophie's smile.

"Doug..." she says, as if she's said my name ten thousand times, "it's great to see you."

"Hey Sophie," I return the smile, stepping over the threshold to wrap my arms around her without considering whether it's appropriate or not. Her ribs are prominent beneath my fingers; they seem to tremble slightly, adrift somehow within the frame of her body. She drapes her arms lightly at my shoulders and we float like that for a moment, eddying hesitantly in a pool at the edge of a fast moving stream.

I take a step back, balancing my gift forward: "I brought you a present."

I extend the spaghetti squash I'd found at the Safeway. She laughs and takes it from me.

"Come on in," she says, backing from the door so I can enter the room. "Thankfully, you arrive when I'm too exhausted to be embarrassed by how I look."

I step into the cool of the house. "You look great."

She waves away the comment, her hand low at her hip.

"The bandanna really sets off the whole ensemble."

"Yeah," she smiles again, this smile turned sideways, partly to herself, as she studies the squash. "I want the Angel of Death to be able to find me. Hate for Him to go to the next house over, pick on someone else."

Her eyes come up to mine. She shrugs, her fingers lightly touching my arm. "I'm sorry. I didn't realize I was using my out-loud voice."

There's nothing to say. So, we don't say anything. Until I think of something.

"There was a guy pulling out of the driveway when I turned in." Everything about this is a question.

Sophie nods, her eyes brightening.

"That's Randy, he's a Hospice nurse. I can't afford Hospice anymore but he still comes by to check on me. On his lunch hour, or after work. He's a really sweet guy, a saint really. I don't know how people do things like that day after day."

She's testing the weight of the squash, her hand rising and falling. "Anyway. Let me show you around my humble hovel." She explains the house had been her mother's; not the house she'd grown up in, but one her mother bought later in life when she needed something smaller.

"Thank God it's paid for, 'cause I'd never be able to afford it. Lord knows where I'd be, if not for Mom."

She tells me the neighborhood is good and quiet and she's become friends with many of the neighbors, most of whom are quite a bit older. Ruby, just down the street, stops in at least once a week. Marybeth, on the other side of the road, sometimes brings her a chicken pie or a cobbler, and her grandson Toby mows the lawn once a week for ten dollars.

She used to love the yard and, before she got sick, she'd had lots of flowers and a small vegetable garden, but she'd had to let that go. "Mom was the gardener. She'd work out in the yard until the sun went down, sometimes in the dark. I'd just try to take care of what she started." The backyard was still nice and she was hoping we could have tea there after lunch.

I stand beside her as she sweeps her hand over the living room. It's bright, the sheer curtains at the front windows diffusing the light to a warm cream. A large, puffy couch, also cream, and a matching love seat at an angle around a wide table. There's a small television on a stand stuck in a corner of the room. There are cut flowers in delicate vases on every table alongside swathes of fabric or a mound of colored pebbles, dried leaves, or bits of wood, objects Sophie found interesting or beautiful. It's something about Sophie that hasn't changed.

She points out paintings on the wall and mentions the names of the painters as if I should know them but I don't. They're abstracts in different styles, some in simple, still geometric shapes. Others are wipes and shades in grey and white. We stand before the one she says is her favorite: rows of squares stacked upon each other, grading gently from white to grey to black. She tells me she often comes to rest within it for a moment, listening to its quiet simple music, settling back into herself.

Behind the living room, at the back of the house is a pass-through; on the other side is a tiny dining room then a small kitchen, much different than the dank alley of her kitchen so many years ago. This one is brighter, cleaner, with wide windows over the counters and sink. A small pot simmers on the stove, its lid rattling discreetly, puffs of steam escaping beneath.

I'm watching her as she describes the kitchen before she remodeled it, watching the flash in her eyes, the curl of her lip. Her hands fashioning the room before her, conjuring an old image and bringing her own form to it until it takes shape before us. Suddenly I'm in her space, in our space, in this remembered never-forgotten location of our intimacy.

The heat of her and I, of our past, rises into my face and I want to touch her, want to kiss her. My body has its own logic. I swallow hard, holding my self in place. My body backs down, shuffling into the distance.

She takes me down the hall, darker than the rest of the house. She turns on the overhead so I can see the framed pictures lining the walls. We stop before them, shifting right then left, our bare arms bumping now and then with a dim spark as we move one to another.

"It was a project I took on a few years ago," she tells me, her fingers lingering over the smooth ridge of a frame. "I started before Mom died, but she didn't get to see it finished. She had all these old pictures, jumbled up in shoeboxes, pushed to the back of drawers. All this kind of invisible history shoved into nooks and crannies."

My body remembers her, it won't be still. She aches in my legs, my chest. My body moves up close, the heat of memory palpable.

Her finger stops at a large old lady in a shapeless patterned dress standing before the door of a farmhouse. Her long hair is white, braided then knotted atop her head. She wears a faded apron. Her hand is a blur, coming up as if to castigate the photographer.

"This is my Mom's grandmother, Cassie Mae. I never met her but I hear she was quite a piece of work. Twelve children, drove the tractor, helped butcher the hogs. Lived to be 92. I think this picture was taken some time in the Twenties."

Sophie lingers there, giving me time to study the photo, the eyes peering out from a completely different world, knowing things I would never know. A hard world brimming just behind the image, everything out of frame reflected in the cast of the eyes and the gaze.

We spend time in the hallway, anchoring ourselves to a more distant history to distract us from our own. I can feel its pressure behind me, I can see it now and then as Sophie's eyes slip from mine, shifting instead to an older photo. As we talk about history, our own keeps leaking in, as a sudden flush and warmth or a nervous catch in our voices.

Sophie introduces me to various members of her family, both threads of her genealogy finally meeting, winding around one another through a blur of faces to arrive at: Sophie in a high chair, face smeared with birthday cake; Sophie eight years old, tiny and grinning atop a huge chestnut horse; Sophie and her mother, arms circling waists in the center of the room at her first gallery show.

"The past becomes important now," she says, "in a way it never was before."

At the end of the hallway where the photos give way to doors on either side, Sophie seems momentarily confused about how we have arrived. She turns up the hallway again, a cursory toss of her wrist into one room, then the other, as if she's lost interest.

The master bedroom, at the front of the house, has been converted to her studio. In one corner is a desk, its surface covered with stacked papers and books, the large flat screen of a computer. The rest of the room is open: an easel against the longest blank wall, canvases resting against the opposite wall, some blank, some just begun or in various stages of completion. Small shelves are lined with re-used bottles and small buckets, two jars of brushes, a stack of stained cloths. A roll of newsprint lies on the floor with a folded plastic sheet.

"I haven't been able to work in a long time...." Her fingers touch my arm at the threshold and I know she doesn't want to go in.

We turn to the bedroom behind us, again without entering. There's only a wide bed with a thick white duvet. A small bedside table, littered with bottles. Here too, the walls are bare.

"I like the white," she tells me, as if it explains everything. Maybe it does. We turn and make our way back up the hallway.

She leads me to a dining room chair with a view of the kitchen and brings me a glass of water: "You just sit here and talk to me while I get everything together."

"Sure there's nothing I can do?"

"Nope." She pulls an apron over her head. It's black, with large orange clown fish. Beneath the bandanna, the orange makes her look like a large cartoon flame. "It's nothing complicated. Just some stir-fried vegetables with a little chicken. I made a peanut sauce too. Not too spicy."

"Sounds great."

"I did learn to cook eventually."

"Not me. If I learned to cook, twenty people would be out of a job."

Sophie gives me a laugh, opening the fridge and withdrawing several plastic containers of cut vegetables and chicken. She's put a flat saucepan on the stove and turned off the rice. I watch her lace a thin stream of oil into the pan.

"You shouldn't have gone to so much trouble, really."

"It's no trouble." She tosses a bit of chopped onion and garlic into the oil. There's a tense sizzle, the pungent scent filling the room. "For the longest time even the smell of food made me ill. Now, it feels good to cook for someone again."

She stirs the vegetables with a wooden spoon, several swift turns. She shakes the pan by the handle and spins to me.

"It's really nice to have you here. It makes me happy."

It's an old smile, rooted in something far away, bringing a certain light to her face and eyes. I'm warm again, feeling myself flush, as if years were simply another room I'd just stepped away from.

Sophie turns back to the stove to break the moment, returning us both to our memories. She adds the chicken, dropping it into the pan from the plastic container, stirring again, the food noisily protesting the heat. Memory has a different weight with Sophie in the room; it changes texture and depth. It's not image, but the sensation of her hand in mine, her head at my shoulder, the scent of her neck, a presence and a need, the emptiness she once occupied. Now and then, the occasional fear ripples cold across my shoulders. It's a fear of us, of falling into the well of us.

She's talking about running into Roger at the grocery store, staring a bit too intently at the pan before her. How he stood to the side of the aisle gawping at her and she'd been unsure whether he simply wasn't confident he recognized her, or was too terrified to approach.

"Finally, I had to go over to him," she says, still watching the vegetables. "I was afraid he'd just stand there until closing time in some kind of catatonic stupor. When I said hello he broke out of it. He was Roger again and could talk to me. Of course, then I had to explain myself as best I could, the diagnosis and all that, and Roger had to figure out an excuse to get away as soon as possible."

"I'm glad you ran into him. I might never have known." I wait until she makes eye contact: "You could have called me, you know. When I think about you going through all that by yourself..."

"I know I could have called," she sighs. "I just felt like I couldn't. I mean, how do you call up after years and years and say, 'Oh hello. Just thought I'd ring to say I have cancer, and how are things with you?'"

Sophie adds carrot then, green pepper, stirring briskly. She has some kind of spice mixture she crushes between her fingers, sprinkling it over the pan.

"How could I ask you, when I needed so much?" There's a sound like a short gasp. She doesn't give me time to respond.

"Besides, I had a boyfriend then. At the beginning, anyway. Zack."

"Zack?"

"Yeah, Zack-the-Asshole. Zack, the 'this is too heavy and I can't be around this kind of negativity right now' asshole. He never returned my best photography books either."

"Bastard!"

Sophie chuckles. I like to see her chuckle. "Yes! Bastard!"

"Well, you could have called."

"I know I could have."

"I would've liked that."

"That's good to know."

"I should have called you," I admit.

She shakes the spoon in my direction. "You should have."

"Well, I did," I remind her. "Eventually."

Sophie nods, stirring the pan. The windows behind her are fogging slowly and a feather of hair at her temple has grown damp. Her body is sloped into the apron. I can see the curve of her back, the bare flesh of her neck.

"I've been stalking you for years, you know," I confess. It's a way of not saying something else.

"It's you at my bedroom window on Thursday nights!" she squeals. "I always thought it was Toby."

"It probably is Toby," I tell her. "I'm more sophisticated than that. I use the inter-nets!"

I take a sip from my glass for dramatic effect. "I raid your Facebook page on a regular basis to see what you've been up to. I google you, find articles about your shows. I drove up to D.C. a few years ago for that big gallery show. It was a beautiful thing." I continue while she stirs, stealing glances in my direction, "I just stood there in the center of the room with all of your work around me. I was so happy; I mean I was happy for you and the show. But it was more than that. I don't know, I'm not saying it very well. It just did something to me."

"Well, thank you. That's sweet."

I cock my head, suddenly moody. "No, it's not sweet. I'm not saying it to be nice. I'm not patting you on the head. I'm saying, in my completely inarticulate way, that it really meant something to me, something wide and deep and lasting."

Sophie gives the pan a stir, laying the spoon to the side. She marches to stand before me, looking down. "You're absolutely right. It just made me nervous, that's all."

Her hand comes out toward mine. "Forgive me?"

I take her hand. "Alright. I guess so."

"You're not the only one who's been devious," she tells me, returning to the stove and the spoon. "When your first book came out, I was dancing like a schoolgirl, bragging to everyone about it. I'm all over your website all of the time. Sorry to tell you, but most of the traffic is just me. It made me proud, every time you published something, sometimes proud like I was your mother, which was weird, and sometimes like I was your friend, which was a lot better."

"It's good to know we each have at least one fan," I reply.

Sophie turns to glower at me. I throw up my hands. "You're right, I know. I deflected just like you."

She continues: "I came to a reading a year or two ago. In Everton. I sat at the back in disguise. Floppy hat and raincoat, like a matron or a bag lady. I didn't want you to see me. I didn't want the reading to be different because I was there. I wanted to see you as if I wasn't there." She pauses for an instant. "You're different when you read. More you than usual."

"Good thing you didn't come a few years earlier," I reply. "Impossible to hide when there's only two people in the room."

I'm up and beside her, without thinking, my hand on the back of her damp neck. I turn her toward me, because one of us has to. The pan bubbles behind her. I slide a palm along her cheek and kiss her lightly on the mouth. Her lips are cool, her smell familiar. Her lips soften with mine. I lower my lips to her bare neck and she extends her arms, gently edging me back.

She puts a finger to my lips and we look at each other for a moment, so close I can feel the thin heat rising from her body and the denser warmth of the stove. I'm sure I'm blushing, with a kind of disassociated embarrassment but I don't look away, unsure of what is being decided and by whom.

Finally I take a step back, my hands sliding from her neck yet not quite wanting to let her go; they inch over her shoulders to her upper arms. I rub them a few times as Sophie studies me.

She leans in, her hand curling around the back of my neck and she kisses me, a single long, deep kiss, my head cradled in her hand, my hands resting on her forearms, and then she pulls away. Because one of us has to.

We take a deep breath. My hands slide from her arms. "Anything I can do to help?" I ask, so I don't say something else, something unnecessary.

"Yep," she says, turning back to the stove and clicking off the burner. "Why don't you pull out the plates and stuff. They're in the cabinet behind you."

I remove the china and cutlery with exquisite care, my body light and unreliable, aware of the dull clack as they rub against each other and the way the sound hangs in the stillness of the room, ringing momentarily like a faraway bell before fading into the low sizzle of the vegetables. In the center of the table is a large glass bowl, half-filled with water. A sunflower floats there, its petals wide and open, nearly orange, surrounding the tight, dark pack of seeds in the center. It seems to give off its own tone, another note lingering in the air.

I set the plates first on her bright straw placemats, already in position at the sides of the table. I puzzle over the spoons and forks for a moment before remembering the correct position for each.

Sophie stirs her sauce in a small white bowl, whipping it with a fork like raw eggs. I watch her pour a thin stream into the pan, circling it twice. A wonderful spicy aroma fills the room, something sweet and hot. She puts down the bowl, picking the pan up by the handle, rolling it forward and back from the wrist, tossing the vegetables over themselves.

"Pretty fancy move," I nod appreciatively.

She winks. "I have a lot of time to watch the Food Channel. Maybe next time I'll make a dessert with raw oysters and Kobe beef."

"I don't think I'm that adventuresome."

Sophie prepares our plates while I sit at the other side of the table. She spoons the vegetables over the fragrant jasmine rice, positioning melon slices to the side of the plate and handing it over the table to me, placing the white bowl with extra sauce nearby. She puts much less food on her own plate, sitting down across from me, scooting her chair toward the table, then resting her hands in her lap, taking a breath, before she looks up with a small, wan smile.

"This looks really great," I tell her. And it does.

I eat in silence for a moment. Sophie's fork flakes her vegetables into the rice, creating little mounds at the edge of her plate. She takes a small bite, chewing carefully, her hands lowering to the table after each one, resting there, her fingers loose.

I'm telling her about the Family Dollar in Barwick and its bins of cheap Chinese product, the sixteen-year-old girl at the register bobbing to her iPod, punching in numbers without making eye contact or speaking to me. I tell her about Beaker, older now and more curmudgeonly, constantly stretched in my windowsill as if engaged in some mysterious yet vital purpose. I'm talking about random things, studying my food with more attention than it warrants, trying to avoid noticing her increasingly small bites and the effort it takes her. She seems exhausted and I'm feeling guilty for agreeing to the visit, the lunch. I tell her again how wonderful the food is.

Her attention has softened. I can't tell if she's paler than a few moments ago. She rests her fork along the top edge of her plate, dabbing at her lips with her napkin, then taking a sip from her glass.

I'm watching her, some emptiness opening in my stomach, some cold heavy place making itself apparent. She notices me watching and, strangely, we are not embarrassed.

"Do you want to tell me about it?" I ask.

Her eyes lower to the table and something begins to unwind in her shoulders. She sighs, but it's not sad or resigned. There is a release there.

"I'm all out of people. I don't have anyone I can really talk to. Not in the way I used to be able to talk to you."

"You can tell me anything," I say. I'm not convinced it's true, but I say it.

She begins with the discovery of the lump and the first doctor. Sitting in the waiting room, alternating between dread and calm. She remembers the magazine with photos of a celebrity wedding. She remembers sitting on the crisp paper of the examining table in the baggy gown, staring down at her feet dangling above the floor.

The doctor prodded her for a moment, asked a few questions, frowned over her open chart, then sent her to the emergency room for an MRI. "Quickest way to get this taken care of. Otherwise, you'll have to wait a week or so for an appointment and I'd really like to see what this looks like now."

She'd called Zack from the hospital parking lot but he was at work and it would be evening before he could get away. "Don't worry," she'd told him, "I'll be home by then." Three hours passed before she was taken back to the examining room where the intern palmed the note from her doctor, prodded her again, then asked her to wait.

There was a television in the room, mounted high on the wall, but she didn't want to watch it. She lay back on her gurney and pulled the thin sheet to her neck. She listened to the activity in the hallway, playing a game, trying to discern what was going on with the elderly man in the cubicle to her right or the young woman she could sometimes hear to her left. After two hours, a nurse told her they needed the room and wheeled her into the hallway, pushing the gurney against the opposite wall across from the open doorways.

The elderly man was sitting at the foot of his bed, shaking his head slowly side to side. The young woman lay on her back, her sheet askew, one foot protruding. Her breathing was shallow and her feet kicked out gently now and then, but she never made a sound.

The exposed foot worried Sophie. She wanted to get up and draw the sheet over it, tuck the sheet around the woman, keep her warm, but it felt too intrusive somehow, a violation of the distances the hospital observed. Thankfully, in a few minutes, a nurse returned to the woman's room. She straightened the sheet, covering the foot, even folding a blanket over the lower half of the bed.

With nothing else to do, Sophie dozed in the hallway, at one point opening her eyes to see a man holding a small girl, perhaps two years old, standing by the woman. The man and woman were speaking in low whispers, his lips close to her ear.

"Everything after that night eventually blurred into confusion," she tells me. "One doctor or nurse after another, one room after another. First this test, then that test. There's so much about it I can't remember. But, that night. I remember everything about that night. And the thing I remember most is the little girl. She was wearing a blue sleeveless dress and shiny buckle shoes, as if they'd just come from church or a family function. Her legs dangling at her Dad's waist, her arms around his neck, her cheek on his shoulder so she was facing me, eyes closed tight."

Sophie's eyes are bright now and color has returned to her cheeks. "There's nothing more beautiful in all the world than a child asleep in their parents' arms. She was completely trusting, completely relaxed. She wasn't afraid of anything. And every now and then, her little fingers would loosen, her hand flattening on her father's shirt or neck, or she'd shift slightly, licking her lips and muttering to herself. And he held her. For hours he must have held her. While I dozed. While she slept.

"She stayed with me, that little girl. There was something about her sleep, her trust. The way her hand would clutch at her father every once in a while. And then her fingers would relax---in her sleep, this all happened while she was sleeping---her fingers would relax again, once she knew he was there.

"I'd bring her back to mind. Through all the things that happened, over the last months, she was something I held on to. It's funny how that happens. The things we hold on to."

We sit quietly for a moment, Sophie's gaze trained to vision or memory while I allow my eyes to slip toward the window and the angled light in the treetops just visible at the bottom of the frame, fringing the pale blue sky.

I'd been watching Sophie's hands, lying still upon the table or beating like soft wings before her as she spoke. Her hands have always been important to me, the essence of who Sophie is. Something in Sophie's hands binds me to the present, refusing to allow me to slip into the past.

She turns, giving me a shrug and the self-deprecating smile I'm becoming accustomed to. I stand up and clear the plates from the table, setting them to the side of the sink, bunching the silverware beside them.

"After that, Doug," she begins again once I return, "things got pretty bad."

She stares at the surface of the table, one finger fashioning wet streaks from the empty ring of her glass. "God, you don't want to hear all of this." She looks up, her eyes wet, sniffling, suddenly anxious or shy.

I don't really want to hear it but she needs to tell me and that's okay. "No, really, it's alright. Don't be silly. Don't worry about me."

She runs the back of her hand under her suddenly red nose, sniffing again, and something in the gesture reveals the old Sophie, someone light and clear and unselfconscious. I'm glad to be here, glad to be with her.

"I felt like I was always in the hospital or the doctor's office, or on my way back and forth. You get to a place where you can't think. They bombard you with so much information, so many brochures, so many possible procedures. You don't have time to be quiet. I'd come home, just exhausted.

"Mom left me a little money, fifty-sixty thousand. And the house. It seemed like a lot, until I got sicker. Bless her, she was always wondering how I was going to make it in the world. Well, I didn't have insurance. I mean, I'm a painter, I feel happy when I can buy groceries, a twenty-dollar bottle of wine. I watched her money vanish over a couple of months. Chemo, radiation. Tests and tests and tests.

"I was a mess too. Sleeping too much, not sleeping enough. Weak, fainting, throwing up every hour.

"Zack the bastard disappeared one day. He left me a card, he wished me the best. Can't really blame him."

"You should have called me," I interjected, without thinking, leaning across the table for her hand. "I should have called you. I could have helped...with the money." Immediately I'm sorry I've interrupted her.

"You don't have any money, either. I mean, I'm sure you manage to hold your world together but I noticed you're not exactly driving a Maserati." She squeezes my hand, letting it go. "I didn't want to become one of those people. You know, my picture wrapped around some jug on a restaurant counter or plastered on some GoFundMe page, please give for cancer treatment.

"I mean, I did what I was supposed to. I talked to every agency and foundation. I've applied for Emergency Medicaid but I'll be long gone before I'm ever approved...and I...and I."

She stopped and I waited for her.

"And I wanted to paint, just wanted to feel the brush in my hand, the pressure on the canvas, but the smell made me vomit, so I tried watercolor but it felt like the strokes were just fading to white on the page and I wanted to make something but I didn't know what, and I looked all around at all these paintings I have stacked everywhere and I started to think it was just a game I'd played with myself all these years, painting, as a way of believing I was doing something and it didn't make sense anymore.

"Nothing makes sense anymore. It doesn't seem to, anyway.

"It's so hard to see the rest of the world some days; I'm just watching my body for signs and signals."

Sophie taps the table with both palms, the way a magician might test the soundness of a trick cabinet. "It's quiet here. I keep it quiet. I listen to my body molder. That word. It came to me the other day, like I'd heard it somewhere, and I had to look it up. So, now I use it. Molder. I am proudly moldering."

I'm feeling a little addled, just trying to keep up, trying to find a thread in the words as she bounces one sentence to the next. This silence is a fumbling one and I'm aware of not filling it, of having nothing to say. Sophie taps the flat of her hand lightly on the table before us, moving on at a renewed pace.

"Okay, I know. What do you say? Don't worry, you don't say anything. There's nothing to say. There's only what is. And that changes every day: a little less every day. That's all there is."

She takes a deep breath. "Okay, I know. Let me just get it all out there so it's said, you know, then we can move on to something else. I did the chemo, I did the radiation. It seemed like they were just trying to kill me in new ways. I watched the money slip away, the doctors telling me this was possible, or that. A new test, a new procedure. The nurses coming in to keep me warm, to give me water or ice chips, or just to say hello. I lost my appetite, lost weight, lost my hair.

"I was a good patient. I did my research. I asked questions. I weighed options, gave informed consent. I listened to everyone, talked to everyone. I was always on the internet. When I wasn't stalking you, I was considering avocado cures and quantum balancing and meditating toward wholeness. All because one little cell got frisky and ambitious and convinced its friends to join the party."

My eyes are welling but Sophie is nowhere near tears now. Something has fallen into words within her, carrying her forward in an articulated rush. She holds herself erect, her eyes trained on mine, her face light and open, her gaze somehow inward yet not distant from me. I slide my open palms across the table toward her and she clutches my hands with a strength I wouldn't have imagined.

"So, I listen to my body. These days, I listen. And it doesn't usually tell me things I want to hear, but I listen anyway. Trying to become familiar with its voice. 'Cause my body is doing its own thing in there. It's got its own thing going on and I'm just riding on its grace.

"And, one day I'm out of options and I'm out of money. Not necessarily in that order. And the doctor looks at me and he doesn't say 'You're dying' or 'We've run out of options and money.'

"He says, 'We're referring you to Hospice.' Sort of like it was a country club. I half-expected a wink, a handshake, a 'job well done.'

"They'd given me a bear. When they first diagnosed me. A whole cancer gift set, with a bear and a bumper sticker and a picture book of inspiring stories of fighting cancer or beating cancer or overcoming cancer, like cancer was a magic dragon or a traumatic childhood, a bad mood or an inconvenient ear infection. But I didn't want their stuffed animals or their happy thoughts. I wanted to know what was going on with me, and one day I kind of closed around myself, tight like a fist, and when I opened again…

"It's not that everything is okay, not that I'm happy about it, or that I go to sleep imagining walking into the light or reuniting with Misty, the kitten who died when I was seven. It's just that I'm alright. Not great, but alright. Knowing that there are no more beginnings.

"Now, everything is end."

Sophie releases my hands and draws a long, slow breath. I'm trying to swallow. I pull my arms in, turning my palms flat on the table before me. They're slick and I know once I move them I'll find small damp rectangles of heat beneath. I listen to Sophie inhale and exhale softly, unaware whether I'm breathing at all.

"That was bad, I know it," she says, her tone even with a sense of relief. "I just kinda threw all that stuff at you and now you're sitting there, feeling like I shoved you into the deep end of the pool and held you under. And I did, so how else can you feel?"

Her forefinger scuds toward a piece of rice left behind on the table. She pries at it with her nail. I can see her hand from the corner of my eye. "I just think that was the best way. I mean, I could've dropped little hints over the course of your visit, doled out everything in discrete doses. That's what I do, of course, that's how it works with everyone else. I just thought with you I could actually do the hard part all at once. Get it over with."

She slides her chair back along the linoleum floor; there's a single gentle squeak which echoes. Her voice is quieter, settling low in her body. "So, I'm hoping you can sorta catch your breath over there for a few minutes while I wash dishes and make us some tea. Then, I'm hoping we can go out into the backyard with our tea and you can tell me something about yourself. Something personal or private or secret I could never learn from your website or your Facebook page."

I've found a way to breathe again, but it makes my chest hurt, so I take it slow, drawing shallow breaths. "I'd like that," I tell her. My voice sounds pretty normal when it reaches my ears.

7

I study my fingers, floating in relief above the surface of the kitchen table. They've always seemed short and heavy to me, nothing as articulate as Sophie's, tapering long and elegant, moving delicately, always carving shapes into the air around her as she speaks or thinks or hums to herself. Her hands are always a further definition of herself while mine, when not at cross-purposes, are mere appendages.

I can hear the slow slosh of the dishes in the sink, their delicate clatter as she soaps them, then rinses them under running water in the second sink. I don't look up to watch her.

I keep my attention on my hands for a few minutes longer, listening nonetheless to her progress, aware of her quiet presence and solidity. I'm just trying to hold myself in the moment, trying not to slip into the past. I'm just trying to be here with Sophie, to find a new place with her. I'm trying not to turn away while feeling the pull like an undertow.

I am wide, far between, scattered into soft shards. The only things holding me in place: the weight at the depth of my stomach and the pressure in my chest. I watch my hands, which do not move, the weight of Sophie's last six months opening in me, making a space for itself in my body where there has been no space before. A cooling darkness still finding itself, where before there had simply been fantasy and memory.

I want to believe I've grown up in these eight years, that's it not the same old Doug sitting here. But, more than that, I can see she is not the same Sophie. More than anything, I want her to be the Sophie she needs to be. I don't want to drag her into a past she can no longer see.

I can hear her lining the glasses on the wire rack. I shift my eyes to the window. The light is changing outside, growing softer and more oblique along the tops of trees. Sophie turns off the water, drying her hands on the dish towel. Steam escapes from the teapot but it has not yet begun to whistle. The kitchen is warm, from the stove and the teapot, the windows fogging again at the bottoms of the sill. Sophie is taking off her apron. I sit very still.

There's so much grieving we could never accomplish together, falling back instead into our own dark thoughts. So much grief that sank from our awareness becoming dark and heavy, until it was simply a part of us, flowing through us, thick and stale, invisible. We accepted it without thought, until an old wound was struck.

I want to look up at Sophie, but not with a question. I don't want to ask anything of her. I don't want her to feel responsible for me, though I know she already does. I don't want to believe she is more fragile than she is. I can't make the mistakes of my old self. I can't allow myself to turn away; the only gift I can give her is not turning away.

I look up. Sophie is retrieving cups from the cabinet, one hand on the door, the other turning the cups upright onto the counter by the stove. A heavy red cup. And a blue one. She closes the cabinet door, flattening both of her hands on the smooth counter, leaning on them for a moment. Head tilted back, eyes closed. I watch her face; it's as if she's listening for a specific sound, listening intently, filtering white noise and clutter from the insistent world to find a certain frequency.

She looks so alone.

"Dibs on the red cup," I announce, pushing myself away from the table. Sophie turns toward me with a soft smile. She draws tins of tea from the cabinet, offering me a choice. The kettle begins to whistle and we busy ourselves with the assemblage of tea as if it were a complex operation requiring the full extent of our attention.

We balance our cups out the back door, down three stone steps into the wide backyard where two white Adirondack chairs await us, side by side near the tree line. She catches me studying her clothesline, hung with what I'd believed to be sheets or quilts when I turned in the drive. I now see they are painted canvasses, fastened to the line with clothespins and weighted like drying skins with twine and stones.

"Oh, those," she says, then continues as if explaining the position of a garden gnome. "I wanted to see how they'd age, wanted to watch them change. But the damned things won't do anything. Six months they've been hanging there, and nothing."

I can't help but laugh. "How many are on the line out there?"

"Twenty or so. I'd put more out if I had the space. Lord knows what will become of them…you know…eventually. I guess I think I'm returning them to the wild."

We settle into our chairs, sliding back while cradling our cups. The air cools as the sun slips behind us. We look out over the flat expanse of her backyard, the grass nicely trimmed. Trees rise at our sides, exhaling a different coolness, earthy and rustling. The green, in a thousand shades, is startling, some leaves tinged blue-white in the light.

Sophie blows across the surface of her tea. "So, I've just been talking and talking. It's like you've found me on a desert island after years of having only a soccer ball as company. Now, it's your turn."

I sip and talk. It helps to have something in my hands. It helps that our chairs are angled beside each other, not facing, so we can spend much of our time gazing vaguely at the trees or the lawn, or the canvases swaying heavily on the lines.

I talk. It's easy after what has come before, more comfortable now because the things we might have tried to avoid Sophie has dragged into the light, so their presence is palpable even if just out of frame. I tell her about where I live and how Beaker grudgingly shares the apartment with me, about how the town has changed over the years, the art theatre and used bookstore gone, the new roads and abandoned strip malls. I tell her about old girlfriends, some I haven't thought of in years, tracing their chronology like a root system winding through dense earth leading nowhere. I tell her about Emma, and Sandy. Janis and Sarah.

I tell her about Kathryn, the only other real romance. Sophie listens, turning her blue cup between her palms. She watches me while I talk or she stares into the trees, the trace of a smile sliding from one side of her mouth to the other and back again. Kathryn, who played guitar and wrote songs about railroads and tobacco barns and lost loves; who lay on my sofa, one leg thrown over the back, her long hair spilling to the floor, her guitar resting along her lower leg, plucking out notes over and over in tiny variations until she found the ones she liked. Kathryn, who sang in a low growl which could occasionally rise to a lilt with such unexpected force that it took my breath. Kathryn, whose songs might have been corny if I hadn't been in love.

I tell her about Kathryn and me, the way everything fades, washes slowly to a paleness over time and takes on the rigidity of habit until it has no meaning and I might find myself standing in a kitchen or a hallway and wonder how I arrived and why. I tell her about the things I cannot hold, the things that change in my hands, becoming other things.

"Do you still see her?" she asks.

I shrug. "We talk once or twice a year. To catch up. She'll call me or I'll call her." I place my cup on the ground, in the damp grass by the foot of my chair. "It's always nice when it happens."

The light is tinting blue around us at the early edge of dusk. I'm slanted in my chair, legs extended into the damp grass, staring toward Sophie's stand of distressed paintings. She's drawn her legs beneath her, turned herself toward me, her cup resting against the top of her thigh, her head tilted to the back of the chair.

"Tell me about the writing," she asks, as if the question has waited a long time. Her voice is quiet, it drifts from a dim past.

"When we were together," she explains, "I always felt you couldn't quite get there, you couldn't make contact or hold on to what you wanted. I watched you struggle. And approach and recede, approach and recede. Like you were preparing for an epic battle that might never come.

"Nothing I could think of to do ever helped."

"No, it didn't."

"You wouldn't talk about writing with me then."

"I couldn't. The connection with it was too tenuous. Or non-existent. I was superstitious, I guess. Or neurotic. Everything seemed so delicate, like a secret whose magic might vanish if I breathed a word."

"Some parts of you were so folded in on themselves."

We sit quietly for a moment, her watching me while I stare across the connecting lawns.

"After," I begin, pulling myself upright in the chair, still not meeting her gaze, "...after you left...I felt homeless, with no center. There were all these empty spaces in my life. Like the place where your clock used to be on my mantle, the moments in the day when we always talked on the phone. The places where you lived in me. Everywhere I turned, empty space with only thin strands of connective tissue holding them together.

"I kept trying to put something in those spaces, to fill them up somehow or make them into something else. Different strategies. Different plans. It never worked. Not for the months and months I tried.

"Finally there was just desperation, the feeling I couldn't go back and I couldn't inch forward. In the end, the fear of going back became worse, much worse. And everything fell away. Everything I thought I was.

"I had to leave the ground before I could find a place to stand. Leaving the ground felt like falling for a long time. Endlessly falling. Everything was loose. Nothing had weight. I had to leave the ground to escape the story, my story of the past. It was choking me.

"So, it wasn't a great battle, when it came. It wasn't making something. It was a falling apart. A disintegration. And the terror in anticipating it turned out to be greater than the terror of confronting it. Once everything actually collapsed, I felt hope. I could make friends with the space around me.

"So, I felt writing in a new way. It wasn't a thing I did, it was a part of my body. A part of me. I haven't explained this very well but I think it's the best I can do.

"I'm not sure I ever would have gotten there. If you'd stayed." The last sentence feels like a confession.

"You found a home," she says.

"It's like that." I nod slowly. "And there are times when I don't understand how to reach that place at all. The space of writing, the sense of self, seems impossibly distant and alien."

I stare into the rustling trees for a moment, Sophie silent and attentive at my side. It's suddenly very important to bring something to words, to say something real to her about this thing I find myself doing.

"When I step outside of the space of writing, I can't imagine how a thing like that might be accomplished. I look at my own work and I don't understand how it was done. Standing outside of writing, writing is just impossible. Outside, I'm locked within words and the words have no flex, no skeleton, no motion or meaning. Away from that space I don't understand writing at all.

"Driving over here today I had no idea how I would, how I could, talk with you. It seemed false or impossible, regardless of the scenario I came up with. It couldn't be done. And we were awkward and afraid, both of us, together, and we didn't know what to say. Until suddenly we did, until suddenly we found where and how we fit, we found our own space, a space that had never disappeared.

"But, with the writing, well, I learned from having watched you wait. I'd watch a certain stillness come over you like a cool wind, watch it lift you just above the ground. I wanted your stillness, thinking I could get by without finding my own."

I turn to look at Sophie. She's curled deep into her chair. Her head is on her hand at the back, her eyes are closed. In the bluing light of dusk her skin appears even more pale and still. There are goosebumps on her forearm.

"I'm sorry," I tell her, "I was just going on and on."

"No," she whispers, "I liked it."

"Hey Soph," I ask quietly, hesitant to break the mood. "Are you cold?"

She keeps her eyes closed, her lips curling into a faint smile. She nods almost imperceptibly.

I reach down to take the cup from her hand. "Why don't we go inside. It'll be dark soon."

I turn back to retrieve my own cup, hearing her stir, uncurling her legs and sliding into a sitting position. I thread my forefinger through both handles, extending my free hand to Sophie. She takes it and I pull her upright, moving a discrete step back as she comes up. Her hand is cold, hooked loosely into mine. I drop my arm and she doesn't let go.

"I was just listening to your voice," she says, leaning into me, her bare arm against mine, a band of cool along the side of my body. "I like listening to your voice."

We wobble across the lawn together in the near darkness. The single light over her kitchen sink, visible through the window, draws us forward. I feel her tremble.

"How is it now?" she asks. "Writing, what is it to you?"

"It's the way I know I'm alive."

She accepts this silently, leaning heavily against me. Or perhaps there's a nod.

I grin. "It's the longest, most stable relationship I've ever had."

We're at the back steps. I open the screen door.

"Do you write about us?"

She knows the answer; she's read my work. There's another question here.

"Every time."

She wavers without my arm to lean on. I help her up the stairs.

The house is dark save the kitchen light. It's warm inside after the cool evening air. I help Sophie to a dining room chair and get her a glass of water, feeling awkward and unsure, staring at the glass, wondering if I couldn't manage something a little better.

Her hand on the tabletop is little more than a shadow. She doesn't glance up when I place the glass beside her. Her mood has darkened, or perhaps she just needs sleep. I sit next to her, looking at everything but her.

"This is what happens," she tells me and from the sound of her voice I know she's still staring at the table. "My energy just bottoms out all at once, everything falls into itself and I have to lie down."

"It's okay," I reply, feeling stupid for allowing her to apologize. "I've stayed too long."

I feel Sophie nod.

And yet, neither of us make any motion toward the door. We sit together, Sophie's breathing shallow, her body limp in the chair while I stare out the window, a strange quietness overlaying the chaos of emotion just below my surface.

It feels good to be in the same room with her, to know her at the other side of the table. I hold to our easy exchange and the way we found each other again after so many years, above the concern and guilt. When it begins to slip away, giving itself up to the riot of emotions so near, that's when I know it's time to leave.

I stand up, moving around my chair and sliding it under the table. "I should be going. I know you're exhausted."

She nods, then looks up, a small smile curling as she licks her lips, slipping through her darkened mood. "Okay."

She turns off the overhead. There's only a nightlight, glowing low at the baseboard. She leads me into the living room without turning on another light. She moves slowly, tentatively, and I match my pace to hers. It's a formless departure conversation, not exactly dishonest but oblique. We say how much we enjoyed getting together and promise to do it again; perhaps I'll call her or she'll call me. Maybe we could even go out, to a park or a movie, if she felt up to it.

And because we are already generating our own distances, and because of my earlier mistake, I decide not to kiss her at the door, taking her cool and nearly formless hand instead, squeezing it. She squeezes back. She thanks me for coming and I assure her I had a good time. I tell her I love her, hoping I make it sound casual and light with no attachments, a thing from the past suddenly and pleasantly recalled. Turning toward the door, I tell her I'll be in touch.

"Doug..."

That's when she asks me. At the door, as I'm leaving, seemingly as an afterthought. That's when she asks if I'll help her kill herself.

"You can say yes or no and I'll love you either way. But I just can't argue about it."

I turn back into the house, closing the door softly behind me.

8

I turn; I think I turn. I jolt back into myself and I am turning. Away from the door and into the darkened room toward Sophie. My hand remains on the doorknob.

The only light is dim in the kitchen behind her, she's a vague silhouette before me. I can't really see her face. Her head is canted downward. She might be looking at the floor.

I almost speak. Then I don't. In a moment, my hand slips from the doorknob. Sophie is a shadow in motion; now she's sitting on the edge of the sofa, her hands between her knees. In the stark silence, I sit near her, on the loveseat.

I'm quiet. I want to be quiet. Not to avoid the question but to sink into the bedrock of it, to find the core. Believing that through stillness I might drop, unencumbered by words, to the idea at its center. I don't want to avoid Sophie, I simply want to find the center. I feel strangely calm. I'm quiet. I wait.

The room is suddenly hot. Sweat trickles down my back. The refrigerator clicks on in the kitchen with a soft, wing-like whir.

She has collapsed into something firm and unwavering. I can feel her dark matter burning in the stillness, and a kind of relief in her as if a pressure were quietly draining off, first in words, then in silence.

"Sophie..."

"It's happening anyway," her voice is low and even, "always a minute closer." Her gaze shifts to me. "I just want to decide myself."

She adds, in a near whisper: "I'm not going to change my mind."

I can't find a complete sentence. Just a swirl of words around a cold ache, just the sound of her breath in the room and the memory of her hand. There are times when words don't work, when words can only come later, after the gesture or the glance, to simply articulate what has already happened, and what could never have happened through words alone.

She is crying. I am crying. Soft, formless tears, hot and silent.

"Sophie..." I begin.

"Doug," she interrupts, "Doug, tell me a story, tell me one of your stories." There's a plea in her tone, an anxious rush of words to stall my own. She's apologizing, but it's difficult to say what she's apologizing for.

"Sophie, I can't..." I'm trying to hold my voice in place.

She nods slowly, a shadow in the darkness, her eyes on the floor. I can't find a way to speak. I can't find a place to begin. Words roll loose in my mouth and won't cling together. There are no thoughts that might push them to cohere, only a dim hiss in my ears like the lost signal of a phantom radio station. Only weight, the pull of a dense gravity, and a sadness so complete it's nearly abstract.

"Tell me..." she begins again, self-conscious now, tentative: "Tell me about the last beautiful thing you saw."

And an image comes. A little girl, maybe four or five, who has obviously dressed herself in her favorite mismatched clothes, glittery scarves flowing behind her. She's following the red cobblestones in the downtown square, weaving away in diagonals from her mom and back again, concentrating, eyes on her feet, arms tightrope straight from her side. An image comes to save me and I tell Sophie. Her laugh is low and breathy. She asks questions about the scarves, the mother.

She tells me about a chipmunk she finds on her windowsill most mornings. Absolutely still save occasional flashes of his head, his bright eyes. She describes the luster of his coast, his delicate feet, his stoic rodent intensity.

The stories remind me of years ago: one of us rushing in the door to tell the other of a new wonder in the world. The new chocolate shop to open, the mural on the abandoned building downtown, the way an old woman stopped to tie her shoe. It was a way of sharing magic.

I feel her eyes upon me. She says: "It makes me sad we never had a chance to grow bored with each other." It's like an outtake from a previous conversation, a deleted scene. It's a private joke between us told for the first time.

Her eyes drift in the darkness. I tell her about sitting in a coffee shop, a couple of months ago. I'm working, glancing up from the computer now and then as I often do. A young woman, at a table in front, faces me. She's pretty, with wide blue eyes, and I enjoy seeing her every time I look up. She's reading her Sociology or Biochemistry, textbook and notebook open before her.

Her phone rings. She answers it and her face lights up. Her head tilts downward into the phone, her sandy hair falling on both sides to frame her face. Her eyebrows arch and she smiles. Her foot edges out to the empty chair opposite and hooks the rung, sliding it toward her as she leans back, phone to her ear.

"It was the way she accomplished both things as a single gesture," I explain, "the rising into the conversation and pulling the chair toward her, as if drawing the invisible person in closer."

"What about after?" I ask in a moment. "Do you believe in anything after?"

She knows what I mean. The tears have stopped by now as we concentrate on our stories, our voices, our dim outlines. They're drying on our cheeks, our hands, they're wet between our fingers. Her voice has taken on more substance, found its place again in her body. She is no longer tentative.

"I wish I could. I can believe in my work. I believe in us, you and I, as...I don't know...a thing. Everything else is just wishful thinking."

In a moment, she tells me about Chess Man: "I'd go to the Barnes and Noble to read the art magazines I couldn't afford. Before. You know, before all this. Every Monday, there's this old guy, must be eighty. Overalls, boots, long scraggly beard. And he's bent over, something wrong with his spine. It's hard for him to walk, painful, but he doesn't use a cane or a walker.

"The first time I see him, he's just standing in the parking lot midway between his truck and the door. He's standing there, body bent, motionless. I ask him if he's alright, I go up and ask, and he kinda growls at me that he's fine, he doesn't need any help.

"I don't believe him, of course, so I watch from the store and eventually, it takes about thirty minutes, he makes his way, one painful step at a time, to his battered truck. The next time I see him, weeks later, he's sitting in the truck, preparing to get out, and by the time I leave he hasn't managed it yet. So I wonder what he's doing, you know? What's so important about the bookstore?

"It's a month or so before I find out, before I find him at a table in the cafe, bent over, studying a chess board, his beard sometimes brushing the pieces. First, there's a middle-aged woman across from him, later in the evening a young kid. It's an informal chess club and he goes through all this to play.

"I believe in futile gestures," she decrees, as a kind of spontaneous revelatory coda. "That's another thing I believe in. That's all art is anyway, right?

"What about you?" she asks, as if it's just occurred to her. "Do you believe in anything? You know, after?"

"No," is all I can honestly say.

Both the question and the answer make me uncomfortable, the shadow of a large object looming overhead. So, I'm talking, wanting to find a new story; I'm delaying, when she stops me. Her hand rising from her knee and floating there in the dark. "Doug, I need..." I feel the shadow of her fear in the room.

I slide onto the sofa beside her; I'm halfway there before I know what I'm doing. She leans over and into me. I wrap an arm over her shoulder.

"Can you just hold me?"

She settles into me, head on my chest, something light and intangible with the heat and the chill of fall weather. I want to bury my face in her hair, to turn her toward me. Instead, I take in her weight, her bare arms along my own. The scent of her hair, with an undertone, slightly acrid and metallic, yet still her scent.

We're crying again now. I can tell from her breathing. My own tears slide from my chin to my shirt. It's impossible to know whether we're crying for beauty or for pain. It's a conversation in tears we pass back and forth to each other.

"I'm right here, Sophie. I'm not going anywhere." I don't know what I'm promising. I just need to make a promise.

I hold her. I tell her about Bill Jane. We worked in construction together, years ago.

"He was a few years younger than me. Maybe nineteen or so. Cursed more than anyone I've ever met. Every sentence, two or three times, at least. It didn't matter if he was overjoyed or pissed, telling a joke or ranting about something, there were always endless strings of goddamns and motherfuckers in there.

"I think the fact that I didn't curse, didn't seem to get too upset, I think it really bugged him. So after a few weeks of working together, he began cursing for me. I'd drop a nail and he'd throw out a 'Goddamn it!.' Anything that might conceivably warrant a curse, he'd supply it.

"And I started to be grateful that he took on that job. There was a comfort in it, in a way."

We take turns, our images of beauty becoming stories. At some point, I begin to make things up. It doesn't seem to matter.

Sophie turns back to me, sniffling, wiping her eyes with the back of her hand. I can't see her face, tucked into her chin. She pulls at my t-shirt, tenting it toward her.

"Can you just...you know...with skin."

I pull the shirt over my head and drop it to the floor. I slip into the corner of the sofa, legs extended. She leans back into me, her blouse against my bare chest. I'm aware of my own heat against her coolness and the slow build of warmth between us. I link my hands over her stomach, the skin loose there where she's lost weight.

She tells me about Toby, mowing her lawn on his grandmother's riding mower. How careful and conscientious he is. How he wipes the mower down after each use. How he takes such pride in the straight lines of his cut and often sits atop the rumbling mower, at the edge of her lawn once the job is done, just to survey and appreciate his work.

"So what do we do?" Sophie asks. "Two people who don't believe in anything."

"Maybe, this is it. This is what we do."

We're quiet for a long time. Sophie gently rubs one bare foot into the sole of the other. I can hear the faint rasp, feel the slow friction along her skin. She adjusts her body along mine and I'm aware of how slight she has become, her shoulder blades sharp at my chest, her pelvis at my hips, her body somehow unsure of itself and its place in the world.

After a moment, she's upright again. She unbuttons the first buttons of her blouse, sliding it past her shoulders to the top of her breasts. Then she leans into me again, her cool skin against mine now. Her head is at my shoulder, breath falling to my collarbone, low and regular when I'm speaking, in tiny gusts when she speaks.

I know she's crying again, slow silent tears, perceptible in the darkness only as warmth near her face, until they drop to my bare chest.

I tell her about the park last winter after the snowstorm. The empty field blanketed in snow, the muffled stillness, the hush, as if the earth were sleeping a contented sleep. The dog barreling past me into the pristine snow. A retriever, running hard then burying his nose and skidding to a stop, leaping up, raising his head, snapping at the snow on his head, his nose. He dances as it falls around him, snuffles deep into the snow by his feet, then turns to run in the opposite direction.

Between the unpredictable tears, I feel her limbs loosen over my chest and I know she's asleep. I continue to talk, in the way a parent might continue a storybook even as the child nods off by their side, believing the sleeping self awaits the resolution. I talk the stories of a parent to a drowsy child, stories leading to dream.

I tell her what she's meant to me. When we were together, when we were apart. I try to describe the place she holds in the world for me, an open door always in view. I try to say how important it is. But she knows all about that.

I tell her what I learned from her, from being near her. But she knows all about that.

I tell her I'm sorry. It's the opening lines of a conversation we should have had years ago, or perhaps we couldn't have until now. Perhaps it's the kind of conversation that can only happen in a dream. An apology for being young, half-formed, confused; for being uncertain, overwhelmed, afraid. An apology for the clutter within myself which obscured something true.

I tell her I'm sorry. The tears come but it's not sad when I say it. Not anymore.

I wrap my arms around her more tightly. She's snoring softly now. I talk to hear my voice in the darkness. I talk until there are no further words. Then I watch the darkness because the darkness needs to be watched. Until sleep comes.

9

The hands are kneading, fingers curled into one another, curled around themselves, nearly a fist, fingers tightening, pulling the canvas taut, curling into the frame for leverage. The fabric rasps against the wood of the frame, dry as breath, the sound brittle and frightening. The knuckles turn into the hard edges, over and over until the skin reddens and begins to crack, until there are traces of blood at the edge of the frame.

I wake up alone on the couch. The light is blue in the gauze curtains, the sun not yet breaking the horizon. Sometime during the night Sophie had covered me with a blanket and I'd cocooned myself in my sleep, turning to face the back of the couch. My bones have settled into the lowest latitudes of my body like tossed kindling. The dry scape of the dream fades in my ears.

I immediately know where I am, remembering the couch, the room, the conversation of the night before. I remember Sophie in my arms and falling asleep with feathery strands of her hair in my mouth.

I lie still for what seems like a long time, nestling into the angle of the couch with the blanket at my chin, attempting to slip gently back into sleep, but my awakening has been too sudden and too complete. Instead, I feign sleep, watching through the slits of my eyelids as the blue at the window drains off, shifting to a light gold which is almost no color at all.

In a moment I'm standing. I simply find myself upright where once I'd been curled into the blanket. I've picked up my t-shirt and pulled it over my head. My mouth is dry. I stretch my limbs against my rumpled clothes, trying to become friendly with my arms and legs again. The clothes feel stiff and clammy, my body some shapeless thing draped within them.

I stumble into the kitchen. The light is brighter there, the windows wide and inviting. It's only after I have a glass of water and stare into Sophie's back yard for a few moments that I begin to feel semi-conscious. I check my phone for the time, which is a mistake because I have four calls I don't want to return and twelve emails I don't want to read. It's just after seven.

I could leave. Write a short and sincere note to prop on the kitchen table then slide out the front door, backing the car over the crunchy gravel, accelerating gradually once on the road. It would be okay. Maybe we could even talk again in a couple of months when she might be feeling better.

I remember last night. I'm not sure how last night fits into anything. I'm locked outside of us again, watching through a window without understanding what happened or how. I can't enter the space again, the space where we were together.

And, there's something else: an idea, a belief. A faith that always keeps me engaged long after I know I shouldn't be, keeps me believing in possibility no matter how dim or ridiculous; a faith always in the next moment. It's a thing that plagues me, the belief something might be revealed the instant I turn away, that the real thing might occur the moment I abandon it. So I lose the ability to take a new step, waiting instead for a revelation that never comes.

I could leave. But in the end, I stay. I still don't know what to do with myself. I putter in the kitchen. I find tins of green tea and Earl Grey, but no coffee. I find the teapot and the cups. I consider the making of tea. I hate tea.

I consider that she didn't spend the night beside me; that she made her way in the darkness to her own bedroom and returned with a blanket before going to sleep.

I feel weird standing alone in her kitchen, weird opening cabinets, as if I might uncover some hidden part of her she wouldn't want me to know, secreted between the dry pasta and the oatmeal. The house seems too quiet, fragile in its way, and any noise I make might wake her. I put the teapot on, thinking perhaps I should check on her, make sure she's alright.

I pad down the hallway, past the museum of her family. Her bedroom door is open but I know it's not an invitation, simply the habit of living alone. Her bedroom is darker than the other rooms of the house. The curtains are heavier, the light dim and soft. A space heater glows, its thickening warmth evident even from the doorway.

Her body is a diagonal across the bed. She's lying on her stomach, her face and one arm hanging over the side toward me. The bedclothes are at her waist. She's wearing yellow pajamas and a dark woolen cap. There's a band of naked flesh where the pajama shirt has pulled away from the pants. Her face is at the base of the pillow, nearly overhanging the bed. On the floor, beneath her head is a red plastic bucket, the kind she might use for mopping. There's a thin thread of vomit at her chin.

I back away from the threshold, not wanting to embarrass her, not wanting to wake her. The kettle begins to steam.

I sit at the kitchen table, ignoring my cup of tea, not staring out the window into the brightening yard. Not noticing the Adirondack chairs facing each other at a slant and the abandoned canvasses hanging slack from the clothesline. Trapped within some kind of frenzied nostalgia, as if bringing everything back in a rush might change the present.

I'm trying to find the melody of the night before, the way I might try to place a song from a thread of overheard music. I'm trying to find the things that seemed so sure then, but all I can find is memory.

Our parties, our old apartments, our bodies slung across the floor together on a Saturday morning reading magazines or books we'd bought at Goodwill. Watching her sleep, feeling her behind me in the next room. Just knowing she was there. The sense of presence that develops in a relationship; the awareness of her, two steps behind or three blocks away, the continuing assurance of her place in my life.

Our friends then: Alex and Sasha, Maggie and Jim. How long had it been since I'd seen any of them? The images whirl up and rush away, dry leaves caught in a sudden gust, all the motion and activity working hard to prevent me from remembering one thing.

The Naked Scrawl. The door thrown open to the office. The large man in the mask against the threshold. The man they never caught. The image burning at the center of all the others, its presence inescapable.

I sit at the table a long time before I hear the bathroom door open down the hall and close, then the sound of running water. My tea is cold. I get up and put the pot on again, but it's steaming long before Sophie comes out so I turn it down, taking my seat at the table, almost noticing that the sun has heightened the lawn to a high shade of green.

I decide to make Sophie breakfast. Checking the refrigerator I find a few eggs, a little cheese, half a loaf of rye bread. It's the least I can do, make her breakfast. This time, she'll sit while I cook. She'll nurse her cup, stretching, yawning.

Placing things on the counter, I try to come up with funny stories to tell her. About Beaker, maybe.

When she does appear, her body is closed around itself. She shuffles into the room, head down. She's still wearing her loose-fitting pajamas, her toes protruding from their puddle at the floor. She scuffs past my chair to the cabinet by the sink, removing a large bottle of something and turning back toward the bathroom.

As she passes, she doesn't really look up, but her hand slides across the width of my shoulders: "Morning. I'll be back in a few minutes."

"Want me to make you some tea?" I call after her into the hallway.

"Not yet..." her voice trails, the bathroom door closing behind her.

I wait for her the way I waited for her after the robbery: wondering if I would ever see her again, the Sophie I knew, the Sophie always two steps away or in the next room, wondering if there would ever be a way to struggle back toward a present from a past so bruised and gaping.

Wondering at my own anger, the rage I tried to avoid. The rage of powerlessness percolating up from my shame. Someone had hurt her; I had done nothing. It was humiliating to feel shame, as if somehow my pain was as valuable or as deep as Sophie's. As if I were insinuating myself into her tragedy. It was something I couldn't do.

Wondering if her pain would ever clear, or if it was so large it would swallow us both, and always wondering if there was something I could do, something I hadn't seen. A gesture like a spell, or a word, that might suddenly change the weather.

Holding her when she would let me. Listening to her cry in the bathroom, in the bedroom, behind a closed door. Then, watching her force the tears just below the surface, pinning them there beneath the skin.

I saw her fashion a smile for public use, a skewed version of the original, to cover herself, to hold back the questions and explanations so others wouldn't have to be bored or burdened by her grief. After a few months, there was only that smile. It was the only smile she had left.

I'd tried to keep an open space for both of us, a threshold we might pass back through together. I tried to hold a clear, unlabored breath we might share. As if memory possessed some key for undoing the past or negating its power, instead of reinforcing it at every turn. Feeling all the while that I grasped something already vanishing in my hand, yet still not willing to allow it to slip fully from my fingers.

Sophie slides into the chair beneath the window, offering a weak smile. The bandanna is blue this morning, her face scrubbed, skin nearly translucent. Her body is ghostly within her voluminous sweatshirt. She seems nervous, her gaze flitting over the table and along the wall, so suddenly, I'm anxious and awkward. We're like a couple who's found themselves together on the morning after a particularly dubious and drunken first date, each entertaining ways to extricate ourselves.

"Too much excitement yesterday. I'm not used to it." Her voice is hoarse and thin. "Sorry you had to see me." Her hand flutters at her chest, "I'm a bit of a mess in the morning."

"Maybe I should have gone."

"Glad you didn't."

10

I'm at the counter where I've laid out the breakfast items. I have a mission, a plan. I want to do something for her. I draw a pan from the cabinet near the stove.

"I thought I'd make breakfast for us. Nothing fancy. But you can just sit there while I..."

"Nothing for me, thanks. You go ahead."

"Aw, c'mon, it's not often I offer to cook. I'm really not that bad at it. Breakfast, I can do breakfast." I grin, placing the pan on the stove, slicing a pat of butter into it. I find a small bowl for the eggs. "I thought we'd just have a little something before I leave. And maybe we could get together later next week, for coffee or something. Or, you know, tea."

"I really can't," I hear Sophie say, from someplace far away.

"Well, maybe the week after then."

"No, breakfast," she tells me, trying to engage my gaze as I spin nervously between counter and stove. "It's just...with the chemo and the medications. I usually can't have anything at all, even tea, until well after noon."

"I just wanted to...do something," I tell her, still holding the bowl in my hand, forward, toward her. "I thought we could, you know, take our time."

"I know. I do appreciate it."

"Breakfast," I hear myself say. "It's something people do together."

Sophie is quiet. She folds her hands into her lap. There's something in her pallid complexion, the ghostly nature of her body lost within the sweatshirt, the stillness around the words we can hardly form, the way the hard edges of the world are heavy against our spectral bodies.

I hear her inhale softly. I place the bowl back on the counter, unsure of the next step. I stare at it for a moment, but it continues to be an empty bowl on a counter.

"You were really sweet to me last night," I hear Sophie say, her voice drifting into her lap. "It's a long time since someone held me. You didn't..." She stops looking for the right words, waving away the thought with a raised hand. "You could've but you didn't."

She smooths the sweatshirt at her waist. Her hands have no weight and it seems to take an effort of concentration to accomplish the task. Her hands are red and chapped, thinner even than last night, each knuckle pronounced and vulnerable.

"Mornings aren't good for me, I'm sorry," she continues. "It takes a long time to get all the parts in place. Lots of times I'm just really sick." Her shoulders tilt in the suggestion of an apology. "I don't mean to put all this on you. It just feels like I owe you an explanation or something. I mean, I'm not some wounded bird you have to take care of. But I have my...limitations."

I've turned away from the bowl, leaning back against the counter, arms at my sides. I'm finding parts of the room to stare into: a corner of the ceiling, the edge of the table, a slat of sunlight lengthening in the hall. My eyes return to Sophie and she looks up, perhaps aware of my gaze.

She smiles, but it's an occluding smile; it hides her. And I stand on the other side, having already lost something, having already become a stranger again. She smiles and I fade in its wake, a distance opening up between us.

Outside, the day has sprung. There's a slight breeze visible in the trees, branches swaying with each other. The grass looks warm and soft. The empty chairs. Maybe we could go into the yard.

"I don't know what I was thinking," I hear her say. She might be talking to me. "Inviting you over here like nothing has changed. But sometimes...sometimes it feels like nothing has changed. And maybe, right now, I need something to believe in. For a minute or two anyway. Do you know what I mean?"

My voice, when it answers her, is hard: "Not really."

She's watching me stare at my shoes. When I look up, her eyes are wet. Her hands are on the table now, empty and forgotten. There's a faint tremor of exhaustion in her fingers that makes me angry. My hands grip the edge of the stove.

"Even if it's just the past," she tries to explain. "Even if it's just knowing something did happen, something actually *was*, years ago. 'Cause the past is something, at least, and there's not much to hang on to right now."

I'm watching her fingers turn, one hand within the other, trembling at the tips. New hands, separate hands, that don't connect to Sophie but float just before her body.

It's as if we're ghosts, spirits attempting to take more solid form. The room shudders, waiting for us and our nearly transparent shapes, everything shuddering, before we come to life or vanish forever.

"What happened to us, Doug?"

"You left me, that's what happened." My voice is loud, the anger in it surprising me. "Went away to Denver and never came back."

Sophie straightens in her chair, eyes locked to mine. "I didn't leave you, Doug. We...left each other. I just noticed first."

"You gave up first." I work to keep my body still, the weight of the counter at my back. I work to hold myself in one place, disoriented by the burn in my limbs, comforted by the pressure of the walls enclosing me, a bystander. "It didn't have to go that way. I mean, it's all over and done now, but it didn't have to end like that."

"We just lost each other, I guess," Sophie whispers, to no one in particular.

"I mean, it's okay, I'm over that part of it," I continue. "You went to your life and I went to mine and that's okay, I guess. But there was something else in it, something I guess still pisses me off since here I am, yelling at you."

"I didn't know what else to do. We were just hurting each other. You remember that, don't you? I'm not making that up. It just went on and on. We couldn't help it."

I drop into the chair across from her, my hands flattening on the table. "But..." My fingers splay at the surface for purchase. I press the tips into the bright wood. "There was a time when we believed in each other absolutely. And that was enough."

After I've said it, I can't think of anything else to add. It's a ridiculous and pointless sort of confession, yet it seems to have burned away all my words.

She goes on: "Something got all messed up and muddy in me. By the time I came back to myself, my self had changed. I had to figure it out all over again. But now..."

I stare through the window behind her. I can only see the featureless sky and the tops of trees. I know she's already inside me, full-breathed, that she's awakened there again. I could walk out the door now but I can't walk away. Something old and raw holds me, whether I like it or not. Whether I want it or not.

And I know she'll ask the question again, that she's trying to find a way to manage it. I don't know what I'll say.

Sophie is working her language back in my direction, but she can't look at me yet. We sit across from each other, gamblers practicing our bluffs. The teapot whistles and I get up to turn it off, circling the kitchen randomly, coming to rest by the stove. I have no plans or answers.

"I thought I could do it alone. Thought I could just curl into this house and disappear. 'Cause I'm so tired now. I don't want to be but I am."

I lean into the stove, my palms flat along the warm surface. I notice my eyes have closed. I feel Sophie's attention turn toward me.

"I'm being selfish, I think. I've forgotten how to be selfish. I only know how to be alone."

I face her: "You can't just..."

"I know how to do it." She allows herself a sardonic smile, as if this is an old joke between us I've forgotten. Her voice is low and even. "The internet is loving and non-judgmental. I've been saving up medication."

"Suicide." I want to make the word as sharp and heavy as possible.

But she's ready for me. She offers a true smile, her mask falling away to reveal the Sophie I know, a glittering spark in her eye. "No, they call it 'self-deliverance'. Makes it sound sort of masturbatory, doesn't it?"

"It's not a joke, Sophie." I sink into the chair across from her. "You just..." I begin, running a finger along the smooth surface of the table as if tracing a route on a map. I say what people say in these situations, and I immediately feel stupid saying it: "You should just listen to the doctors, take the treatments. You fight, Sophie, that's what you do.

"You're not the kind to give up." I try to sound definitive but it seems more a plea.

"Doug, there's nothing they can do." She's watching me earnestly, her head tilted slightly to the left.

"There's nothing to fight. If I go back to the hospital they'll just keep me there, farm me out to a nursing home or a hospice center. I mean, I could stay alive for a year or two. But why? Can you tell me why?"

I stare at the blank table.

"I don't have any money left and they'll take the house soon and...I don't know. I don't want to die in a hospital, somebody just pulling a sheet over my face one day."

She reaches across the table to take my hand but thinks better of it, her fingers fluttering back toward her chest like the wings of a trapped bird. "You think I don't know what I'm asking. I know what I'm asking and I'm sorry, but I'm asking anyway."

"It's not something you can ask. Call me up and say, c'mon over. We'll have tea and you can help me kill myself."

"You called me. I didn't call you..."

"Not for this," I whisper.

"I know," she sighs gently. "I hung up the phone after. I'd been thinking about it for weeks, of course. I was frightened. I didn't want to do it alone. I thought you might understand. If anyone, you, maybe."

"Well, call some other old boyfriend. There must be a few. Work on a couple of them. How about the goofy guy in the driveway?"

"You're the only one...and you're not an old boyfriend."

I glance up. "What am I then?"

Her voice catches and she waves words away. There's a lump in my throat and I can't look at her. Can't allow the moment to dissolve into tears that might drown us.

"You're my spotter. You're the one who holds the ladder, the one who stands to the side when I do the heavy lifts. The one I can trust."

"Sophie, you can't be serious. I can't believe you've got me talking about this like it's a real thing. You can't have thought this through. Things just don't get that bad."

I'm pacing again, two strides from the kitchen table and back, my arms flailing, flapping around my body. I don't know what I'm saying, I'm just saying it.

"Do you have any idea how much of you I've carried around all these years? How long I've tried to get the memory of you out of me. We, this whole memory of us, a memory I can't separate any more. I don't know what's real and what's imagined until it takes me by the throat and even then I don't know.

"I carry us like a weight. Sure, I can go for days without thinking of you, of us, then something triggers a memory and I'm yanked backward into it again."

I'm standing over her now, adopting a weird accusatory tone I don't understand. "And every woman after was just another part of the same thing, just me trying to re-enact something or figure something out. I said the same things to women after you. Maybe I meant them, I don't know. But I kept it up, year after year, because you were so goddamned deep inside me I couldn't get you out. I just had to learn to deal with it. A part of you, always there."

I'm standing over her now. Her eyes are on me. Something in her suddenly relaxed and softening, and I almost stop speaking. There's an instant in which I could stop and take her hand. But I don't:

"And me, I'm the last person who should help you. I'm the goddamned last soul on earth who should be here."

Sophie holds up a hand, trying to block my rage. Splotches of red are rising in her face.

"I don't know how you think you can do this. What gives you the right to do this?" I go on and on, pacing the box of the kitchen, listening as my voice rises and falls. After a moment or two, Sophie stops making any effort to speak. She's motionless, staring into a disc of sunlight on the table.

Minutes pass as I lean back against the kitchen counter. Trying now to come back, to gather the shattered pieces I've scattered back into myself, to find a place within my body after the spin of my fury. There's a slight machine buzz in the kitchen, a distant bird twittering outside, and the slow rise and fall of Sophie's breath. My fingers curl and uncurl over the edge of the countertop.

Finally, Sophie's voice, low and deliberate: "This is about me. Not you. Me. You cannot make it something else. It is what it is and it's mine." Her tone softens yet she continues to stare ahead. "Can you let this be about me?"

"I'm very aware it's all about you."

"I'm sorry. I can't fight with you, Doug. I don't have it in me. I can't make you feel better about what's happening, I can't heal the past. I am doing all I can do. Right at this moment, I'm doing all I can do."

I know she's telling the truth but it doesn't help. I want something from her and I don't know what it is. Or I want her not to want something from me.

"Make yourself some tea. I can't manage or I'd do it for you. I'll wait right here."

"I hate tea," I say.

"I know you do," she nods. "Just make it anyway."

I make tea. I pour out the stale water and fill the pot again, placing it on the burner, clicking it to high. I lean back against the edge of the stove. "Are you ready yet?"

Sophie tilts her head, scrunching her nose. "No. Not yet."

Something is playing behind her eyes; her face has lost some of its tension. When she begins I can't tell if she's called the memory for my benefit or her own.

"I woke up this morning...I must've been dreaming, I guess...I was thinking of the bench on Trade Street, near the corner, the place we always sat together. And I could see down the streets in all four directions. I think it was just before daybreak, because there was no one there. You were there but you weren't. I mean, I felt you there, in the dream, but I couldn't see you. It was spring, I think, and the edges of the buildings were beginning to glow in the sunlight. All the shops and stalls, full of scarves and paintings and jewelry, but no one had arrived yet. I was the first."

She turns to me and she doesn't need to lead. I'm already there.

"Remember how, sometimes, after a late one at the Scrawl, you'd meet me and we'd sit on that bench, three four in the morning and we'd hold each other, watching the shadow of the stoplight swing on the red brick of that old warehouse. Talking, watching that stoplight click from red to green and back again. Now and then, a police car would crawl by and we'd wave at them, they'd wave at us."

She closes her eyes. "I woke up with that inside. Because it's a thing that happened, do you see? It happened: you and I on that bench. I was happy that it happened. I felt like crap, but I was happy."

Suddenly Sophie has fully arrived and the room has lost its hard edges, its light more fluid, and I can feel myself only a few feet from her. The heat from her body, and her scent. And we are who we are, and were, as if some magical filter has been lifted from the frame revealing a crisp, pristine image. She's come into her body. I can see her form through her baggy sweatshirt.

She enters the room in a flood. She comes into me as she has in the intervening years, complete and unpredictable; only now she's not a memory. She's here. We're real people in an actual room. She's here, and I want to spend the morning in aimless conversation, a range of memory rising warm onto my skin.

I want to tell her my dream and the memory that arose from it: I'd borrowed a video camera from someone at work. Back then, it was bulky and cumbersome. I didn't have a tripod so I had to push the camera into my shoulder and chest, press it against my cheek, to keep it as still as possible, framing Sophie's hands working the fabric, wanting a record of her hands, always her hands: at the canvas, with a brush, resting on a table or entwined with mine.

I'd watched her stretch the canvases before, the long process of preparation: stretching tighter and tighter, the stapling, the gesso, the sanding one layer after another. I was enthralled with the process, the tedium and the constancy of it, the amount of work required simply to reach a place to begin.

She talked to me, to the camera, as she worked, explaining each phase of the process, her conversation casual, demonstrating the work step by step.

"There's always a space," I remember her saying, "a pause between the moment the canvas is ready and the first stroke. All that time the thing just waits. It's quiet, patient." I remember she smiled. "It's resolute.

"Then the first color comes," she said. "Every color has its own smell, its own texture. If you listen you can hear them. You know it's the right color by the way it slides onto the canvas."

I recorded it diligently, not knowing why, knowing only that there needed to be a record. Back then, I was always doing things like that: wrestling with projects that had no beginning, middle or end, that never found a way to hold together.

I want to tell Sophie what it meant to study her hands but the rasp of her fingers on the canvas returns from the dream. The rasp and the clutch of the canvas and the torn skin at her knuckles and the thin streaks of blood.

I pour the steaming water into the cup I don't want. I stare into the cup, catching my breath. My chest is pitching wildly. There's an annoying lump in my throat. I ask the question to the floor but manage to force myself to look at her after.

My voice is quiet, someone else's voice. "Why do you want to die, Sophie?"

Her body turns in my direction and she winces with the effort, placing both hands at the corner of the table. Her limbs are trembling, but her eyes are clear. "Oh, baby. I don't want to die. No one wants to die."

"But then..." The lump in my throat is larger and my eyes are starting to burn. There's a rushing in my ears, the muscles in my arms tightening, my mouth dry.

The ceramic cat drops to the floor, shattering, and I have done nothing. The man leans in the threshold for a moment before disappearing. All I can do is hold her.

Her face is turned toward me, her fingers clutching the kitchen table. I recognize the tone of her voice as intimate. She's trying to tell me something but I can't hear her.

I don't want to have this conversation. I don't want to hear her answer. I don't want to have known. We have cried too much and too often and I have done nothing. If she'd known how easily I'd betrayed her, she'd never have forgiven me. Yet, she did. Immediately, without any doubt. It's her forgiveness I cannot bear.

My hand is trembling around the cup. Scalding water sloshes onto my fist and I draw it away quickly. I spin from the counter, shaking my hand, bringing it to my mouth, blowing on the reddened skin.

"This is bullshit," I hear myself say, "all your 'remember-whens' jumbled in with 'just do what I want'. Maybe it's your medication, or something. But this is crazy and you need to get a grip. There's got to be someone who can help you. Not me, someone."

Sophie's face goes blank, her eyes cold, and it's a relief to see her distance. She draws herself upright again, dropping her hands into her lap, leaning slowly into the back of the chair. Her words are clipped and jagged: "Just say no then. Okay? Say no and be done with it. Say no and leave me the hell alone."

I lean into her, inches from her face. It's the closest we've been all morning.

"I can't help you."

I turn without another word, storm through the living room and out the front door without looking back. On the porch, nearly blinded by the sun, I stumble down the steps toward my car. I gun the car from the driveway, spraying gravel, only truly breathing once I see the road fall behind me in the mirror.

I glance back at the house but it's a blank face. I knew she wouldn't follow me, stand at the door, or peer from a parted curtain. I knew she'd simply remain at the kitchen table for a very long time.

The road is a relief after the box of the kitchen. There's the sense of motion as the landscape blurs by. My body loosens into the seat, my fingers around the wheel; I settle into the car, onto the road. For a long time it doesn't matter where I'm going, though I'm vaguely aware of signs urging me toward the highway. I keep them in sight, not wanting to find myself adrift on unmarked country roads.

The countryside is soothing, unfolding in greens and browns and miles of unbroken road. A large tractor groans along a fence line, churning dark earth beneath it. Cows stare from the shade of an overarching oak. There's a hawk spiraling endlessly above the road like a kite floating in clear sky.

And then I'm crying. Hot tears on my cheeks, in my lap. Tears streaked along the back of my hand, erupting now as if my entire body has held them for years and they have finally found a means of escape. Crying now, because I'm hurt, again. Because I've allowed it to happen, through some idiot trust in something between Sophie and me. The fear is all over me and there's no way to push it back. Larger than us, larger than anything.

I slam my hand hard into the wheel over and over, pounding at my own inability to extricate myself from the past, until my palm stings and I notice I'm accelerating, the car at nearly ninety now, tunneling blindly forward.

I ease off the accelerator, push back into the seat, try to calm my wired limbs. The sobs come, wrenching upward from my gut, nearly doubling me. I'm gripping the wheel, clutching at it, holding my place in the car, holding the car in the road.

Then I've stopped and I'm climbing across the seat toward the passenger door, pushing it open, struggling to escape. My feet hit the soft shoulder and I'm away, door open behind me, the car chiming incessantly to remind me of keys abandoned in the ignition.

I run into the trees, into an old and dense plot acres deep between two mown fields. I run as I did as a child, into the trees, toward something old and clean and immovable, toward something that, though silent, might somehow slow and contain me. To escape a terror I can never name, have spent my lifetime unable to name. A rage and terror so irreparably linked, so massive and impossible as to be unapproachable.

The sobs ache now, the muscles in my abdomen cramping with them, the tears a simple hot stream. I'm running, branches whipping my face. Deeper, further. Away.

I stumble and crash into an old oak. I flail at it with both fists, my body resounding with each blow, the impact pounding up my arms and into my shoulders as I hit it again and again. Chips of dead bark fly away while others embed themselves in the flat sides of my fists; I pound and kick until I'm spent, bloody, sliding down the trunk, legs splayed outward onto the twisted roots, where I catch my breath for a moment before pushing myself forward into a kneel.

The sun is blocked by the canopy of branches. The trees are quiet. With no breeze, they stand silent, unwavering. There's a coolness seeping up from the earth, clinging in the low branches, a damp just below the leaf bed. I can feel it wicking into the knees of my jeans. I hear my own ragged, pacing breath, a voice or a dog far away. I push my fingers into the leaf layer at my sides, down into the dark earth, feeling it give at my fingertips. Its heavy scent rises into me.

I am silent, still. Cold and empty. My breath rattles through the empty drum of my chest.

I cry again. Different tears this time. I'm crying for us, Sophie and me. For our fragile, broken hearts. I ease onto my side in the leaves, my fingers damp with earth, my cheek along the rooted arm of the tree. I bring my knees up, my arms flung over the ground before me and I cry again. Slow, still tears forming like patient clouds.

Now there are no sobs. My body has receded. There are only eyes, staring across the forest floor, and a mouth, lips working without word or sound. My tears bleed out as sunlight filters through the branches above me, choosing to collect now along this stone at the edge of this leaf then flickering out, only to reappear a few feet away at the base of a sapling.

I know Sophie is at the kitchen table. She's wearing her oversized sweatshirt and her blue bandanna. Wisps of hair curl outward at the edge of the bandanna, looping back over its lip. Her face is clear but her eyes are red-rimmed and wet. She's staring down into her hands on the tabletop, her fingers clasping and unclasping slowly. She looks up, her eyes a deeper green in the afternoon light.

I lie at the base of the oak for a long time. I stare, unblinking, across the width of the forest floor.

I heave myself into a sitting position and fall back against the trunk, gathering whatever energy I have left in order to stand. I pull myself to my feet, embarrassed, glancing around, ridiculously concerned someone might have been watching.

But I'm alone. I brush the dirt and leaves from my damp clothes, wipe the debris from my cheeks, and try to remember which way I'd come. I set off in that direction.

I know Sophie is already leaving, already moving from me, and there is nothing I can do. She's straining from shore, all the ropes tugging, and I can't change it. Everything ends before it ends. I'm always catching up.

The car is still chiming optimistically when I return, the door hanging open. I climb into the passenger seat and click the door closed.

I pick up the phone from the seat beside me and poke it awake. I stare through the grimy windshield, into the open, empty road, waiting for the connection.

It won't be a relief to say it. There'll be no inviting lightness as after the break of a fever when, finally returning to my body, my limbs feel more supple and welcoming. In the open landscapes that surround Sophie and me, there are arguments. Inside there is only one answer.

The selves we once were, still are, are aching and broken. I will not leave her. This time. I will not turn away. Maybe I can choose a self for the next months, as I choose the right tool to fit the job, as I choose the correct word for the sentence.

There are times when words don't work, when words come later, after a gesture or a glance, times when words simply articulate what has happened, and what could not have happened through words alone.

It's not a decision, but an acceptance, the announcement of another departure. The pressure will not ease. It will simply settle like a thin fog.

It's ringing on the other end of the line. Perhaps, I think, she won't pick up.

I'm watching the road through the windshield. It doesn't move. There is no traffic on this road.

"Doug?"

THREE

11

I've dropped my flashlight. I don't really need a flashlight. The emergency lights are always on, throwing intervals of grey to the bare floor. They resemble stones for crossing a stream. I could play a game of skipping one pool of light to the next but I don't. I stand watching the beam of the flashlight skew to the side and bump against the edge of a far wall, muddy and diffuse. I stand there a long time, unsure of what else to do.

I drop things a lot lately. My grasp simply gives way and anything in my hand slips out. It's become commonplace. I roll my eyes then look around to see if anyone has noticed. Sometimes, I snatch the object up quickly; at others I just stand there staring at the thing as if blaming it somehow, the way people on the street look back when they've stumbled over their own feet, wanting to find a crack in the sidewalk or a loose stone. Wanting to find a reason.

The building is vast and heavy around me. There's lots of empty space to guard. The hallways are long and sullen, the rooms empty. The walls give off a lazy warmth, the sun having seeped through the high windows all day and trickled down the brick. There's a tone to these open spaces in the middle of the night, a low roar like underground water. I have to be very quiet to hear it. I have to be motionless.

I watch the flashlight for a long time. I reach down to pick it up. I click it off and slide it into my belt. I continue my hourly inspection of the building. What else is there to do.

Since the robbery it often seems quieter at work. I tell myself I'm calmer here, more useful. I can feel I'm doing something, even if that something is utterly ridiculous: protecting emptiness from any intrusion. Constantly on guard against those who might want to steal nothing.

The robbery. That's what we call it. Sophie doesn't want to talk about anything else that might have happened. She clenches or cries. I know she talked to the police. To the doctors at the ER. But she can't talk to me.

"Give her time," Maggie says, her voice low and close. She's sitting beside me on the steps of my apartment building. The beginning of a fall chill is in the air, with a high rustle as the leaves begin to turn and curl.

Maggie slips her arm around me, pressing her cheek to my shoulder. There's the scent of her hair and a slight perfume. There's the heat of her against me and the tenderness of her touch. Something distant warms with the contact, something far away flickers like a beacon.

"These things, God, they're not easy," she tells me. "It's not you. Not something you've done. It's because you're so close. It's easier to talk to strangers. For a long time."

"It feels," I begin, without knowing what I'll say next, "like there's nothing I can do. And, like doing nothing is so wrong."

I don't tell her about the nightmares, the images strobing through my mind in endless loops. Of what might have happened behind the office door. Of what probably did happen behind the office door. I don't tell her I can't control them and that each time they come I feel I've betrayed Sophie just a little more. Again and again, day after day.

I sit beside her on the step, my arms between my knees, my knuckles slowly scraping back and forth on the rough brick beneath.

"This is so bad," Maggie says, almost to herself, "so wrong." Maggie's head rocks against my arm. "Oh, Sophie."

Her hand tightens on my shoulder, pulling my body gently to her. I'm surprised by the kindness in her voice, surprised that I notice it. I want some gesture or word to let her know I've noticed but can't find one. I don't say anything. I don't do anything.

In a moment, Maggie sniffs and raises her head. Her arm loosens, uncurling around me, her hand coming to rest on my knee.

"Still not ready to come inside?" she asks. There's no trace of judgment in her voice. But I feel stupid, like a child who can't stop sulking.

"No. There are plenty of people in there. She doesn't need me."

"She does, Doug. She just has to find the way again. You have to help her."

"I..."

But there's nothing to say.

Since the robbery, Maggie has come every day. She brings food, every day; Jim comes when she can't. They've done this for two weeks. Sometimes it's a casserole, soup, or a salad she's made herself; sometimes it's pizza or take-out from a nearby restaurant. She drops off the meal, stays just a moment then politely excuses herself.

It was Maggie I called from the hospital, borrowing quarters from strangers in the waiting room because our phones were gone.

"How is she?" she'd asked. I could hear her slipping out of bed, I could hear her starting to get dressed.

"I don't know," I'd replied.

"How are you?" she'd asked next.

"I don't know," I said.

"I'll be right there," she told me. I held the phone to my ear. I couldn't think of anything else to do. "Doug," she said, her voice firm yet comforting, "I'll be right there." Then she hung up.

Since the robbery, Sophie has lived with me and there are always people in the apartment. Which is good, I guess. Artist friends, folks from the Scrawl, people I've never met. Someone stays with her while I'm at work; I could only afford to take two days off and none of us wanted to leave her alone.

Someone drops by to say hi. Often they'll sit on the side of the bed and I'll leave them alone with her. The murmurs through the partially closed door become difficult to bear and I put on my headphones, listening to music I can't actually hear.

Everyone asks about me too, but only for a moment. Which is fine with me. I can't maintain eye contact for very long anyway. I don't want a conversation. I have one going in my head already:

You were there and..?

How could you let him...?

Why didn't you...?

I hear their questions. Even if they never ask them. Even if they've never even considered them.

So I stay on the couch, pretending to read, pretending to listen to music, pretending to write. I get up to answer the door, to answer the phone, to answer their questions.

"How's she doing?" someone asks, before tapping lightly on the bedroom door and going in. We'll be standing near the kitchen or at the end of the hallway. They'll be close, sometimes with their hand on my forearm or shoulder.

"Better," I say. "I think she's doing better," without knowing if I mean anything at all or if I'm simply talking to keep more questions, or a certain silence, at bay.

When nothing more is required of me, I sink back into the couch or a chair by the window. Now and then, usually at someone's urging, I go for a walk, but it feels worse being away from her. As if I might return and she will have faded in my absence, her body slowly growing transparent before vanishing altogether.

Last night when I came home from work I found her on the couch in the living room. It's the first time I've seen her outside the bedroom since it happened. Her back is straight, her hands flat on her knees. The skin of her face is drawn tight; it seems to take all of her effort to remain in the room.

She's wearing sweat pants and a bulky sweater. Her feet are obscured by thick socks. Her hair is pulled away from her face and tied behind. She's staring into the television, soundlessly flickering blue and white shadows along her face and the wall behind her.

She turns slowly when she hears the door click shut behind me, a memory of a smile suggesting itself at the borders of her mouth.

Natalie is asleep, curled like a child at the other end of the couch. She'd stayed with Sophie tonight.

I slide my keys into the dish on the bookshelf by the door, pull off my jacket and hang it on the corner. I walk to her side of the couch and let my hand fall to the armrest.

"How're you feeling?" I ask, holding my voice quiet and steady.

Her eyes track me from the door, but drop as I approach. She glances up when I speak and the tiny smile returns for an instant. She shrugs, her shoulders hardly rising before releasing. Her skin is waxen in the light of the television, bluish, her eyes swollen and red-rimmed, her mouth small and tight. She lifts a hand slowly from between her knees and pats the open space on the couch beside her.

Since the robbery it's been difficult to touch Sophie, even to hold her hand or smooth a stray hair from her cheek. She might flinch or pull away, both of us embarrassed and apologetic, or she might quietly acquiesce. Even then I'm never certain if the touch means something to her or if she's simply bearing it for my sake.

Gradually I've learned to keep my distance. We slept in the same bed for the first two nights but after that, it seemed better for me to take the couch. Sophie's tossing and muttering, my betraying dreams. It was easier to be apart, easier to have time in the morning before we saw each other.

I settle beside her, Natalie's feet overlaid an inch or two to my left.

"What're you watching?" I whisper, close to Sophie's ear so I don't wake Natalie.

"I don't know," she whispers back. Her voice is soft and dreamy. "It seems to be about a guy building a rocket in his backyard. I turned the sound off. I just try to imagine what they're saying to each other."

In a moment, her head lowers to my shoulder. I hold my body still as if bracing against a storm, staring at the flicker of the screen, listening to Natalie's rhythmic sleep-drugged breathing.

"Did you eat something?"

Sophie nods.

She leans into me. I drape my arm over her shoulder, drawing her close. Her body is light and delicate beneath the sweatshirt, as if filled with air. She's a ghost, a whisper. I can't find her warmth. It's only the pressure of her bones that lets me know she's there.

Then, after a moment, her breathing appears in my arm and along my side. Before, it seemed to be circling loose within her but now it settles in her chest. It happens gradually, as if she's pouring herself into form in a trickle, accomplishing it silently so no one might notice.

"Sophie," I begin, my face nesting in her hair.

"Sshhh..." she whispers.

We tremble like baby birds on a branch, weak and still startled. Her ghostly body beside mine, her tepid warmth hardly noticeable. In the past weeks she's seemed not broken so much as empty; as if everything about her has pulled away from her skin and her bones, knotting itself tightly somewhere dark and out of sight. Whenever I've touched her, she simply wasn't there.

I could feel her presence in the room as a shuddering light but it no longer seemed housed in her body; it floated like smoke and shadow around her, just above her head, at the tips of her fingers.

Constantly having others in the apartment means I've had little opportunity to be alone with her while she's awake, to be aware of her absence, to feel her absence when she glances at me or when I touch her, to realize how fully her body has been vacated.

I'll stand in the other room or heat soup in the kitchen and be aware, instead, of her presence in the apartment. Away from her, out of sight, I can feel a whisper of her, and this is soothing until it occurs to me it might simply be memory; her muscle memory in my limbs, thrumming like the rippling vibrations of a bell rung long ago. Then I'm terrified again.

I just want her to myself. I want her the way she was. Before.

The morning after the robbery, Maggie drives us home from the hospital. It's after 11 a.m. and we're all far beyond exhaustion. I see Maggie hesitate on the street after opening the car door for Sophie, see her eyes play over Sophie's face and slide to mine, watch her decide she'll let us climb the stairs alone, enter the apartment together without her. She squeezes Sophie's hand, kissing her on the cheek.

"I'll drop by this evening," she says. "I'll bring you both some dinner." And she's gone.

Somehow we make it up the stairs and I fumble the door open. The apartment is quiet. The light hangs at the windows, the air is heavy. Beaker raises himself from the sofa, stretching with great care and concentration, then padding over to us, winding himself between our legs.

I touch Sophie's hand and wish I hadn't. Not because she pulls away, but because she doesn't notice. Her breath coming short, her gaze darting around the room trying to locate something familiar. It's a look of shallow terror I'll grow accustomed to.

"Hey," I ask quietly, "can I get you something? Water or tea. Something to eat? I don't know what I have."

My voice locks her into place somehow. Her eyes focus on the window, then the coffee table. She looks down to Beaker, then reaches to pick him up. His legs splay across her chest as she clutches him there. She still can't take another step into the apartment.

"No, Doug," she tells me, lowering her swollen cheek into Beaker's neck. I try not to notice the purple bruise by her left eye shading to green at the edges of swollen flesh. "I don't need anything. I just…I just want to take a bath and lie down. Is that okay?"

"Sure," I tell her. I want to take her in my arms, but my touch doesn't matter. I want to say I'm sorry again, but my apologies are meaningless. I want to tell her I understand but I don't. I can only make petty efforts that don't amount to much.

I move into the living room, away from her, straightening books on the table, collecting socks and dishes, acutely aware of how disheveled the place is. When I look back she's no longer by the door. In a moment, I hear running water.

I give her space, knowing she hasn't been alone since yesterday morning, knowing there have been questions and physical exams, many repeated again and again. I make the bed while she's in the tub. I draw back the curtains and open a window. I toss dirty clothes into the basket and push the basket into the closet.

She stays in the tub a long time. I wash the dishes and clean the refrigerator. I even sweep the floor. Anything to keep moving, the activity holding something at rest as I slowly become aware of my own exhaustion.

My body grows heavy and jangling. There's a dull buzz at the back of my head. My movements are erratic, my fingers twitching. I flatten my palms on the kitchen counter, splaying my fingers then leaning into them with all my weight like a child pressing handprints into wet cement.

She's sitting on the side of the bed, swathed in her heavy bathrobe and my socks, staring vaguely at the open window. Beaker lies in the center of the bed, cleaning his paws. On the dresser beside her is the amber bottle of sleeping pills they'd given her at the hospital. I watch her from the doorway as her eyes shift from the window to the pills and back again.

I sit down beside her. Not too close.

She pulls the bathrobe tighter, her hands smoothing it over her legs.

"Sophie, I just want to..."

"Can we..." Her hands stop moving. "I just...I need to not talk." She's stifling a sob. "Can we just not talk? Just for tonight."

"Sure," I whisper, not knowing why I'm whispering.

Sophie glances at the bottle again, reaches for it, hands it to me. "Would you get rid of these please."

I stare at the bottle in my hand. There are many things I could say. Instead, I tell her: "I'm going to make you some tea. It'll help you sleep."

Sophie allows a tiny smile. "Tea would be nice."

She's already asleep by the time I return, in the middle of the bed, curled around Beaker, a tight ball of fur at her center. I sit for a long time in the chair by the bed, as if she might awaken at any moment in desperate need of tea.

The cup grows cold. My hands begin to shake. They shake so violently I place the cup on the floor. Then I begin to cry. Thin, hot tears that won't stop. They turn in my stomach, shudder in my chest, curl in my throat then drip down my cheeks. Sophie is turned away from me, wrapped around the cat. I watch her sleep and I cry.

I jolt awake to Sophie's shriek. She's sitting up in the bed, panting, her eyes closed, fingers gripping the comforter. I'm already beside her. She folds into my arms. I can't tell if she's awake, but she's sobbing. Her body is spread across my lap.

"It's okay, Sophie," I tell her, stupidly. "It's going to be alright." I know I'm lying. I don't know how to be honest. I can find no honest place to stand. I want to be honest. I say nothing now, so much of the time, because it's the only way to keep from lying.

When she's nearly asleep again, I manage to get her beneath the sheet and comforter. I slide into bed beside her, flat on my back, staring at the ceiling, wondering how we will ever be okay.

I'm awake by five, the afternoon sun throwing long shadows through the open windows. I'm sitting in the living room, absently stroking Beaker when Maggie knocks.

"Hey," she says when I open the door. "I'm not going to come in. I just wanted to drop this by. Some soup and bread. For when you get hungry."

She hands me a bag and I take it without looking inside.

"How's it going?" she asks. It occurs to me that she actually wants to know. So much conversation lately has been vague or frightened. Her eyes watch my face.

"I don't know. I'm just…I'm just here."

"Sophie?"

"She's been sleeping."

"Sleep is good." Her eyes remain on me. I should feel uneasy but I don't. Her eyes are bright and deep. There's a steadiness in them; some kind of soft assurance that's alluring. I feel the endless tears again, but I hold them low and boiling.

"You get through it a few minutes at a time, Doug. That's all you do."

I nod.

"You're doing fine," she says. "I'll be by tomorrow, but if you need anything before then, you've got my number."

Sophie has taken form on the couch beside me. She slopes across my lap in the flicker of the television. She has a shape, her arms and legs gathering weight as her body rests upon mine. I drop my hand to her head, her hair beneath my fingers. I listen to her breathing. I can't see her face but I don't think she's crying.

In a few minutes she rises up again, sliding back into place beside me. My hand drifts from her head, following her spine down her back, coming to rest in the open space between us. Her hands are turning gently in her lap, her palms upraised. She takes a deep breath.

"I think I want to go back to the studio, Doug." She turns to look at me. "Will you go with me?"

I nod. "Of course."

"I don't think I could go alone."

"Do you want to paint?" I ask, trying not to press her, trying to want nothing.

"I don't know. I don't know what I want to do. I don't think I *will* know 'til I'm there."

She takes my hand and places it in her lap, kneading it between her warm, damp palms. "Do you mind?"

I shake my head. "I'm off on Wednesday. Want to do it then?"

Her fingers lace into mine. She's staring straight ahead.

"I know it doesn't seem like it," she tells me, her voice low and distant, "but I'm trying to find my way home."

She turns, our eyes meet, and I'm startled. It seems so long since we've seen each other. "I know my trail of breadcrumbs is around here somewhere."

"Damn birds..." I reply.

"...always eating my breadcrumbs."

She leans in and kisses me, placing her palm on my chest. It's a soft, quick kiss, her hand both an intimacy and a barrier.

All I can do is watch her. She's trying not to cry, swallowing hard, holding my gaze. I feel a single tear on my cheek. She offers her crooked smile and wipes it away with her thumb.

We are so lost, Sophie and I. We're almost non-existent, struggling just to breathe. Our bodies are holding a place in the world for us, but we can only occasionally make contact with them. We struggle to push our awareness into our eyes and see, into our fingers and touch. We struggle for the strength and the will to guide our awareness anywhere, to gather it like the shards of some delicate vase we believe we can repair if only we can find every piece.

We're still standing open-handed and agape, as a child does when something has been snatched away so suddenly and completely that there's an instant of disbelief before the tears or rage. Despite the tears we've already cried, the loss hasn't yet been felt. We can agree something has happened, but not that something has fallen away, and not that the loss has changed us. We haven't yet closed our hands to find nothing there.

I watch her until I can't any longer. Until we understand we don't know what to do next and we turn from each other to stare blankly at the television or the wall behind it.

There's a scream still hanging in the air, one that hasn't yet been found. Not the scream of a week ago, when Sophie's wail from the tub had instantly frayed every nerve and sent me careening into the bathroom without a knock or a word. This scream, if it comes, will be longer and deeper. It might never be found; it might never end.

I burst into the bathroom without thinking. Sophie is naked in the tub, fists clenched, her body rising in the wail. She's tiny and pale, her face flushed with the effort, her fists dark and tight. There are green bruises on her left breast and purpling bruises high on both arms. Bruises I hadn't seen before. Her hair is wet and glued to her head. Her eyes are closed. She doesn't know I exist.

She's slamming the water with her fists, spraying it into her face and onto the floor. Her voice is deep and ragged, an old voice newly found, or a voice not hers at all but borrowed, drawn from some arcane current, billowing into the room in a heavy cloud. She strikes at the water, her tensed face tilted upward, eyelids pressed tight, everything in her jammed into the fists and somewhere deep, where the voice is found.

I'm on my knees by the tub. I pull her into my arms and she fights me, fights the water and the world, fists crashing downward again and again, then flinging out against the wall with sharp thuds. She fights until I've pinned her between my arms and the side of the tub.

I'm saying something. I don't know what I'm saying. I'm holding her, terrified, with no clue what I'll do next, her naked skin against my soaked shirt. I'm holding her slick limbs against mine as the water in the tub rocks one side to the other, spilling over the lip with every return.

She doesn't so much relax as drain away. She's not crying. She's staring directly ahead, into the white tile of the shower as she slowly falls back from me, from herself, from the world. I hold her trembling body as she tumbles through it. I lift her out of the water and she lets me. I dry her and dress her and get her into bed again, accomplishing it quickly to avoid the body I miss and the bruises I don't want to see.

One evening, Jim delivers dinner. Sophie is sleeping in the bedroom and I invite him inside, no longer able to bear the loneliness. Jim places the bag gently on the kitchen counter and takes a chair; I sit on the sofa. He tells me about his new project, a low-slung walnut coffee table. He'd just bought the wood a few days before from a guy tearing down an old house. He leans back into the chair, arms relaxed on each armrest, and explains the grain, the beautiful weight and shape of it.

For an instant, I'm not ghostly. I'm a normal person having a normal conversation, listening to a man talk about something he loves. He hadn't started woodworking until after the baby died, when he found he needed to do something with his hands, needed to make an undeniable object. We talk for a few more minutes before he stands and moves toward the door. He shakes my hand there, his other hand grasping my shoulder, dark eyes locked onto mine. He nods toward my notebook he'd noticed on the sofa. "You've got to find a way to use it. If you don't, it uses you."

When the scream comes, it might be hers or mine. Either way, I don't know what I'll do.

We don't talk about that, of course.

We stare at the blue-white flicker of the television, Sophie still cradling my hand in her lap and, on Wednesday, we go to the studio together.

She's wobbly, like a young colt, blinking in the sunlight and the noise of the street. She steps back once she pushes open the door and the room hisses in a sudden intake of air. She steps away from the cool darkness inside and the thick scent of oils and turpentine and old dust.

I take her hand. "C'mon. You'll feel better once you're inside."

I lead her into the middle of the room where I drop her hand and make my way to the switch on the back wall. When the light comes on, she gasps.

It's one part fear and one part joy, the shock of beauty followed by something overwhelming: responsibility, or some kind of response because beauty always makes its demand. A burst of color and form, a silent crescendo high in the brain. A gaping astonishment mixed with the desire to turn away or narrow the vision to only one object.

I recognize myself. This was my response in the art museum we'd visited on our third date. I'd been to art museums before but only in school. This museum, this night with Sophie, left me shaken. I was speechless and Sophie laughed, but only for an instant, before she took my arm and squeezed it, leaning into me. Sophie has that expression now, in the midst of the studio, taking in her own work. I imagine it seems personal but also distant, as if these paintings were accomplished years and years ago, instead of months or weeks.

She's staring at a self I pray she recognizes. A self that's finer and clearer, composed of different materials than our life together. She's not looking for clues but I'm hoping she finds them in the tone of a color, the texture of a stroke, or some wisdom she'd secreted in the past for a now impossible future.

At first, she's motionless before the painting directly in front of her; in a moment, she begins slowly turning, to take everything in. She makes three revolutions, each a little slower than the previous, coming to rest in her original position, arms loose at her sides, eyes wide and clear.

Bright light streams in from the open door behind her, a light more golden than the overheads or the skylight above. Leaning on a post, I watch her. Leaning, likewise, against the wall near me, are blank canvases she'd prepared the week before the robbery. There are four, each a different size, the largest four by six feet.

I'd watched her for hours working the canvas over these frames, pulling and stretching, kneading her knuckles into the wooden frames until the skin broke and bled, so fascinated by the process I'd filmed it. Once the canvases were stretched and mounted, she began to gesso and sand them, one layer after another. Day after day, layer after layer; she worked for an empty space from which to begin.

Maggie smiles when I tell her Sophie's been back to the studio. There's a deep breath in her smile, different from the others over the past weeks. She turns to me on the apartment steps. The sun is slipping behind the roof of the opposite building, the light sifting low to the ground.

"She stood there for a moment like she'd never seen it before," I tell her. "She didn't even know I was there. She just turned in a circle, over and over, and every time she came back around something in her face had changed. I can't tell you what it was. I don't know. But something changed. We only stayed ten minutes or so. Then she was ready to go. She didn't want to do anything, she said. Just wanted to see it."

Maggie nods; it's a gesture she extends with an air of contentment. She pats my leg confidently. "It's gonna be alright, Doug," she tells me.

And for a moment, because she believes it, I believe it. A spark of hope catches in me. I rock gently in the wake of her grace for long enough to draw a deep breath.

She stands up, her hand sliding to my shoulder as her legs unfold. I miss her beside me. I miss, already, her hand on my knee.

"You should go in to her, Doug. Sitting out here, it's not good for you. Or her."

"In a minute," I promise. "I have to be at work in a bit. I'll go in before I leave."

I go in just long enough to collect my uniform and shoes. I nod to Sophie from the other side of the room. Natalie is there, and Abby, and two others I might have met before. Sophie's hand comes up in something like a wave as I edge to the door.

I know how it will be at work. I know every moment of the night, can almost number the steps from one room to the other, one building to the next. I know the fine grey dust that shudders on the floor when I pass. The stale, damp air. The stones of light thrown to the floor by the emergency lights. I know I'll walk and walk, wishing I'd spoken to Sophie, wishing I'd willed my heavy limbs to carry me toward her, put my arms around her, or that I'd taken her hand and drawn her to the porch to watch Fall arrive.

All night, I'll try to believe it is her pain that keeps me away.

12

I blink awake on the sofa. The dim square of the window hangs before me. A threshold. The rest of the room blotted to grey.

It's the middle of the night. Or almost morning. The heavy, deep blue falls on the other side of the sheer curtains Sophie bought in the summer to blur the thick sun of midday. I lie still, uncertain for a moment, overtaken by a kind of dream vertigo.

I know I won't be able to go back to sleep. The nightmare is too itchy and hot. The behind-the-door images. Glimpses of skin. Fingers pushed into flesh. Bruised limbs flailing. Sophie's hair tattered across her cheek. Sophie sliding to the floor in my arms, too late to matter. I can't close my eyes without seeing the shadows and I can't just lie here and let them crawl all over me. I wait for the room to take shape but I know I have to get up.

I pour a glass of water I don't want and stand by the window, staring through the gauzy curtains to the empty sidewalk and street below. Everything's hanging in early morning stillness, each brick and lamppost resting gently against the other. There's something pliant in the features of the world at four in the morning. The juxtaposition of building to street, tree to sky; it all seems provisional.

I remember the feeling as a child. The surety that somehow everything changes shape behind me once my back is turned, slides into a different aspect as soon as my attention shifts. The world is a puzzle, teasing me with secrets.

All week I go to the studio with Sophie, who doesn't want to go alone.

For the first few days, she moves things around, one corner to the next and back again. She dusts, she sweeps, she scrubs at ancient spatters of paint on the wall. I sit in the corner on a stool with my open notebook. She doesn't want my help, she says. She just wants me to be here. Sometimes I pretend to write, others I help her anyway. We move canvases or shift easels. Or I just watch, not wanting her to catch me in the act, but unable to keep my eyes from stealing toward her.

Her jeans are clean, not her usual painting clothes. She wears a white blouse, open at the neck. Red Chuck Taylors. It's good to see her in real clothes again, good to see her freed from formless pajamas and billowing sweat shirts. She's finally returning to physical form.

She sweeps the floor, shifts canvases, collapses easels and unfolds them again. Takes down sketches, rolls them, leans them in a corner. Hangs others. Tests her brushes and chemicals. She's silent and focused, some quiet confidence taking hold, allowing her to move again.

On the third day she positions a blank canvas on a black metal stand. I can see her through the maze of easels and the sketches hanging from the stretched wire. If her gaze shifts in my direction I stare at the nonsense in my notebook, but in a few minutes she's forgotten I'm here. She stands before the canvas, hands abandoned to her body turning left now right, a step forward, a step or two back. Her fingers are limp. Her hands hang loose as her head tilts, bent askew toward her shoulder. She holds that position as if studying a ray of light I can't distinguish.

She hasn't picked up a brush. She hasn't mixed any paint. She's simply dropped the canvas onto the easel. She stares at it for a long time.

Each morning she's waited for me to wake up. Already awake herself, she'll be in the living room with a cup of tea, sitting by the window. She's ready to go as soon as I am.

She's given up her apartment. It's both a practical commitment and a hopeful decision. She can't go back to work at the Scrawl; she can't think about work at all yet. We didn't have enough money to pay rent for both places, so I began moving a few things at a time into mine before Sophie could really help.

We want to believe the decision is more than just practical, want to believe we've given each other a firm glance and taken a step. We choose not to talk about what we might imagine the future to be, other than a magical retreat into the past. But, with Sophie back in the studio, I can feel the light changing, a heat lacing my body, a circuit between us newly opened.

There's an exhilaration, a hope, just at the edge of vision. I can't afford to look at it directly. It feels like something I would frighten away by devoting my attention. So, even though she's been in the studio for over a week now and her hand occasionally touches my shoulder, I stay on the couch and leave the bed to Sophie and Beaker.

When the night comes I'm alone, and the nightmares are waiting for me to slip far enough away that I can't protect myself from glimpses of her body smudged with someone else's fingerprints, twisting and turning in other hands like wrenched sheets. I curl and buck in the dream, fingers grasping. I call out but I don't know what I say. I hear the slap of something like a blow then a moan. I see her eyes through the veil of hair.

I wake up, struggling for breath in the cloud of my idiot jealousy and loss. The hard edges of the room hot around the dream. I tell myself again there was nothing to do. I remind myself of the gun. I turn into the back of the sofa, forcing away the rest of the room, all I can see is my own body standing in the middle of the Scrawl's empty dance floor staring at the closed door as if seeing it could make a difference.

I restrain the rage rising around me. I restrain myself from throwing the water glass across the room or punching my fist through the night window. I hold myself motionless at the curtain, my shoulder against the frame, the street blue and empty beneath me.

The blue changes things somehow, sets off some string of images deep behind my eyes. One blue spills into another, back and back, water tripping over stream stones until it's the first night at Sophie's studio and she's standing beside me as I study a painting, not quite sure what I'm looking for. The blue on the canvas is a note she hums over and over, her fingers rippling at her thigh in a pool of color. The blue and its memory make my night bearable and I return to the sofa, nested in the climate of her studio.

She stands beside a covered easel held together by wire, the loose ends budding from the top in sharp fronds. One hand is at the stained sheet thrown over it, the other on her hip. She blows a few strands of dark hair from her face. She pulls the sheet back, her bare arm settling along the top edge of the canvas, her attention fixed on me while my eyes dart from one corner of the canvas to the other, spilling across the image.

A smile sweeps her face. I can see it at the edge of vision not overwhelmed by paint, light and shadow. She watches me, one leg bent at the knee, her foot resting on her toe.

I feel myself flush, unsure, while she remains patient, learning as much from my body as any words I might find. Finally I let go, tumbling somehow into the painting and a place without words, a place where there is only her and I and this thing she's made. I smile, a different smile with each new canvas. She knows something then, but I never know what. She lowers her eyes to the floor. Perhaps she's smiling too, her head slightly declined, but I never know since I'm caught in the motion before me, one color and stroke flowing around the next, changing the light in the room.

Memory folds itself around me. Something fragile I'm careful not to disturb as I extend my legs the length of the sofa, pulling the blanket to my shoulders. I lie still and quiet so as not to frighten this memory away. Both of us before the easel, her bare arm along the top. As if any sudden gesture might tear the visitation from me and leave me alone with the night. I drift in the moment, I sink away into something warm and calm.

I open my eyes. Sophie is standing before me. She's naked, the blue light of the window dense around her. She looks down to me, her head tilted slightly, her hair curled behind her ears. Her skin has an ivory sheen in the light; her features seem cut from cool stone.

The past has not yet arrived. I reach out to touch her. I place the back of my hand against her thigh. I turn my hand, feeling goosebumps along my palm. It's then that I blink fully awake.

She's watching me curiously, waiting, perhaps, for me to wake up. Her mouth is set in a quiet patience and determination I've seen before. I can make out the birthmark on her thigh. The constellation of freckles just above her breasts. Her legs are apart, her nipples are hard, her arms limp at her side. I rise on the sofa, shifting my hand to her bare arm. The skin there is taut, warmer than her thigh.

Her arm slides away from my hand. She rests her palm upon her stomach, rubbing it gently in a light circle. The room is blue and quiet except for a low hum from the street and the brush of her palm along her abdomen. There's the smell of her soap with a hint of eucalyptus, her shampoo. The heady scent of her skin.

"I want to fuck," she says, her voice low and even.

Her voice is distant but familiar. Her eyes haven't moved from my face. They flash in the dim light. There's something brittle in the air. I touch her arm again, leaning forward, my fingers sliding over her wrist to take her hand, reluctantly leaving her stomach.

"Sophie..."

"I want to..."

I try to draw her gently toward the sofa but she doesn't shift, merely leans forward to follow the direction of my hand. I pull myself against the armrest of the sofa, drawing my legs toward me.

"Sophie, sit..."

She studies me for a long moment, then turns to sit beside me. I lose her hand in the movement. Her gaze has left me now. For an instant she stares directly ahead, her eyes trained to some vague section of the opposite wall.

In profile, it's easier to look at her. In the last weeks, it's only been while she's sleeping I've felt I could look at all. I followed her features, still so afraid to touch, yet remembering touch. Her cheekbone became the bridge of her nose. The line of her chin, the cup of her ear. Her hair fanned across a cheek. I could study them as she slept, their presence in my fingertips, their past traveling up my arm. I'd sit beside her, often in near darkness, the invisible threads of her body drawing tight around me with the easy knowledge we had of our skin. I never let her know; it seemed intrusive somehow and often I felt guilty, as if she'd been so ripped and torn that even to look was a violation.

She turns back to me, hands flat and still upon her bare thighs.

"Remember when. Sometimes. We could just fuck." Her voice remains low. There's a flatness at odds with her words, an intimacy almost there. "Not thinking. Not saying anything. Not even having to love each other. It was just our bodies. It wasn't making love then and that was fine. It was something else. It was great. Fucking."

The word narrows into my body, settling low and turning there, a tiny gear, some part of us in quiet communication. At the same time, things are sharp and dangerous; I can feel myself pulling away in a cautious gravity. I'm watching the clean slope of her back in the dim light, the tilt of her breasts.

She's not crying. She hasn't been crying. Her eyes are dark and clear. Not swollen at all. Her body, where it's seemed diffuse over the last weeks or, alternately, an artifact of the past, now appears totally present and completely real and she seems almost true within it.

"Don't talk like that, Soph. I don't even know what to say to you."

"I just want not to think." Her eyes are burning, her body motionless. "I want out of my own head. I want my fucking body back. I want it to be mine again."

"It's too soon. I think." I hear the plea in my voice. "Isn't it too soon?"

She's trembling. I can see it at the ridge of her shoulders against the light of the window. It's a tremor, a subtle current, in her bones. I can see it in her nearly imperceptible shrug.

"I don't know how to wait. I don't know a when."

She's so naked and near. I want to hold her, everything in my body leaning in her direction. I don't know what to do. I hold my hand in my lap to keep from touching her. But not to touch her is even more of a statement.

I slide my palm along her shoulder. Her skin is warmer than a moment ago, her skin settles around my fingers. I stop myself from pulling her toward me.

"You just need to go back to bed," I tell her.

Her hands remain on her thighs. Her eyes are wide and clear and do not release me.

"Are you afraid of me? Why is that?"

"No, I just…"

"Or is it something else?"

It takes me a moment to realize what she means. I shake my head.

"No, it's not that. And I'm not afraid of you. I want us…I want to be… Sure, I guess. I want to be sure."

"How do we ever get sure?"

"Yeah." I have to admit it. "I don't know."

Her hand is on my leg now, moving beneath the flap of the blanket, her fingers tracing the ridge of bone, shin to thigh, to the waist band of my boxers. She's leaning into me, fingers pushing beneath my t-shirt, hot on my skin, arm resting along my thigh, her palm flattening on my stomach.

"I don't know either."

"Don't you think it's better to go slow? Take your time?" I don't move. I don't stop her. "I mean, it's just… I just don't want to hurt you. I don't want you to be hurt."

Sophie nods solemnly, her eyes dropping from mine to my chest. She gently kneads my stomach. Her head is close, the pale skin of her shoulders. The curve of her neck toward her ear. The hinges of bone just beneath the flesh.

"You haven't kissed me in weeks," she whispers, not looking at me. I feel her breath on my chest, then lower. "Not a real kiss."

Her eyes meet mine again. Her eyes are close and deep. Her lips are close. Her other hand rests against my thigh.

"I worry about it. Obsess over it, because I can't get it out of my head. When I'm not crying or aching, I'm worrying about you. About us."

"I'm sorry," I try to explain, feeling some rush of relief in the speaking, "I didn't know if you wanted me to. It's not you. I wasn't sure. Not really."

"Oh, baby..." and the words are a sort of echo, some frayed bit of memory drifting past us in a slow current.

I know she feels the erection tightening my boxers against the flesh of her arm. It's the sudden assurance of her body. It's the light in her voice I haven't heard in weeks. It's every moment of her my skin remembers.

She's leaning into me now. Her face is strangely motionless, an occasional flash in her eyes. I rise to kiss her, it really takes no effort at all, and when our lips meet, her mouth opens. I taste her breath. I brush my tongue against her lips.

"I miss you," I tell her.

"I miss me too," she says, her voice barely audible.

My hands on her shoulders, I pull her toward me and she slides in my direction. I take her in my arms, curling her around me and down the back of the sofa, coming to rest on the cushions beneath. I hold myself on my elbows above her, reaching back to pull the blanket over us.

She sighs, a soft exhalation, both of her hands at my chest now. "Take this off," she tells me, tugging at my t-shirt. I pull it over my head, tossing it to the floor. She draws me down to her, her arms wrapping my body. My head sinks to her neck.

And she is here. I find her again, intact, her skin and smell more than a memory. I kiss her neck, and her hands rake my hair. My lips come to hers and I kiss her, like the instant before, a slight brush of lips and the tip of my tongue. She smiles, pushing my head to her neck.

"I want you inside me," she whispers. "Now."

I fumble to extricate myself from my underwear, my face buried in her hair. She shifts beneath me, dropping one leg off the side of the couch, her foot resting on the floor. She opens herself to me. I press into her, gently, entering slowly. She adjusts her hips, her back arching from the cushions.

"Go slow," she says, her lips at my ear.

I do. I enter, then withdraw, moving deeper with the next push. She's tense but not resistant and in a moment the thrusts become easier.

Her hands rest on my buttocks. "Now, all the way in," she tells me. Her hands guide me, her pressure on me, fingers digging in as I reach my full length.

"Now. Just a minute." She whispers urgently: "Be still."

We pause, our bodies taut and straining one against the other. She presses against me from the hips as I push into her, her fingers clutching, her back arching. She draws long, slow breaths. Slowly she releases, her hands sliding to my shoulders. Her hips lower her back to the cushions. She takes my head in her hands, looking me full in the face. She's tightening into my body as she kisses me, her legs winding my waist, a deep full kiss that I know is Sophie's.

"Now." Then she adds: "Gently..."

For the first time in weeks, I think maybe everything will be alright. With Sophie's arms folded around me, I begin to think there's a chance. I want the memory of her. I want who we were. She wants that too. We want it together.

My thrusts are long and measured as Sophie's body closes around mine. She's turned her face after the kiss, tucking my head again into her neck. Her pulse is at my lips, her breath in my hair shifting slowly from deep exhalations to something shorter, shallower. I try to be careful. Not too forceful, not too demanding.

I leverage my weight to one shoulder against the back of the couch so I can see the plane of her body beneath me in the light of the window. I follow the ridge of her ribs with a finger as I move into her, then flatten my hand along her stomach. Her face presses my arm to the back of the couch. I feel her breath on my skin. She kisses my forearm, then bites it gently. I cup her breast with my free hand, fingering her nipple with my thumb. I take her breast in my hand and squeeze.

Sophie freezes, her body rigid beneath me, her heat draining away.

"What is it?" I'm frantic and confused. Her face is pressed into the back of the sofa. Her hands come to my shoulders.

"Stop," she says. "It's okay. Just for a minute." She doesn't turn to look at me. She's fallen away from her bones. I feel her loss in the empty skin.

"I'm sorry, I..."

"Don't talk," she whispers into the sofa, "just give me a minute."

I raise myself above her on both elbows and move to withdraw but she holds me inside her, silently, with one hand. The fear is cold and hard in her body, her breath muffled gasps. She holds me inside her, and in a moment, turns to me, her face set, her lips thin.

"It's okay, now," she tells me, attempting a smile. "Just go slow, Doug. Alright?"

"Sophie, we can wait. Let's..."

"I'm here," she says, her palm at my cheek. "I'm right here. I want to. I want you. Let's do it now."

We begin again. We balance our bodies on the narrow sofa, her leg dangling off, one foot on the floor or wrapped around me, mine angled back, foot to the floor for leverage. She draws my head to her chest, guiding our rhythm one hand on my back and one in my hair. And we find each other again. Not the same as a moment ago; more tentative, more cautious, giving ourselves by increments.

I'm self-conscious touching her, kissing her. I hold myself still for her, my head and hands immobile, only the slow gentle thrusts and the warm press of our bodies against each other.

I lose myself in our skin, our heat, our smell, in some open space of the past, and forget for an instant the last weeks, the solitude and silence. When I return her hands are fists at my shoulders and I stop. She turns to me as I rise from her, her eyes wide with fear, her lips thin and pale.

I want to take her in my arms and hold her and tell her everything will be fine. We'll get through this. But I pull away instead, her arms dropping from my shoulders to her sides with a damp slap. As I feel myself rise I extend the moment as best I can, my hand sliding from around her neck to her collarbone, two fingers tracing the line from her neck and between her breasts to her navel.

I withdraw, sitting up in the space between her parted legs. Her arms wind across her chest.

"Sophie, can we talk..."

"No" And that's all she'll say.

I pick up the blanket from the floor. Standing, I lift her leg to the sofa and draw the blanket over her, her arms still across her chest. She won't look at me, her face curled into the sofa. I tuck the blanket in around her. She's motionless, hardly breathing.

I reach under to find a hand at her breast, winding my fingers into hers against her cool flesh. She stiffens her fingers, her arm, but I take them anyway. I sit on the edge of the sofa, holding her hand loosely until her fingers allow mine.

Later I'm sitting on the floor, my back against the sofa, still holding her hand. She might be asleep. Later still, I wake up in the same position, my face turned into the cushion by her thigh, our hands still clasped.

The next day we don't really talk about it. We go to the studio together and I watch Sophie stand before the same blank canvas she's stood before for the five previous days. I watch her, motionless, arms taut at her sides. I can't tell if she's completely focused or absolutely lost.

I'm scribbling in my notebook, writing something; I don't remember what. Another story trailing into silence, another borrowed idea in someone else's style, another angry screed against an imagined injustice. I'm writing to feel I'm doing something, pasting a fragile meaning into my life. I'm writing to claim myself as a creative person, separate and special, knowing it to be a lie. I'm writing, hunched over the bound notebook Sophie had given me months before. A slurry of words, page after page.

Sophie has changed position. It's been minutes, or hours. She's closer to the easel now, her arms loose, her palms open to the canvas. Her arms come up and away from her body as I watch, her back arching just slightly, her head tilting back. She exhales quietly, arms lowering to her sides, her long, pale fingers twitching.

Then she's at the work table, mixing paint on a piece of board, her body confident and known. I can only see the shape of her back as she works there, the occasional shift of an arm through the camouflage of the canvases. I'm quiet. I don't move. I'm not sure I breathe.

On my stool by the sink and the ancient gurgling coffeepot, I glimpse her through the shutter of easels as she returns to the bare canvas, turning this way and that. The brush begins at her shoulder then slips to her waist, rising an inch or so then sinking away again. She sways before the canvas as if finding a breeze.

Her body is full and real and taut as a bowstring. It's an engine in the startled hum of the room, its memory spilling into me like the remembered chorus of a forgotten song, the kind I can't help but sing along with because it connects my life, a tectonic layer beneath the days. Something in her new presence startles me, a jangle in my own skin as she turns before the canvas, brush in hand.

With a single stroke her body lightens, one foot lifts from the floor for an instant. The fingers of her left hand, raised a few inches from her hip, curl and she holds absolutely still in the posture of an exotic bird.

From my stool I watch as she waits, brush arrested an inch from the canvas. I watch her find the stroke and accomplish it, a sweep of color I cannot see. A gesture to my vision, an instance of dance divorced from result. I watch her settle back to earth, one foot touching down then the other.

She covers the painting before we leave. It's weeks before I see her new work. She doesn't need me in the studio anymore, so I de-camp to the coffee shop nearby where she collects me when she's finished, or I wander off to a movie and we meet up again at the apartment.

When I do see her new work, it surprises me. The canvases are light and spacious. The strokes wide, vibrant. They're assured in a new way, inasmuch as I know about any of these things. She doesn't know what to say about them, even to Maggie, but I catch her glancing to them now and then, as if some drift of communication is still open. As if they continue to whisper secrets.

Secrets she can't tell me. Or won't. In the weeks after they become almost a physical presence, like another figure in the room mediating what can be said, the way we look at each other, the way we touch. Conversations take place I cannot hear. They alter her.

As time passes, she develops a code of new expressions that resemble those of the past but with a tender distance, a nearly imperceptible fissure between her skin and the body beneath. She is fully within herself but that self is somehow held back.

I watch her practice a new smile in public when meeting a friend on the street or stopping to talk to a child in the grocery store. It's much like the one from before. But not quite. I watch her craft a distance between herself and the world that she never had. There's a pause when she speaks to others that didn't exist before. Her body tilted just one fragile degree away. Her laugh is shallower. I watch her grow more assured in her new form.

Then the letter comes from Denver. She's been awarded the residency. Finally we can say that something is changing, is about to change, has already changed; we can talk about plans, the residency. Finally, we can talk about something.

In an alternate history, the kind that supposedly exists for everyone in some veiled corridor of the universe, this is a cause for joy and celebration, the first real recognition of her work. We would be excited, leaping around the apartment in congratulation. I might even have talked about going with her.

But too much has happened and the letter is simply the unavoidable diagnosis of everything that's come before. A final artifact of separation affording us some care and civility. I take her to the airport. I pull over on the way home. I cry in my car as traffic flashes by. I open the apartment door and enter the shell of the place.

There are holes in the apartment where her things have been. A blank space on the wall where a sketch once hung. An open stretch of the bookshelf that belonged to her. The empty drawers in the dresser. The other side of the bed. It's a room like a sieve, full of open spaces, draining light and substance.

In the warehouse, I step between the dull pools of light, my flashlight tucked in my belt so I don't drop it again. The rest of the building falls away. The walls have vanished and there is no ceiling. Only one pool after the next, each alike in their muddy light, dimly yellow and wavering. The world filters away beneath me, far below my feet.

I picture myself falling asleep atop a pile of her clothes like an abandoned cat.

I stare at the bound notebook she'd given me after repairing the first. I consider tossing it into the street or ripping it in two. Instead I move the kitchen table by the window and press the notebook open on its surface. I leave it there. I sometimes pretend I don't notice it.

Weeks after she's gone, I'm still taking long circuitous walks, building my own maze from city streets and alleyways. I can't be still. I spend the rest of the days forcing myself to the chair and the open notebook. I do it until I'm motionless at the table, glancing across the blank page and out the window. Hands, palms down, framing the notebook.

I stare at the paper. For days. It looks back with a damnable blankness. It can wait, in silence, forever.

Nothing of me remains. No thread of self to anchor me. We find faith when there is nothing else left. I put down a sentence, then another. I imagine a landscape, then place a figure in it.

Each word stings. My blood slow, my lungs aching. It's like breathing underwater: a panic, a flailing about, a gradual surrender. Over and over.

13

"You were sweet," Sophie tells me, adjusting her bandanna, tucking wisps of fine hair beneath it. I'd made the mistake of asking what she remembered most about me, way back when.

"Right," I reply, rolling my eyes. "Not sexy. Not brilliant." I sigh. "Sweet. You never want a girl to say you're sweet."

She chuckles, eyes flashing. "You were sexy too. Still are. Not like me, all bald bones."

"You're..."

She curls her open hand on the table. "Blah blah blah..."

I'm silent. She grins, tilting her head in a silent thank you.

"So, about this cake."

I'd decided Sophie could have anything she wanted, at least for the next seven days. What she wanted was food. I'd call ahead on my way over each evening to ask what I should pick up. The first day it was a hot dog with slaw and chili. I could see, when she unwrapped it, that the smell alone made her queasy. Still, she managed two bites, which she chewed with an astonishing slowness. Today it's chocolate cake.

A few weeks after I said yes, Sophie set the date. She needed six weeks she said. "To finish things up." It's pointless to pretend we're not aware of these passing days, one by one. A gift each day, like the chocolate cake, feels like more than simply waiting.

She's begun to live posthumously, with a sense of gentle erasure. Most of what's going on I can't see and she doesn't talk about. The less I know the better, she tells me, and I suppose she's right.

She'd told me she'd been stockpiling medication, researching drugs on various websites. "The time to hoard your meds," she confided, "is before you tell the doctors you're stopping treatment."

She was quick to remind me she'd spent months considering this before I ever called her and nothing I could say or do was going to change any of that. She'd actually talked to a couple of people, on the internet or the phone, who'd been through the entire process with a loved one. They'd offered advice, added details she hadn't found anywhere else.

She'd been making plans. She'd begun to give away her things. She'd donated her easels and materials but they hadn't been picked up yet. She'd completed her DNR and her will, copies made and mailed. She'd managed to get more pills from her doctor.

We hadn't talked about much that was practical over the previous weeks. We watched television together; I rented the occasional movie. We cooked small dinners together, shared a bottle of wine. We even played Scrabble a few times.

In the meantime, we meander through stories of our lives in separation. She tells me about art shows and the classes she's taught. I share the middling life of a mid-list writer, my supplemental job driving seniors from one doctor's appointment to another. Idlewild Press had picked up my novel and were actually offering me a small advance, but it wasn't like real money.

"Hire a publicist," they told me, "and someone to design a website for you. The one you have now sucks."

We spend most of our time at the kitchen table instead of the living room. There's more light and the space seems larger somehow. Airy and warm. Sophie, wrapped in a sweater, in the chair under the window, a small pillow at her back, me in the chair to her left.

The Rescue Mission had come by that morning to pick up books and her mother's old chest freezer. And because she's stopped the chemo she feels a bit better and can enjoy at least a couple of bites of whatever she requests.

I'd bought the largest cake I could find from a local bakery. Four layers, it's almost a foot high, crusted with white chocolate rosettes and dark chocolate piping, a five-pound monster. I'd planted candles randomly over the top and she fingers one as she contemplates the cake.

"We have to light them," I say, "and you have to blow them out."

She withdraws the candle at her fingertips and places it on the table beside the platter. Then she removes all but five, lining them on the table beside the first. Five days left.

She flattens her hand over the spare candles. "You were so shiny and earnest then. On your stool in the corner of the Scrawl. I loved your wonder, your innocence."

"We were kids," I tell her. "We were both innocent. Or just stupid."

"I know. It's just..."

Her eyes lose focus just slightly, the way one adjusts to study something in a middle distance. Her lips pursed, her eyes wistful. She's trained to a different time or place.

"You had this thing you wanted and that's all you knew. You were so tortured and ecstatic."

"Melodramatic and pretentious, that's what I was."

"Yeah, that too. But there was something clear about it. Being so fired up and frustrated. You were always working, somehow or the other."

A curl of a smile. "You could just never manage to get much done. But you started again over and over."

"I wasn't very good at anything."

"But that's just it. See, I'd always painted. I was always doing some kind of arty stuff. I never thought about it. I was like the kid who grows up around horses then doesn't understand why every other kid can't cinch the saddle or hold the reins. It was second nature to me.

"But you. You were the kid who'd never even seen a horse before, yet climbed up and held on for all you were worth. You'd hit the ground and get right back up.

"You had this light. Everyone knew you'd figure it out. Everyone knew you'd do it eventually. Everyone but you." Her hand drops to the table near mine, her forefinger following the grain of the wood. "I know you didn't feel that way, but everyone else could see it."

I can't imagine this was true but I don't interrupt her, partly because I like the vision of the past in her eyes. It's simpler, clearer, than my own.

She tells me who I am. It's not a command. There's no obligation, but she describes a person I can barely discern.

"Some nights I'd find you gnarled in a ball, just desolate with frustration. Some mornings you'd stare out the window for hours. And you'd be holding your pen over the blank page. You were waiting. And even though the waiting tore you to pieces, there was some part of you that was patient. You had a relentless patience."

"You make it sound like I knew what I was doing."

"None of us ever know what we're doing." Sophie pauses, drifting away a bit. "I kept on painting. You know, until recently. They've sold, people liked them. I liked them. But there's always that feeling of never quite reaching it, you know? Never quite getting there. I always wish there were a way to paint one more, just one more, but now, it's impossible."

Sophie rolls her palm along the lined candles. I wait, wanting to change the subject, knowing she'll catch me if I try. I choose to believe soon she'll soon veer off onto another tangent.

"Remember your notebook?"

I remember it: the stiff cardboard cover in my hands and the clean, bleached smell of the pages, the tension as I wrenched it in both hands, twisting until the covers began to part at my knuckles and, once begun, the tear spread easily along the pages to the binding which broke loose in strands of fabric and glue. I remembered flinging the halves at the wall, the dull slap as they hit the wall then the floor.

I remember something I never actually saw. Sophie kneeling on the floor to pick up the upended halves. She'd arrived at my apartment while I was at work, to surprise me. She fell asleep warm in my bed where I found her the next morning; she fell asleep, but not before taping each page together again, reassembling the entire thing and returning it to my desk.

"I still have that notebook. It's standing on a shelf near my computer. Where I see it every day."

This makes her happy. She nods slowly. I was thinking I could cut the cake, arresting the current conversation in exchange for chocolate. But she anticipates me, sliding a finger along the side nearest her, shaving a splinter of icing and popping it into her mouth.

"When I had to start over," her finger rests on her chin as she eyes the cake, "I could only do it from having watched you. Your focus, your assurance. You'd decided something and you wouldn't let it go. You had a thread of ecstasy all your own.

"I'd always just done it. It took a long time before I could begin to think about it instead, sort good ideas from bad and zero in on something. But I had you. You were my hero."

A new intimacy has developed over the last weeks. Something that holds a taste of our old closeness, only more fragile and melancholy. It's the intimacy of collapse, exhaustion. The kind that arrives at four in the morning after an all-night rage, or with a wide and thin grief stretching to the horizon. It arrives at times when there is nothing new to fear and the old fear has become exhausting.

"We believed so hard in art," Sophie whispers, mostly to herself.

We have no reason to hide from each other, only from ourselves. The important things we already know, all other secrets losing their shape as one day passes to the next.

So, we talk, and every conversation shades new memories into being, every word resonates with our history. We choose our subjects often in order to avoid others, yet there's a contentment and clarity in talking about them together. We talk to keep the past from becoming too real, placing our words before it as a screen. I have the impression Sophie is losing contact, little by little, with everything that isn't the past, that fragments of it are beginning to push together, and the edges of events are slowly shading to a wash of primary colors.

Sophie shaves another sliver of chocolate, licks her finger. "I thought you'd never kiss me. Way back then."

"Yeah, I know." I shrug, vaguely embarrassed. "I'm not any different now, actually."

She watches me while I study my hands on the table. Her gaze is like a band of sunlight across my face. I glance up to her.

Our hands are close. I take hers.

"Okay," I release a long breath. "Now, about this cake."

Sophie laughs. A full-throated, head-back laugh. It's good to see her laugh.

She's laughing when she opens the door, red-faced and breathless. "I've been up all night cleaning house. Folded all the laundry." She shrugs. "It's a girl thing."

There's the suggestion of a bow, motioning me in. "Nice weather out there," she offers, peering past me into the bright lawn.

"It is nice. Very green." I turn, once inside the door. "How're you doing?"

"Alright, I guess. A little out of breath. Nervous." Her eyes try to hold mine but can't help darting around the room, her fingers skittish at her sides.

The curtains have been drawn away from the windows and the place is flooded with the slanted light of late afternoon. The windows are open, for the first time since I've come, a breeze rustling the curtains near the sill. There's the faint scent of pine cleaner mixed with open air. The house itself is oddly silent: as if silence were itself a sound: low, round, and constant.

Sophie flits around the room, straightening a cushion or brushing an invisible filament of dust from the table. "I need to take a shower. You don't mind waiting while I take a shower, do you?"

"Not at all," I reply, still lurking by the front door.

"I wasn't sure you'd come," she confesses from the corner near the television, her eyes settling on mine. "And I wasn't sure what I'd do if you didn't."

"I said I'd come."

She's at my side, her palm sliding along my cheek for an instant. Her hand is dry and cool. "I know you did."

Then she's away again, off toward the hallway. "Make some of your coffee." Two weeks ago, I'd finally brought coffee, having had more than enough of her thin herbal teas.

"Anything for you?"

"Tea!" She's down the hall by now.

"What kind? You have about a hundred!"

"The one in the prettiest box!" I hear the bathroom door click closed.

"You're forcing me to make an aesthetic judgment," I call after her. "You know how much I hate that," I mutter to myself.

I'm on my second cup by the time she returns, her tea cooling just the way she likes it. I'm holding myself erect in the chair. Formless limbs flicker into existence when I move, then fall away from me again in stillness. There's the weight of the warm air in the room, the light tinting at the windows; they seem more solid and vibrant than our bodies.

I'd slept fitfully during the night, aware of the mass of tension defining my limbs, coiled and knotted in a kind of terrified crouch, my breathing shallow and quick. I'd finally fallen asleep for a couple of hours, waking late in the morning. I'd carried that tension through lunch and the drive over, which I extended by shuttling across the countryside, winding down unmarked roads to discover abandoned barns and rusting farm machinery.

Once in Sophie's driveway my body fell away, as if it were always two steps behind me. Sitting in Sophie's kitchen, I seem to be drifting just above the table.

She enters, tying her bandanna at the back of her neck. She's wearing jeans and a white blouse, open at the throat, sleeves folded back nearly to the elbows. The skin of her forearms, the nape of her neck, are still damp. She smells of lemon and ginger. She sits beside me at the table, plucking rolled socks from the pocket of her jeans and angling her legs away from the table to slowly pull them on.

I watch her fuss with the socks until she becomes aware of the density of the silence. When she looks up, my breath catches in my throat and I don't know what to say.

When I'd brought over the coffee two weeks ago, I'd made the first cup and sat in the same spot, waiting for her to enter the room.

"Sophie, we need to talk."

"Oh, lord," she'd replied, taking a seat beside me.

I raised a hand to forestall complaint. "I promised, I know. I've been very good about it."

Sophie nodded solemnly, folding her hands one over the other on the kitchen table.

"I haven't brought it up once. I haven't initiated any conversations or asked any searching questions. I've let the last weeks be what they were. And I'm really happy about that. About having the time together."

Sophie noticed the tea I'd made and slid the cup toward her with a tiny smile, clasping her hands at the base, wrapping the string of the teabag slowly around her forefinger. Both of us watched this operation intently.

I managed some noise that was supposed to be a chuckle but sounded more like a thin gasp. "I guess, some part of me thought you'd just forget. I know it's stupid. Of course I wanted to believe it, wanted to believe we'd never speak of it again. As if that first conversation had purged the subject somehow."

"I know, you're sick. I'm not pretending you're not. And I know it's bad. Now and then I get some glimpse of how bad it is for you and I wonder how you've managed to go on and..."

I realized I was just setting out one word after another, afraid of what might happen should I stop speaking. Sophie bobbed the teabag in her cup, her head lowered in the aspect of a child awaiting censure.

"It's just that..." The words were failing. It was a struggle to get the last few out. I had the sense I'd broken some kind of vow between us, admitted a breach of trust. "It's just that you're not alone anymore."

"I wish it mattered," she said, her voice even, low. She was watching the cup, anchoring herself to it. I was watching it too; I couldn't bear to look at her. There was a wedge of light at the corner of the table, its borders diffuse with the edges of distant leaves, shuddering as the breeze touched the trees.

Sophie withdrew the teabag and held it between two fingers as she wound the string around it tightly, squeezing the excess into the cup.

"It was never really fair of me to ask you." She dropped the wrung teabag onto the table by the cup and looked up to me. Her face tight, eyes pinched at the corners, a tension in her lips. She curled her hands around the cup again.

"I knew it wasn't but I did it anyway. I took a chance. Because I didn't want to be alone. Something about seeing you again, that first night. I never could have done it otherwise. I wanted to be with you. It's what I wanted. But it was never fair."

We let the silence hold. She took a sip of her tea, her eyes falling to the table. I picked up my cup but couldn't stand the smell of the coffee. I held to the cup. I wanted to apologize, but didn't, wanted to explain that I had to say it, had to object, even though I was no longer sure that was true. I wanted to believe I understood her desire to die though every day I understood less and less. Or wanted it less and less.

We'd talked about it often over the last weeks, both the practical details and the shadowy emotions. We'd struggled to come up with visions of death more forgiving, less final, but we'd failed repeatedly, the conversations gradually winding down to a certain anxious stillness one of us would find a way to break with a digression or a joke.

"I'm not alone anymore," she told me. She waited until I met her gaze, then whispered, "Thank you."

"There are ways we could manage it together. Until the end," I'd offered, but I didn't elaborate. I didn't want to find myself endlessly filling the room with words again. It was a thing that seemed very important, even though there seemed so much that needed to be said. The weight and pressure of the words banked up behind me. A roar in my ears, throbbing around my head, a heat in my hands.

Yet, somehow the words felt like a turning away, a negation of Sophie herself. They were the illusion of doing something, the pretense of mediating what could not be mediated. The words were an excuse for not simply bearing the moment and the coming weeks.

"There are ways we could," Sophie nodded lightly. "But I can't do it. I don't know if it's the right thing, Doug. I don't know if it's moral or cowardly, good, bad; but it's what I need to do.

"I want to be the one to choose. And there's no reason to wait."

Her head tilted to the side, a tiny smile curling just in the corner of her mouth. "I don't know, maybe buried deep somewhere in there, you have more faith than I do."

I shrugged. "Faith and desperation. I always get the two confused."

The more I restrained myself from speaking, the less anything needed to be said. After a few moments, the pressure of speech drained away and the world became very simple again. I was having tea with Sophie at her kitchen table.

Now, it's as if she can see the thoughts pulsing bright and edgy in my head. She finishes with her socks and turns to me.

"You can leave if you like," she says. "I won't hold a grudge."

"No, I'm not going anywhere," I reply. I slide my hand, palm up, across the table in her direction.

She takes my hand and we don't quite know what to do next; she drinks her tea, I finish my coffee. I notice her breathing as it slows, the hiss of a passing car and two finches twittering to each other somewhere near the tree-line.

Sophie finally breaks the silence. "I have our last treat." Her eyes are glittering. "It's really sinful."

Her fingers pull away and she stands. I watch her cross to the cabinet and withdraw something. Her jeans are loose around the hips, her socked feet scuff at the floor. Her arm extends toward the cabinet, her fingers closing lightly. It's an image I know will stay with me for a long time. It's the ordinary that's remembered. I watch her move across the room, the light shifting around her, until she returns with a chocolate bar she places on the table between us.

"Habanero Hazelnut Dark Chocolate. Almost too delicious for mortals. I have a friend who brings them back from Brooklyn, one at a time. Any more would just be too decadent."

I handle it with the solemnity of a holy relic, sliding my thumb under the paper wrapper first, then laying open the gold foil beneath to expose the rich chocolate. I pluck up a tangerine from the bowl on the table and stab the remaining candle into it, balancing it between us as I light it.

Sophie is sitting now. I break the chocolate into pieces, holding one before her in two fingers. She leans forward and I place it on her tongue. She does the same for me.

The chocolate is warm and rich, melting slowly in my mouth with a nutty sweetness and the burn of the pepper as it reaches the back of my throat. It's a raw, earthy taste with a rolling, creamy fullness that hits my bloodstream immediately.

She's talking about Randy, the Hospice nurse, who'd been by to visit earlier that morning. She explains that he's a songwriter and a singer, building up his courage playing open mics in the area, trying to get enough songs together to record a CD.

"When I was still on the chemo, he'd come over and make food for me. He'd put it in the fridge in case I could eat. He'd clean up and check my meds. Now, since I feel a little better, you know, before it starts to get a lot worse, now, we just talk. He tells me about his songs, the audiences. He keeps promising to bring his guitar over and play a few..."

"He's in love with you."

Sophie winks. "Maybe," she teases.

I tell her about Beaker that morning, languishing, fully extended, in the windowsill in a bright band of sunlight. His coat was warm and smooth when I flattened my hand over it, his tail flicking against the pane with a dull thump.

We're halfway through the chocolate, trading small broken pieces that we savor slowly, my sinuses clearing, my nose running, when she edges away from the table.

"I wanted to sit outside," she tells me. "It's nice out and the sun'll be setting in a while. I may take a blanket. Is that okay? After?"

She's standing and, for some reason, I stand too. Her hands fall to her sides and she exhales slowly.

"Scared." She declares this, eyes wide, shoulders sagging. Some broad weight she carries becomes visible for an instant.

I put my arms around her. She sinks into them, hands limp at my waist, head on my chest. Her body is nearly weightless against mine, her bones held in place by her breath. There's a tremor that may simply be her heartbeat. Waves of heat rise into my face from her shoulders and chest, the top of her head. The heat has her smell and something in it of the texture of her skin, the silk of her forearms, the base of her neck.

She sniffs. I let my hands slide to her wrists as she adjusts her posture, then I let her go. She tucks her blouse into her jeans and smooths its front.

"How do I look?"

I can't help but laugh. "You look great."

She laughs too. "Good."

She's still for an instant, both of us motionless by the kitchen table. Then, with something like a start, she's in motion toward the hallway.

"It's probably going to take me a few minutes. To get everything down."

"I'll be here."

There's a moment of quiet in her absence, the quiet we'd found together, but it's soon followed by a rush of panic. I stare out the kitchen window into the flat green of the backyard, newly mown by Toby. The two white Adirondack chairs are in exactly the same position as when I first arrived eight weeks ago, the paintings still weighted on the clothesline at one edge of the lawn. I can see the breeze in the flutter of leaves at the tree-line but can't find the finches I'd heard moments before.

I wash the cups at the sink, leaving them to dry in the rack. I wrap the remaining chocolate in the foil and return it to the cabinet. I pick up the tangerine and candle, realizing we'd forgotten it completely. After an instant of hesitation, I blow out the candle and toss it into the trash. I wipe down the table, then stand by the window, staring at nothing until Sophie returns.

She's flushed. She holds her hands before her, one palm cupped in the other. Her limbs are still, but I can see her trembling in a kind of light voltage, her eyes darting around the room.

"I'll get the blanket. We can go into the yard," she says. I step past her to the living room, my hand sliding along her arm. She doesn't move. I toss the blanket over my shoulder.

"Okay," I say softly. She moves toward the door without looking and I follow, holding it open for her then closing it behind us as we step into the grass.

An elderly lady studies me from Sophie's open door, a soft, round face crowned with tufts of stark white hair, horn-rimmed glasses partway down her thin nose. She has one hand on her hip, the other still on the doorknob.

"Hi," I stammer, "Is Sophie here? Is everything okay?"

"Sure is. You must be Doug. She's sure told me a bunch about you." She pushes her glasses along the bridge of her nose. "I'm Marybeth. I live just up the street. That brick ranch there," she explains, her hand flicking lazily to the left. "You come on in."

Marybeth backs away from the door and I step into the living room. "I just came by for a visit and she told me you two had a date."

Her hand closes around my arm and she leans in close, whispering, "And I think that's a good thing." She motions me to the sofa, assuring me Sophie will be along in a minute, then sits when I do.

"So, you're a writer, huh?"

I nod, hands pressed between my knees.

"What do you write?"

Thankfully, Sophie appears in the dining room, relieving me of the necessity to fumble with an answer to that question. I stand, reflexively, when I see her. Her eyes are wide, her lips a pronounced 'O' of mock surprise.

"Oh my god! A collared shirt. A jacket!"

"I'm trying to make a good impression."

"Mission accomplished."

She gives me a hug, a kiss on the cheek, then turns to Marybeth, who's standing now too. "He's the t-shirt and jeans type. Known him a thousand years and I've never seen him like this."

"You make a very nice looking couple," Marybeth says, offering a wink in my direction. "But I got to be going now. Jeopardy'll be on in a few minutes, you know. 'Bout all the excitement I can manage these days."

When goodbyes are accomplished, Sophie turns to me from the closed front door.

"Stay there," I tell her. "Let me look at you."

In the weeks since I'd agreed, we'd lived out a sort of alternate history domesticity, a day here and there when we planned something together, followed by two or three for Sophie to recover. Those days I drifted, unsure what to do with myself, feeling unable to begin anything. It was some kind of waiting state, where the space of hours stretched and thinned around our plans or the short phone calls she could manage in her exhaustion.

There was a grief already taking hold, something thick and muffling but not yet in my field of vision. The way fall announces itself by the angled light in the trees and a diffuse shadow long before the weather turns cold. My body felt a change while my mind struggled to follow.

The days between seeing each other were malleable, constantly changing shape like the endlessly shifting spaces between us, with their odd rhythms and time signatures. The past was always there around us, sometimes as a pressure or weight but sometimes as a kind of warm gravity, drawing us into the same orbit, the once we were, allowing what we could now be.

The future had a limit. We knew it. For the most part, we didn't talk about it.

Last week, she'd asked for a date. "A real date, you know," she'd explained, "where we get all dolled up and go out to eat. Maybe a movie."

"We could do that," I replied. "Where would you like to go?"

"Oh, no," she answered, hands up before her, "you have to decide all that." She raised an eyebrow, "I might even wear makeup."

And she is. A light band of green on her eyelids, a pale peach on her lips. There's a bright woven scarf around her head, not the usual bandana. It's mostly red, long, veined with glittering silver threads, falling past her shoulders and down her back.

"Have I ever seen you in a dress?" I ask.

"I don't know," she teases. "Maybe not."

She turns before me, modeling with exaggerated gestures, chin upturned, a stiff wave from the wrist. It's a simple black dress, scooped gently at the neck, cupping her small breasts and flowing loose from her hips to just above the knee.

"Well, you look great in one."

She takes my arm. "We make a very nice looking couple," she repeats breathlessly.

At dinner we go the whole hog. I'd picked a restaurant downtown, overpriced but dark and comfortable. I order a bottle of wine. Appetizers. Sophie paces herself, taking small sips of the wine. A bite or two of the calamari. The portions aren't huge so she isn't self-conscious about how little she eats.

She's excited, her face flushed, leaning over the table toward me to whisper something about the older couple toward the back of the restaurant or the art scattered randomly on the walls.

"I knew someone who painted like this," she says. "She could do two or three a month. And sell them too. People would tell her the colors of their living rooms or bedrooms. Or they'd bring swatches. And she'd slap something together to fit right over their king size bed. She made a fortune."

I share idiot details of my day. We trade pointless information as we often do, not caring at all what we talk about but happy to be talking somewhere away from her kitchen table. It seems the world has ballooned around us, or fallen away, depositing us on some mountain peak, the air suddenly clear and still.

She swoons when her fish is delivered, savoring each tiny bite while assuring me she has her eye on the double chocolate espresso mousse for dessert. But her energy is flagging by the time dessert arrives, though she continues her excited conversation. We'd planned a movie, but I can see it'll be too much, so I suggest picking one up on the way back to her place. She agrees with a wink.

The night is warm and damp, a faint skin of mist on the windshield when we get to the car. She falls into the passenger seat with a satiated groan, adjusting the dress over her bare legs.

Then, I'm telling her about a new story I'm just beginning to work on, the phantom outlines of it, the details without shape.

"I like to hear you talk about your work, the process of it," she says. "There's a light in you so clear then. Or maybe it's that you're lighter. Looser, more yourself.

"It's like you're telling me secrets. I don't understand them but I know they're precious. What I feel most is the truth of it. For you. It's a glimpse, every now and then, of something magical, but it's like a picture in smoke, unique each time but it won't hold. And I so love that. Every time a little different and then it's gone."

So, I keep talking, words freed by her interest, as the damp black road unfolds, allowing the sentences to form themselves, attentive both to what is said and this way of speaking with her. Something musical, or more like music than speech in that a meaning doesn't seem confined.

"Doug, I think you'd better pull over."

"Are you..." I glance at her, hands at her stomach, skin greenish, and slide the car to the shoulder.

She's out the door in an instant, one hand on the passenger side at the rear bumper, leaning over to vomit. I watch her for a moment, then she goes to her knees and I'm out of the car, coming up behind her, holding her headscarf with one hand on her hot, damp back. She kneels in the grey dirt, retching long after everything she's eaten has come up.

It's this image I often remember. The wet slab of my car before us, the pan of passing headlights and the frightening hiss as they go by, the car rocking slightly. Sophie in her pretty dress, nearly doubled over as she retches again and again, food then liquid then nothing, her body continuing to convulse.

I'd known her days were getting progressively worse; it took her longer now to recover from our occasional outings. We'd planned a drive to the Blue Ridge Parkway, only an hour and a half away, but after forty minutes, Sophie had fallen asleep, her head resting against the car window, exhausted. I'd watched her face for an hour as the sunlight strobed through branches and clouds, falling along her pale, blue-veined skin.

"It's gonna get bad soon, Doug. And it'll get bad very fast."

She'd told me that now and then she wakes at night and doesn't know if she's still alive. She'd lie absolutely still and nothing would hurt for a moment; she'd be motionless, not nauseous or cold or flushed, and she'd think she might be dead. Sometimes it's a blissful feeling, she told me.

I remember standing by the car as she vomited. It was one of the only moments she allowed that kind of vulnerability. She didn't like to talk about how she felt, the minutiae of her disease and the tediousness of coping with it.

She doesn't say anything as she reaches for my arm and pulls herself up, leaning back against the bumper, staring into the darkened field bordering the road. I lean with her, my hand finding hers, her fingers closing around mine, if a bit reluctantly.

After a moment, she sighs. "I'm not much of a party girl anymore."

We're quiet the rest of the drive home. I want to tell her it's okay but I know the spell has been broken; the evening she wanted has slipped away and my assurances will only make this more obvious. Sam Cooke comes up on the iPod but neither of us mention it.

I leave the car running in her driveway, turning to her with my goodbye.

"Don't go," she says. "Come inside." Her voice is weak and grainy from the strain of vomiting. In the living room, she turns on a dim lamp.

"Give me five minutes. Just five minutes, I promise." She disappears down the hall.

I wander randomly, not wanting to sit down, feeling I can't be still. To continue to move means something is happening, would continue to happen, not stop. My dress shoes hurt my feet, so I slip them off, tucking them under the edge of her sofa. I curl my socked toes into her carpet, trying to latch myself to the floor.

Sophie's illness, her coming death, isn't real for me. I can imagine it, even talk about it with her, in an abstract way, but it's not in my bones or in my blood. I know death is real for Sophie, that it's been real for quite a while. Sophie is like that; she sees things as real long before they are.

She enters the room with her laptop and places it open atop the television. She's washed her face and hands. I can smell the mint of toothpaste and a hint of perfume. She smooths her dress over her hips.

"I might smell now, but I don't want to change."

"You don't smell."

She turns off the lamp and we're left with the grey glow of the computer screen.

"I want to dance," she says. It's nearly a whisper, her head dropping then rising again, "Will you dance with me?"

"I'm awful at..."

"No excuses. C'mon."

She presses a key on the computer. The music begins softly. It's *Low*, their album *Trust*. Guitar, slow and wide, with lost angel choruses.

She comes up close, taking my hand, her face near mine. Her skin is very pale in the computer glow, a chalk blue that makes her re-applied lipstick darker. I slip my arm around her waist.

"You can't spin me though, or I'll puke again," she says with a wink.

"Okay then."

"How're you doing, baby?" Her eyes are searching mine for clues. "Holding up okay?"

"I'm just fine," I tell her.

Her arms are resting loosely on my shoulders. She lowers her cheek to my chest.

"You don't even know…" she says. "How much you…I know you're clueless, that's why you have to listen to me when I say it. You have to, at least, believe me."

I squeeze her waist gently in response.

What we do then isn't really dancing. We hold each other, my feet shuffling between hers as we turn gently in the center of the room. Her slight body against mine, the vague press of her breasts, my hands clasped in the small of her back, forearms on the pronounced ridges of her pelvis. Her arms are around my neck, her face in my chest. I can feel her breath on my shirt.

What we do isn't really dancing. It's an excuse to hold each other, to be silent, my body to hers. Her skin is cool, she feels slight in my arms. In a moment the computer screen dims though the music continues, and the room is nearly dark. I watch the shadows on a blank slab of wall, lit now and then by a passing car. I close my eyes.

Sophie lifts a bare foot and drops it atop mine, then steps onto the other. She's nearly weightless, only her frame has definition like the hollow-boned skeletons of birds. I lift her feet upon mine, one then the other, one then the other, folding my arms around her more tightly.

14

I lunge awake, banging my head on the roof of the car, hand on the steering wheel. The phone blinks and shouts from the passenger seat. I answer, struggling to remember where I am.

"Hello?" It sounds more like a stunned declaration.

"Is this Doug?" A watery, low rumble of a voice.

"Who's this?"

"My name's Randy Perkins, I'm a Hospice nurse. I'm afraid I have some bad news. It's Sophie..."

It's light outside the steamed windows of the car; the landscape before me is a smear of green. I'm only a couple of miles from Sophie's house in the lot of a Barlow city park. Last night I couldn't stay with her but I couldn't go home. I'd driven aimlessly for an hour or two before finally ending up in the lot, staring from the idling car into the darkened trees.

Randy is telling me the story. He sniffs now and then, his voice thinning to a trickle then rumbling, again and again. He'd been concerned this morning when Sophie hadn't answered the door. She'd given him a key, so he let himself in. He'd heard her talk about me and thought he should call. He'd found my number on her refrigerator.

"Can you come?" he asks me. "I know she'd like to have friends here."

I don't know how long I'd stayed after I lay her body on the bed. I'd placed her arms at her sides, a pillow under her head. I sat on the edge for a long time, staring at nothing, my mind a blank and a whir; images, conversations, memories, flash through rapidly but at a remove, as if behind a screen or in another room. I lay down beside her for a moment, my cheek pressed against her cold and empty face. I'd wanted to say something else but there were no words. None of mine, or anyone else's. It's only later I think of lines from a Neruda poem.

I turn the key in the ignition, swinging the car into the road, back in the direction I'd come.

There are cars lined on the grass in front of Sophie's house. Three police cruisers block her Subaru in the driveway. As I slowly approach, looking for a place to park, an ambulance turns onto the road. I find myself tracking it; I almost turn to follow without knowing why or what I might do should I catch up. It disappears from view as I slide between two cars, one I recognize as Randy's.

It's 10 a.m. but the sun is mild and the grass still damp with the dew. People are gathered on the porch; Randy sits on the step, hands between his knees. A uniformed officer is in the doorway, talking to someone inside, but I can't hear what he's saying. It isn't until I'm almost on the porch that I recognize Maggie and Jim, hardly changed in the intervening years.

Maggie turns, new tears welling when she sees me. I walk into her arms. She holds me tightly. "Oh, Doug," she says, her voice close to my ear. When she releases me, her hand lingers on my arm, clutching me to her side.

"I'm so glad you're here. She was so happy you two were talking again."

I shake Jim's hand; it's firm and cool. It imparts some form of strength that gradually seeps under my skin and into my bloodstream. He retreats to one side, a quiet, stoic presence, while Maggie takes charge: talking with the officers, making phone calls, breaking the news to neighbors as they arrive.

"I didn't expect the police," I tell her, my hand sweeping the scene, "all this..."

"They say it's a suspicious death."

"What do you mean, 'suspicious'?" I ask, an icy thread tracing my spine.

Maggie lowers her voice, leaning in: "She left a note. It's standard procedure, they say. They have to treat it as a crime scene until the Medical Examiner gets here. That's why we can't go in, why there are so many officers."

"You mean, she's still in there?" I ask, incredulously.

Maggie nods. "They can't move her until the Medical Examiner says so. And he's not here yet."

Randy is beside me, his hand extended. He's large and soft, in jeans and a red flannel shirt buttoned to the neck. His hair is red, curly and wild around his head, his beard oddly misshapen. He smiles broadly, momentarily unable to subdue his natural cheeriness in the situation.

"I'm Randy. I'm the one who called you. I'm with Hospice. Sophie isn't officially a patient but I still stopped by now and then to check on her."

I take his hand. "She told me you looked in on her. I know it made her feel safe. She thought a lot of you."

Randy nods. "Well, it was a mutual. I guess we got kinda close. I wish this were different," his hand plays low over the scene, "but I guess I understand."

I can see that he does and that understanding, unnamed and silent, is an unexpected intimacy. It's an awkward, comforting moment between us, broken by a police officer calling my name as he steps from the doorway. He asks to speak to me, motioning toward the lawn.

I follow him. I can't keep my eye from falling to his gun, heavy and relentless at his side.

In the months, even years, after the robbery, I couldn't write anything that didn't include the appearance of a gun. One or more. Brandished or holstered. They were always there. As appendages, deus ex machina, forces of nature. It took relentless acts of will to ease them from the pages, off the border and into some kind of void where they lost their insistent shape.

They don't have the same power now, but I can't help noticing them around me. Can't help noticing the ghost of the sweat they would have caused me years before. Can't help but wonder if one day I will have written Sophie out of my body in much the same way. Each gesture and phrase, each instant somehow stammered into words and then no longer my own.

I follow the officer to a spot partway between the porch and the cruisers where he turns back to me, flipping open a small notebook. He asks if Sophie and I were seeing each other.

"We'd had a relationship years ago. Now we're just friends." I notice the present tense, uneasy in the noticing, unsure now of what words to use. "Is there a problem, officer?"

He looks up from his notebook. He's young, in his early twenties, with no veneer of guile. "No," he tells me, apologetically. "No problem. I'm sorry. I just have to ask a few questions."

I tell him the story Sophie and I had agreed on: I'd come over early yesterday evening and stayed a couple of hours, but Sophie was tired and I'd left around nine.

"Everyone in this neighborhood is in bed by nine except me," Sophie had said. "No one will know any different, believe me."

Then Randy called me, I tell the officer, and I came right over.

"And you were home when you received the call?"

"Yes."

The officer nods, scribbling my responses. I turn back to the porch. Maggie is engaged with another officer, nodding in response to whatever he's telling her.

It had occurred to us that the police would be involved, we knew there would be some rudimentary investigation, but I'd never imagined there'd be so many officers, and their guns, in and out of the house, striding across the lawn to their cars and coming back, their muffled conversations sifting through the open door.

I don't know what they're doing in there, stepping around Sophie, motionless and vulnerable on the bed, ruffling through her clothes, opening her medicine cabinet. I want to tell them they should come back another time, should lower their voices so they don't disturb her. I want quiet for her, a hush like slow water. I want a layer of snow to gently erase the features of the house and the people in it, to bring the cool warmth first snowfalls have and the stillness that comes then.

On the porch, Randy also seems anxious with the activity. He peers in through the open door then turns away. He resists the urge to turn back to the door. He stares at the stone step beneath his feet, his head drifting side to side and I can hear one word echoing in his head: Why?

Only he isn't really asking why Sophie is dead, he's asking why anyone dies, how it happens and what we're supposed to do about it. He, of all of us, should be used to this. He's asking if it makes a difference how it happens, wondering if there's a right way to go about it. He's afraid Sophie had chosen the wrong one, believing in some shadowy distinction between dying as a result of faulty wiring or a gang of cells banding together in the bloodstream with mischief on their mind, or dying as a simple choice. One somehow more tragic than the other.

He apologizes later, at the memorial service. He comes up to shake my hand. "I'm sorry, man. I was messed up that day. I got to apologize. Been working with Hospice for six years and you get used to a lot, you know. But every now and then a case just gets to you and you fall apart."

He's trimmed his hair and his bushy beard for the service. He's bought a new suit and new shoes. All at once I'm achingly grateful for him, for his mellow, goofy energy, for the care he'd taken with Sophie. I squeeze his shoulder and try to tell him. He nods, eyes down.

"Well, she was a special person," he glances up to me with a grin. "I think I...well, I cared a lot about her."

Maggie brings me up to date. "Officer Bradley says the M.E. is on his way. It's all a formality. Once he comes they'll call an ambulance to take her to the funeral home. Then we can go into the house."

"Why would we want to go in?"

At my arrival, I hadn't given a second thought to entering the house, but now, after waiting outside for an hour and a half, the idea fills me with horror. Sophie will be gone and the rooms will be vacant, the place will be an altar of emptiness.

"We'll need to have a memorial service, Doug. Then the funeral. We'll need to go through her things to see if she has insurance policies, arrangements."

I nod. "She showed me where all that stuff was."

There's a delicate tap on my shoulder and I turn to find Marybeth. She looks much different from the first time I'd met her at Sophie's door. She's obviously returning from church. She's wearing a floral print dress, light makeup, a deep red lipstick; her hair is combed and sprayed stiffly in place. She smells of perfume and powder.

"Sophie?" she asks me.

"She's gone," I tell her, eyes on my shoes.

Maggie draws her aside to give her the details. Throughout, Marybeth watches me, her head tilted in my direction, her gaze returning now and then to Maggie when she asks a question, nodding to details. Her lip quivers, her fingers rubbing gently at the strap of her handbag as she listens. Her gaze always slides back in my direction. Her face is expressionless, though occasionally she squints, pushing her glasses up the bridge of her nose, as if to draw me into deeper focus.

In a moment, she embraces Maggie. They exchange a few more words then Marybeth makes her way across the lawn to her house, leaning one side to another with each step. She pulls a handkerchief from her bag and dabs at her eyes. She doesn't look back to me.

I hadn't worried about the officers, hadn't worried that I might be accused of helping Sophie kill herself. I hadn't even considered how I might explain the decision to someone else, knowing there was no language to describe it outside of Sophie and me. There was no doorway through which someone else might enter that decision. We were the last of the dying tribe, all our history passing into silence.

Yet, something in Marybeth's glance brings our intimacy into relief, mine and Sophie's, and the deep and lasting way it has been exposed. Not to the people with guns, not to the officers, but to those on the porch and those in the neighborhood. I feel naked, yet I'm not sure I feel embarrassed or awkward.

I make a deal with Maggie: I'll take care of the funeral arrangements and the service if she and Jim handle the house, what to do with Sophie's things, her paintings and possessions. For some reason the funeral appears manageable to me, all practical details and logistics; the other seems completely beyond my reach.

When the Medical Examiner arrives, a small balding man in a blue suit, we wait another thirty minutes before Officer Bradley returns to the porch. "We're going to be moving her soon. If you'd like to see her before we take her, I can give you a few minutes. I understand you're the closest thing she has to family."

"Alright," Maggie answers for all of us, "just let us know."

She's standing again, by a large pot that once held a plant but is now just dried stalks and loose dirt. Randy remains on the step, silent now, staring across the lawn, hands between his knees. Jim walked toward their car a moment ago to retrieve something for Maggie, who stares at the phone in her hand as if she's forgotten who she was going to call.

"Maggie, I'm sorry I fell out of touch," I tell her. "It's been so long and I don't know what happened but..."

"You were out doing your own thing," she smiles, her damp eyes widening slightly. "And I've seen your thing. It's worth doing."

I nod in a vague flush of embarrassment. "I hadn't realized you'd kept in touch with Sophie."

"We never really lost contact. Sometimes we'd go a few months without speaking, then we'd have coffee together and it was like no time had passed at all."

Maggie drops her head to my chest, bumping her forehead to my ribcage, a sigh escaping. "Lord, I'm gonna miss that girl. Even when I hadn't talked to her, it made me happy to know she was out there, spinning in her orbit."

Jim steps onto the porch with a nod. His eyes are rimmed in red but they are dry. His mouth is set, his hand pushed into his pockets. He's as solid as a fencepost and that solidity is a comfort. In a few minutes, Officer Bradley returns to escort us into the house. There are two officers in conversation in the kitchen, one in the corner of the living room talking into a radio on his shoulder in hushed tones.

Randy smooths the sofa cushions. He straightens a picture on the wall. The house is as vacant as a museum; it has that sense of a stilled, hermetic world where the elements could never intrude. Even though I'd been here last night, stood in the same rooms, it seems like weeks have passed and the structure itself has changed, hardened into place like a cavern calcifying into dry stone.

I follow the group down the hall, past the pictures of Sophie's family, her childhood, but I know I can't go into the bedroom, can't see Sophie again here, motionless and blue-cold on the bed. I turn into the studio to collect her insurance papers and funeral arrangements from the desk where she'd left them for me.

I try not to look at anything else, but the images stay with me. Her lined jars of chemicals and paint, the folded rags with ancient stains, the brushes, papers and books, an empty easel in the corner, the room still ripe with the smell of fresh paint. The walls bare, white and clean.

On the porch, I wait for the others, papers in my hand, turning away from the house to those on the street. I want to crawl into my car, go home and crawl into my bed, but I'm held in place by Maggie and Jim, the police, the ritual of departure. My eyes are drawn to Marybeth's house. I wonder if there's something I could say to her, knock on her door and explain. I don't know what I would explain.

I come back to what is. And what is not.

The gurney has already wheeled past us, bumping over the threshold onto the porch with a shapeless form wrapped in blankets then deposited into the back of the ambulance. We wait in the house, our movements tight and contained as if afraid our voices might shatter something delicate. We whisper now when we talk, but we don't talk much at all. We're waiting for the moment we can say it's finished.

I take as many days off work as I can afford, seeing my grief as a kind of virus that might infect others, but I don't know what to do with myself. I take long walks in the park. I stare from the apartment windows. I make food but can't find a way to eat it. It's impossible to say how I feel about anything.

There's a stillness, a dull quiet intermingled with a churning rage, each presenting itself without warning. They strike sometimes one so immediately upon the other that I feel thrown open, completely vacated. I don't hold these feelings, they hold me. Tossing me, thrashing me, then ebbing at once to leave behind a gasping emptiness.

There are words. A rage of words. I direct them at myself, accusations of weakness and cowardice; I direct them at a God I don't believe in, at a Universe that doesn't notice. A flurry of words spat into the face of the world and a rage at the words themselves, their ridiculous poverty and pretense. As if there were, or ever could be, a formula for describing Sophie and our world together. As if there were the possibility of speaking the pain of her loss.

There's the way the loss overtakes everything before it, wipes away the touch of her, the sound of her voice, blots memory and joy and the casual glance; this loss stains all history, every word ever spoken between us.

At night I drive. Sometimes the dull monotony of a highway, others the swerve and sway of country roads. Often, late, the car comes to rest in Sophie's driveway. Her car is still here. I sit, staring into the dark. My mind churning, wandering. Occasionally there's a memory of soft music, or a phrase from the Neruda poem. Mostly there is quiet. And darkness. I hold myself motionless. As if some fine sediment is settling into my bones and any movement or light might simply stir it again.

I am the sole survivor of our world. The historian, the witness, to the home we made in each other. What can we do but stand with those who suffer when we can do nothing else? A world lost with every death and all we can do is bear witness to the living and the dying, the peculiar slip and sweep of their lives through our own.

Three days after the service, parked in Sophie's dark driveway, I'm startled by a rap at the car window. Toby is standing beside the car. He's twelve or so, shifting nervously. He's holding a pie, wrapped in cellophane, weighing it before him in both hands.

I lower my window.

"Gramma says I should give you this. Says she'd come herself but she doesn't see too good in the dark."

We stare at each other for a moment in the darkness.

"You want to get in?" I ask him.

"Okay."

"Just put that in the floor," I tell him when he opens the passenger door. He does, positioning his feet around it when he sits, then clicking his door closed.

The darkness outside the car takes on dimension as we study it, angles of dim light stretching across the lawn and up the sides of the blank house, light thrown by Marybeth's porch light and the occasional sweep of headlights from the road behind us.

The scent of apples fills the car; it's a full, brown, sugary smell. I can feel the warmth that the crust and metal pie pan bring to the interior. Toby's palms are flattened on his thighs; his breathing is long and slow. He watches the night with me. Out of politeness, maybe. Or the assurance that if an adult is doing it, it must be worthwhile. Or because, like me, he's looking for something in the shadows. We sit together for twenty minutes or so.

He turns to me. "I've gotta go now."

"Okay," I nod. "Thanks for sitting with me."

"No problem," he tells me, opening the door. "See you." He closes the door with a soft click.

I should start the car. I should go home and feed the cat, wash the dirty dishes. I should work on the notes for the new book, re-establish my writing routine. I should begin my life again.

Marybeth's porch light blinks off once Toby arrives home and the shadows that gave the lawn definition are gone. The car is a raft in a windless pool; it's lodged in a plane of glass. I'm not going anywhere.

The green of the lawn slopes toward the chairs like still water. There's the lingering scent of cut grass, the rows of the mow slicing the lawn parallel to the house. The sun is in the trees now, the occasional blaze touching a branch here, a leaf there.

I angle the chairs toward each other, the trees at Sophie's back, the sky and the neighbor's lawn at mine. She stands before the chair, rocking slightly on her heels, hands in her jeans pockets then out again, gazing up and down the line of yards, up and down the treeline. She kicks with a toe at a small mound of cut grass, spreading it evenly before her shoe.

I wait beside her, blanket over my shoulder, until she turns with an awkward smile. I drape the blanket over her when she sits, tucking it in around her waist, then take my place beside her.

Her hands are in her lap, her eyes passing over the yard, the back of the house. She glances at the paintings on the lines but immediately turns away.

"If you close your eyes," I explain, fanning my arm to the side, "the breeze in the leaves sounds like water, like a stream very close, just on the other side there. I like that sound."

I nudge her arm and her eyes come to mine, wide and bright. "Try it."

She turns her attention to the trees. I take her hand, resting both on the wide arm of her chair. She sinks deeper into the chair, her eyes on the trees.

"When I rented studio space for the first time, it was a really big deal." Her eyes are closed now, though her head remains tilted to the trees. "It just came to mind. Just now. It's funny, you know. That I should think of it."

She shifts her weight in the chair, her limbs loosening. She squeezes my hand lightly. "It seemed like a complete change of direction, a new self, but it was absolutely unclear. The place was dirty, dusty; I wasn't sure what I was going to do there. But that first day, after Mr. Arthur gave me the key, I went inside. I just walked around in the room, I leaned against the wall. I remember my hand on the raw brick. The smell of the old dust and the way it clung to my jeans."

She glances over to me, opening her eyes with a small smile. "Don't know why I thought of that."

She settles back into the chair, closing her eyes again. "I like the sound. The trees. It's nice."

"What made you do it?" I ask, quietly. "Rent the space."

It's a moment before she speaks. "It was a declaration, I think. About the future. I was turning away from something, toward something I couldn't see. And that was okay."

She hadn't told me much but she thought I should know the steps, so I wasn't completely in the dark. The first drugs were for nausea, so she could keep the others down. The second were sedatives so she would gently drift to sleep, while the third drugs would stop her heart. I knew she'd taken the nausea drugs before I arrived, finishing with the others after our tea.

"You'll talk to me, won't you?" she asks. "I know it's a bit much. But I want to hear your voice. Don't talk about me. Don't talk about us. I don't want memory. I want you."

She's motionless, her eyes still closed. "Tell me about the new book. You haven't said much about it."

It doesn't matter what I talk about and I know it. I don't talk about the new book, not about myself, not about us. I talk about finding the new book. I talk about the gap between books, the weird purgatorial period of drift when one project is finished and another hasn't yet taken hold. The loss of definition then the feeling of being not quite visible.

The terror of having nothing to work on, as if I've slipped out of existence, eventually replaced by the terror of a new project I'm always convinced I don't have the skill to accomplish. I go on as if she's listening, and she might be.

She's not looking at me, though she nods now and then. Her eyes, still closed, are on the trees, her face gently relaxing. Her fingers aren't trembling, though the pressure changes now and then as if re-affirming my presence.

I talk because she needs me to talk and I know she wants me to talk about life, about the things that will go on once she is gone.

So, I talk about writing. I tell her each new piece is its own space. Each new piece its own landscape and I don't exist there. Each has its own atmosphere, its own weather. My only choice is to write myself into that world.

In that moment, I stand outside of time and I am never more myself.

I move to an idea for a short story, just an image or two really: a house on a wide green hill, the smell of straw, a question about how we know what is real in our lives.

I'm talking now, my voice low and close to her, because I don't know what else to do. I let the words come.

She starts, as if from sleep, her body clipping up from the chair, her eyes widening open. Her pulse is fast in my hand, her fingers tensing around mine. She starts forward, her neck craning, muscles taut.

She's disoriented for an instant, glancing about the yard, to me, before leaning back into the chair. She's drifting in her own body, her hand loosening again around mine.

In a moment, she sinks back into the chair. Her words are slowed when she speaks, but measured and clear: "I'm glad you're here."

"I'm here," I tell her.

She closes her eyes, squeezing my hand again. "You tried to catch me when I fell. But I didn't know what to do. I'd never fallen before."

The light slides from her face to a deeper place, though her fingers continue their soft pressure. There's a deep blue in the sky, the sun having slipped over the horizon. I draw the blanket up around Sophie's shoulders as best I can without letting go of her hand.

I don't feel like talking now. I can't think of anything to say.

A smile curls on Sophie's lips, a soft inward, intimate smile. Her voice is dreamy, the words stretched now and then, or halted for an instant as she remembers. I'm not sure what she's talking about or who she's talking to.

"It was a red, a red I'd never seen before. Purple. A bit of fire. A red with a voice. Quiet, strong voice. Something low. And sexy. And dangerous."

Her body ripples beneath the blanket, her hips tilting, her hand pressing her chest.

"And I wanted it. Around me. Wanted it on my skin. Inside me. It led to new blues and greens. Even blacks. So many new blacks."

Her voice is slowed now, each word long and articulated.

"They'd always been there. They were always there. I'd just never seen them. Until I did. Just like the river in the trees."

I'm not crying. I will not cry. I'd made the vow to myself. I will stand by her side, I will be with her, for her. I will give her what she wants. I can do that for her. The last thing I can do for her.

I know all the things I could say. I'd counted every word, over and over. The confessions, the admissions. The regret and guilt. My apologies. But I know none of that matters to her, only to me.

I say the only thing I can say. "I'm here, Sophie."

She is loose again in her body. Light tracing a limb, a leg or arm, deepening in her eyes for an instant, her eyelids fluttering, her hand again, her fingers tingling around mine.

I watch her face, the muscles slowly slackening. I let my focus slip, as if trying to make out something new, something not seen by close inspection, but from another perspective or in a differing quality of light.

There's a twinge of pain and she winces, her hand dropping from her chest to her stomach, limbs closing in reflexively. It passes in a moment and her body slackens again. I adjust the blanket over her legs and shoulders.

Her lips are moving but there's no voice. Emotion registers in the muscles of her face then disappears. A smile, concentration, a question. Her words are just under her tongue. A private history unfolding.

Then, she's looking at me, her head tilted in my direction. My eyes come into focus on her face as her hand tightens around mine.

She's speaking now but I can't make out the words, only a smile in her voice her muscles cannot manage, an expression I call up from the past without effort and respond to with a smile of my own. But there are no words now. Her lips moving, only an intimate whisper in her throat which won't become words.

Sophie closes her eyes. I stare out across the lawn as it loses what's left of its color to the darkness. There's a light mist just above the grass now. The air is cool.

"Oh," she says. It's a quiet sound, nearly silent. I might not have heard it.

I can make out her face against the darkening trees. Her eyes are wider, her lips full, her mouth slightly open. She's staring into the sky or the middle distance with intense concentration.

I breathe through the weight in my chest, the hard lump in my throat, breathe through it with all the concentration I can manage.

She's entering a slow current, drifting from me. Even as I clasp her hand I feel her more distant. Diminishing.

"Was this my idea?" I ask Maggie. "What was I thinking?"

She simply rolls her eyes and smiles, turning away from the door and into the restaurant to confer with the manager. It's sheeting rain in the parking lot, quick streams inches deep at the curb. I watch the storm from behind the glass door, its rush and hiss filling my ears.

"I want to get people together. For Sophie. Her friends, people who knew her." That's what I'd told Maggie. We'd had the simple memorial service Sophie requested, but I wanted something else.

"Not a service or a wake," I told her, "not a memorial..."

"A remembrance," Maggie offered.

"Okay," I nodded. "A remembrance."

I'd just received the advance for the book which now seemed impossible to finish. It was more money than I'd had in a while. I wanted something more to mark Sophie's passing than people standing around a silver urn, I wanted something like a celebration. Maggie said she'd help.

She still had her gallery downtown, had even expanded it, taking over stores on both sides, but the neighborhood was becoming increasingly gentrified. It was surrounded now by trendy, expensive clothing stores, sushi restaurants and boutique cocktail bars. She told me The Scrawl had been converted into a restaurant, Nouveau Blanc.

I called them up and booked the place for a Monday. I let Maggie talk to them about food and staffing; she handled the particulars, I paid. I also relied on her for help in rounding up Sophie's friends. We compiled emails and phone numbers, we set up a Facebook event page. It was impossible to know how many people might actually show up.

But now, with the maniac rain blowing sideways, flinging itself against the door, it's difficult to imagine anyone coming at all. I turn back to find Maggie, my anchor. She's leaning on the bar with Robert, the manager. He's tall, thin, very pale, with a slight affected indeterminate accent.

Nouveau Blanc isn't a large restaurant; The Scrawl hadn't been a large club. Black lacquer tables with square black lacquer chairs; bright white linen napkins tented at every setting beside tall crystal goblets. The entire decor black and white save a deep banner of red beginning at one end of the bar along the ceiling, above the bottles and the mirror, unfurling across the wall, widening all the way to the front door.

Small black shadow boxes hang every few feet, filled with tiny porcelain tea cups, some white, some blue, some etched in ebony and violet. Sophie would have liked the place, I think.

Robert slips from the bar toward the kitchen. It's at the back of the building, usurping the area where the office had been. Maggie looks tired, still managing her usual wry outlook, but tired at the corners of her eyes and the edges of her mouth. Tired of phone calls, and arrangements for movers, and decisions about what to do with Sophie's things, in the same way I'm tired of funeral directors and their unnaturally hushed offices.

There's a way I go numb with only practical details lodging in my brain; everything else passing into something unfocused and inarticulate, everything else losing its texture to the decisions that must be made, the papers that must be signed.

Time opens up, long stretches of time, bland and barren, between the practical decisions, or the discussions of arrangements, or the meetings with more documents, that place me for an instant like a star sparking in its fall. I pop into being when a decision must be reached, a line initialed, then vanish again, lose corporeality, until called upon for the next.

This will be the last event. I've deleted her messages from my phone, and all of her emails. I know what memory is. I know what knowing is. They're not the same thing.

This evening is the final thing to accomplish before life simply goes on. On and on. Without Sophie.

"They'll be here, Doug," Maggie assures me. "Don't worry."

"You need some wine?" she asks. There are glasses nearby and bottles open on the counter, some plunged deep into ice.

"No, not now. Thanks."

"How was she, Doug?" Maggie asks. "That night? Before she..."

I take her hand. It's odd to be reassuring her. "She was quiet," I say, "She was scared. She was happy."

Maggie smiles, some degree of exhaustion lifting. I remember, still again, that she's a good twenty years older than I am, a fact I struggle with as she never seems to change year to year, her energy hardly wavering.

"Good," she says. "I'm glad." She pours red wine into a wide glass, absently rolling the liquid in the bowl.

I'm sweaty-palmed and itchy, as if awaiting the arrival of a blind date. I haven't seen most of these people in years and have no idea what to say to them. Still another thing I'll awkwardly stumble my way through.

I'd wanted this for Sophie. I'm beginning to realize that, strangely, I always thought she would be here for the party. Moving among the crowd, laughing, making people comfortable, taking the lead so I could hang back. I'd set this snowball rolling, now I stand at the bottom of the hill waiting for it to flatten me.

The door swings open, the clatter of rain and a shuffling at the threshold. Someone fanning an umbrella before bringing it in.

"Man, it's raining like a bastard out there!" It's Josh, looking much the same as he had nearly eight years ago, a few pounds heavier, his face a little fuller, but still Josh. He breaks into a smile of recognition.

"Biff!" he calls out, with a grin. "Jesus, look at you!" We embrace, his arms strong around me, his downturned umbrella dripping at our feet.

I find myself in a new space, some remembered warmth washing over me that carries me through much of the night. The glow of shared memory, of another time, a lightness opening within the room, growing deeper with each fresh arrival, each introduction of a spouse or new boyfriend.

It's by not thinking of my Sophie that I manage to make it through. Of course we talk about her endlessly, telling our favorite stories both in small groups or, one person clinking a glass with a spoon to regale the room with their favorite Sophie.

The Serious Sophie. The Artistic Sophie. The Wacky Sophie. The Sophie in Love with Doug.

Even this last one is alright. I can listen to stories of people finding us making out in a closet, our exotic, penniless diet, our ridiculous private jokes. I can listen because they're talking about a different Sophie, the Sophie I've carried for years. The Sophie of memory.

The real Sophie I hold away from myself as I listen. She's relegated to a place I've made very small, nearly invisible within me. It's a distinction I can't quite get a handle on yet feel nonetheless, the Sophie of memory and the Sophie alive within me.

Around 9:30, there's movement at the door. Sasha stands just inside. I've only seen her once since the robbery. The first week, she and Alex had visited Sophie for a few awkward minutes, and they'd never returned.

She's taking in as much of the room as she can, unsure whether to come in or turn around. The rain has stopped but her raincoat glistens with errant drops. Her glasses are fogging, her hands stuffed in her coat pockets. She's half-turned toward the door.

I break away and come a few steps up the short hallway toward her. "Sasha, come on in. It seems like almost everyone is here."

She's startled, twisting her coat around herself, her mouth working even before I'd spoken. She pushes her fists deeper into her pockets.

"No, I have to go," she says, eyes darting up and down the hallway, around me into the dining room behind, settling at her feet, then darting again. "I wanted to see you, I think. I'm sorry I never came. I...I just disappeared."

"That's alright," I tell her. "Come on in and say hi to everyone."

"I didn't. I couldn't."

"It's okay, Sasha." It doesn't seem right to touch her, to take her hand; it seems she might scream or dissolve.

"No. I wanted to say I'm sorry. For what happened." She takes a short, hard breath, her shoulders rising, dropping. "And what I didn't do. I never said it. Not to you. Not to Sophie."

"I'm sure she knew, Sasha."

Her eyes are burning and fierce, her fists turning in her pockets, bringing the tails of her coat up as she speaks: "No. No, she didn't know 'cause I never told her."

She looks to me, her eyes wide, lips thin and bloodless, then she's gone, the door slapping back into place behind her. I don't go after her.

Soon, Josh brings his guitar in from the car. He's in a band now; they've made a few CDs, been reviewed in Pitchfork. They'd been touring and he'd only been in the area by chance, happy he could come. He props a leg on a black lacquer chair, resting the guitar on his thigh, and strums lightly. The crowd goes quiet, folks gathering new drinks, making their way to tables, as he sings a slow and sweet love song he's written.

Maggie catches my eye, halfway across the room, leaning back into Jim. She winks, then slowly closes her eyes to listen.

Josh plays three or four of his own songs before Roger, wedged into a corner at the back of room, calls out: "You gotta play some Neutral Milk, Josh. For Sophie."

Josh looks up from the guitar and over to me. I can't help but smile. "You gotta," I tell him.

He pulls the chair away from the table into the aisle and sits down, plucking one string then another until tuned to his liking, before strumming the intro to *Oh, Comely*. The room grows even more still. Glasses are gently placed upon the table tops, eyes are closed.

Goldaline, my dear, we will fold and freeze together.

Sophie slides over the armrest of the sofa into my lap as if dropping into the leather seat of an expensive sports car. She has a beer for both of us. The room is a jumble of bodies and noise. She drapes one arm around my neck once I take my beer, bringing hers to her lips.

The room slips past me and I grip the edge of the black table. Some are singing with Josh, their voices low and ghostly, a nerved language of raw desire, yet measured and quiet, as if that desire were a constant, unending current.

Our kisses are loose and wet by now, both of us tasting of beer and stale coffee, our skin oily with the night, our clothes limp. She slips her hand under my shirt and I cup her breast as she curls into me. She growls softly in my ear: "I'll eat you up, I love you so."

The voices in the room are a shadow of the voices at the party long ago, themselves a shadow of the night Sophie and I listened to *In the Aeroplane, Over the Sea* for the first time at her apartment, lying along each other on her narrow sofa, motionless as the music opened around us, nestled together in a moment we could never define.

When the music ended, the last words and final notes lingering, we didn't talk, couldn't talk. We could only stare out in the same undifferentiated direction, while my forefinger slid slowly back and forth along her bare arm, a tear collecting at the corner of her eye, the top of her nose, then spilling over the bridge.

The song finishes itself; there's the sense the world might end now in a sort of hushed whisper as a coda to the last note. No one moves in the room. It might be that no one is breathing, the stillness so ripe and pitched that I don't breathe, wanting to hold this sense of motionlessness, forever.

Josh adjusts himself on the chair, but it's really just to make a little space for one last song. It's like a door opening, throwing a dim wedge of light across an expansive darkness. He plucks a few tentative notes, offers a short cough, then launches into the first chords of Two Headed Boy, Part Two.

Those who know the words sing, low and quiet almost in chant. Those who don't, hum with eyes closed, focused on the ceiling, or blankly directed to Josh. Her scent is around me, something like ginger and apples at the tender slope of her neck. I clutch at my edge of the table until I know it can't save me and I have to leave before the room overtakes me.

In the parking lot I gulp at the air, easing Sophie away. The night is slick and black. I rest against the brick of the building, staring up into the darkness. A police cruiser glides by, puddle ripples bouncing to the curb. A stoplight swings gently on its wire. I can hear it click from one color to the next.

Back inside, Josh has put away his guitar. I order a rye whiskey because I'd seen someone do it in a movie once and liked the way the two words sounded together: rye-whiskey. I keep ordering them and, after a while, the world begins to slip slowly from focus.

In an hour or so, I'm drunk. I haven't been drunk in a long time. Deborah Costellano eyes me from a nearby table and I sit down to talk to her and I follow her to the bar and we kiss in the hallway between the restroom doors, a long sensuous kiss, our bodies shifting and fluid, her hand on my thigh, mine sliding along her stomach, just asserting our blood and skin and bone and the goddamn inconsolable confusion in the face of the ridiculousness of death.

Or something like that. I don't know.

I sit in a corner on a square black chair after kissing Deborah Costellano. In the corner by the kitchen, near what used to be the office of The Scrawl. I stare, bleary eyed, at the group of people I used to know, shaking my head slowly. Confused, resigned, disconnected. Out of place somehow within my own history. Wanting desperately to know if memory can rescue me, lock my life together again once this night is over, or if it will turn back on me with a hard edge.

After a time, Deborah appears, sitting down beside me without a word. We lean against the wall there. I think of taking her hand, pressing it flat between my palms as petals between the leaves of a book. But I don't.

Deborah Costellano takes me home with her. I let her undress me like an exhausted three-year-old, my arms up as she tugs the t-shirt over my head. The angles of the walls drifting toward the floor, the furniture untrustworthy. I stare blankly from the side of the bed as she pulls off each sock, already feeling guilty for reasons I don't readily understand.

I let her slide me beneath her comforter and sidle up naked next to me. I throw my arm over her torso and draw her close, our bodies slipping together. I fall asleep with my face in her hair.

15

"We're dervishes!" Sophie announces breathlessly.

Her forehead rests at my chest, as damp and warm as the night air. The pressure of her breath is on my shirt. I slide my hand down her bare arm and leave it there, just at her wrist.

"Not very good ones," I counter.

She takes my hand, tugging me from the parking lot to the sidewalk. "Well, we've got to start somewhere."

We can see a few of the paintings through the wide, bright windows of the museum. Splashes of color spill from white walls buoyed by shadows in both directions, shadows thrown across the terrace, down the stairs, into the black grass then up the hill toward us.

In the parking lot, Sophie had begun to spin, arms out, head tilted to the stars, and I'd followed. We turned in the darkness, turned around each other, one spinning in place with the other, until we collapsed into each other, panting and dizzy, clutching at each other in the darkness. We're still unsteady as we descend the steps to the museum.

It's our first few months together; the burn of the first blush, a full-bodied warmth between us, blood rushing constantly to my face and hands. There's the impossibility of Sophie: her skin, her touch, her kiss. The long phone calls, the parting and return, the moments on her doorstep just before I turn to go home.

It's our first few months together and she's dragging me to an opening at an art museum. I'm the one who remembers museums from high school field trips as grey, dimly lit and vaguely claustrophobic. I'm the one who knows nothing about art. I'm the one she leads like a small child.

"Ellen Laskow. She's Swiss," she'd told me a week or so before. "I've only seen her work in magazines---I can't believe it's in town. We *have* to go!"

I agree, of course. Enthusiastically.

The memory rises to the surface because of the phone call. Maggie's phone call.

"This Friday," she'd said, explaining it's a gallery hop and it's spring so there'll be a crowd. "Come early."

I'm at my desk, staring out the window, Beaker's tail thumping languidly against the warm glass. The images return: of stars spinning above our heads, the damp pressure of the night years ago, the knowledge that Sophie's presence, even then, was already deep beneath my skin.

In the months since her death I've managed to reassemble my writing routine, the hours at the desk, at the window, the long walks. An array of images, thoughts, bits of conversation; they all tumble past me but nothing has really connected yet. Still, there's some comfort in the discipline, in sitting down, fingers on the keyboard or pen in hand; in scrawled notes soon crumpled and tossed aside; the occasional visit from Beaker who sprawls dismissively across the legal pad or keyboard, demanding attention.

Some parts of a life begin to cohere, from a chaos that isn't really an openness or an emptiness, more a clutter in which no object fits with another. It's a jumble and a tightness, a kind of pressure and closing in as if my experience were searching for some code which might draw the pieces together into clusters or tangents or stories, as if I'm waiting for a secret narrative to reveal itself.

I've tried to allow the memories to come and go as they wish, to neither grasp them nor push them away. I've wanted them free to rise and fall. In their freedom, they have life. In their freedom, they can surprise me, catch me unaware, fill me completely with her scent, the press of her fingers upon my skin.

I have to let them go before they can overtake me. I try to push the memories, gently, away from becoming stories. I want to preserve, for as long as I can, the chaos of memory, to resist the stories that begin to form and in their telling and retelling become the only truth. I resist a narrative line, sentences ending in periods, and the past reduced to photos in an album.

Maggie's invitation reminds me of the museum so long ago, a clean space of meaning, a moment in which I'm placed and real, at Sophie's side. It's still bright and untouched by revision, not frozen, worn, or faded. It's a time in which, for a breath or two, I know who I am.

Because there are people with whom we are more ourselves than we can ever manage to be alone. There are people with whom we emerge from our own shadow, look back on our own features, our own gestures and watch ourselves with a kind of unequivocal appreciation, studying ourselves as an element of their world.

I can't see her, as we turn, my head tilted to the sky. I feel her by my side, feel the swish of her arms as they pass mine, her breathy giggle, and the faint shuffle of our feet scuffing the wet asphalt. I know she's beside me.

Then we're climbing the steps to the bright door of the museum, a wide, white building nestled in a gentle, sloping valley, Ellen Laskow's paintings, a Czech sculptor, and the heady cream of the town's arts community.

"Everyone will be there," she'd said. "Well, everyone who matters. And people like us, who don't."

We're climbing the steps, hands on the rail, still reeling. Sophie separates from me on the landing, her head rising from my shoulder. I reach out to hold the door for her. She comes up close and I think she's going to kiss me there at the entrance to the gallery, and she does, a deep and full kiss. But more than that, she slips her hand into my back pocket and squeezes my ass. She completes the kiss and squeezes again as we enter the museum, sliding into place at my side.

In the parking lot, I remember rotating around her like a car on a carnival ride. I remember watching her paint from the corner of her studio, her stance before the blank canvas, the work changing shape one day to the next, layers applied, then scraped and applied again, gathering and burning off one after the other.

She'd stand beside a covered easel held together by wire, the loose ends budding from the top in sharp fronds. One hand at the stained sheet thrown over it, the other on her hip, blowing a few strands of dark hair from her face. She'd pull the sheet back, her bare arm settling along the top edge, her attention fixed upon me as my eyes darted from one corner of the canvas to another, spilling over the image.

A smile would spread across her face. I'd see it at the edge of my vision not overwhelmed by paint, light and shadow. She'd watch me, bending one leg at the knee, resting her foot on the toe.

I'd feel myself flush, unsure, while she remained patient, learning as much from my body as any words I might find. Finally I'd let go, tumbling somehow into the painting and a place without words, a place where everything vanished and there was only her and I, and this thing she'd made. I'd smile, a different smile every time.

She'd know something then but I never knew what. She'd lower her eyes to the floor. Perhaps she was smiling too, her head slightly declined, but I never knew since I was caught in the burn before me, one color and stroke flowing around the next, changing the light in the room.

For an instant, I know faith is something that's already happened, something I only catch up to afterward. It's a simple gesture or a few words sparking a flicker of recognition then vanishing again into the folds of life. On this night it's Sophie, only Sophie, climbing the stairs with me, just before the door and after our spin in the parking lot, our bodies still lurching into each other in the remnants of vertigo. She finds the gesture, completes it. Then she sweeps into the room like new weather, changing its shape and its horizon line.

In the doorway of every gallery and museum since, the moment passes into me like a ghost moving through on its way to another visitation. Some slip in awareness and time loses hold. In the doorway of every museum, there's an instant of Sophie.

We storm into the museum as a single organism that night, fingers and toes all aflutter in the bright light and the neutral carpet and the evening gowns and dinner jackets with Sophie in her red silk dress, towering in her heeled alligator boots, trailing various glittering scarves. She looks like Ziggy Stardust's orphan sister. I follow, a satellite in her outer orbit, as she sweeps into the crowd, scoops two glasses of red wine from the table and spins back, offering one in an extended hand.

"Welcome to the world of Art!" she declares, and she's only half joking.

"I mean, look at this," she exclaims, turning the stem between her fingers, "they use real glasses."

We parade through the exhibition, lingering for a second or two before each painting, continuing on once she's managed a grunt of appreciation or a moan. She holds her glass precariously between two fingers, arm rising and falling with her attention, taking small sips between pieces. I watch her study them, head tilting to one side, light rising in her eyes as she takes a few steps back or edges closer to inspect a twinge of color.

We haven't gone far when someone shrieks her name from the other side of the room. She spins in the direction of the voice, leans toward it instinctively and away from me, fingers sliding from my arm, head angling back as she mouths, "Just a minute," then sails away to throw her arms around a tall elderly woman with even taller hair. I hum in her absence, a top left to wobble in place.

Circling the gallery alone, I uncover a gentler stream that brings me near one painting after another. I linger there, bringing her attention to each piece, trying to enter her joy in color and shadow, the feeling she has with a brush in her hand. There are times I turn back to the black glass, and cross the room to gaze over the dimming rise of the hill toward the parking lot, aware of the wash of color behind me, the shudder of the crowd and the drone of indistinct conversations, aware of Sophie coursing through the room like some wild virus of light.

I can see her behind me, all hummingbird flutter and laugh, bobbing bloom to bloom. Now and then, her hand returns to my back pocket and she kneads my cheek for a moment like a kitten settling into a purr. Lips near my ear, she whispers, "They don't know what we know."

It's the kind of thing she says when we find ourselves doing something that makes sense only to the two of us: spending our last few dollars on theatre tickets, or driving nine hours in one of our dubious cars to see a band.

Now and then, she kisses me, always bringing me back to the doorway. Her hand slips in my pocket just as I draw the door open, her fingers tightening. It's an act so casually intimate that all motion ceases and I stop, jolted from my body somehow, watching as we linger in the threshold.

Weeks after her death, the mourning has changed. In the car as I drive, in the produce section of the grocery store, or at my desk staring past Beaker's flickering tail and across the lawn, it is no longer an aspect of rage, no longer anger or remorse. Now it is a clean and pure sadness like a Bach fugue playing softly in the next room. I can turn my attention and listen, or allow it to fade into the background, but it's always there.

It isn't a forgetting; it's something more subtle and moderate, something liminal I can discern only by ignoring. A new form of remembrance. There is a true forgetting, the sinking away of the moments and details of the past into obscurity; then there is the forgetting that is more a change in who we are.

I notice her language or gestures in my own: the way I throw up my hand to say goodbye, the phrases I use when annoyed. It's the syntax of our intimacy nesting into my bones, the way a conversation with another can slowly become a conversation with oneself.

I don't have to think of her to include her, she is always a part.

Sophie put off the largest gallery, that night at the opening. The gallery with Ellen Laskow's work. Perhaps she was nervous she might be disappointed, or suddenly wished she were alone. Maybe she felt intimidated. Or perhaps she was simply relishing the anticipation, extending it, treasuring the moment just before.

I don't say anything. I watch her, fingers nervously plucking at her scarf, head tilting, birdlike. I retrieve new glasses of wine and we wander the other galleries still again before arriving at the Laskow exhibit.

She squeezes my hand and releases it, pushing into the room the way one pushes into waist high waves to reach calmer water. I come in behind her, sliding along one painting after another. I'm thirty feet from the door before I realize I've left her behind and turn to find her.

She's just inside the threshold, leaning against the white wall at her shoulder, legs angled out, the left bent at the knee so one boot balances at the toe beside the other. Her hands rest at her waist, cupped as if capturing something delicate. She's peering down the wall toward a huge painting at the end of the room. Her eyes are streaming tears; she makes no effort to wipe them away. They pool at her chin, dropping to the floor at her feet.

She's smiling her crooked smile, her mouth curled one side, lips pressed gently together. Her eyes are wide and intent. I know the room has vanished around her, her body has vanished; there are only her eyes and the painting. It seems she's motionless, but she's not motionless at all.

I want to believe I fulfill some function, standing silently in the gallery, watching her cry. Guileless, innocent. Ecstatic.

I want to believe my witness makes something more real or nurtures the moment somehow. At my desk, nine years later, Sophie gone now, I want to believe this memory matters and that my carrying of it, the savor of it, burns a certain thing into the world: a thought, a feeling, a location like a marker. Something.

I handle these things tenderly. Judiciously. I want so much to believe that to witness is to create.

So, I return to my desk, over and over, to the blank screen, the blank paper. The routine and the part-time job hold my life in some kind of order, even though both are nearly transparent, with hardly any shape or force. Often, they more resemble the dream of a life rather than any form of living itself. They are actions I move through on the way to something I can't discern.

Some days, it's a relief when Beaker extends himself along the keyboard, random onscreen windows opening, the nagging sound of a single depressed key iterating one letter again and again. Some days, it's a relief to find a sentence, and then, perhaps, another sentence to slide beside it.

Some days, there is only silence. And waiting.

One morning, finally, I wake with the idea for a project, more like the atmosphere of it, its weather. This idea doesn't emerge from any of the meandering work I've been doing. It's completely new. An instant of grace.

There are no images yet, no characters, and only the thinnest thread of an arc. But there's something. An opening, a presence. Like a change in temperature, as if I might envision a long journey from the simple acknowledgment of a horizon.

I stand before this horizon line, colorless land separated from colorless sky by the thinnest of borders. A dark, constellating world. The slightest beginning.

It's dark and I can't make out the features of Sophie's face in the light of the distant half-moon. It's a pale waft at my side. I don't want to disturb her so I remain still, charting her drift through the hand in mine, the pressure of her fingers slowly giving way, the pulse lightening.

We'd talked about what to do next, about carrying her into the house and placing her on the bed, about Randy's return in the morning and my phone number on her fridge.

"I've told him about you," she'd said, "told him you were a friend."

We'd talked about waiting for the phone call, and even though some part of me wanted to believe she might change her mind, I'd known she wouldn't. That wasn't Sophie.

I'd considered the steps, considered the chores required of me. In tiny cut scenes, since I couldn't hold myself before the thought for long enough to imagine completing it. I'd separated it instead into the completion of a single task followed by a kind of blankness or void, then the accomplishment of another.

Sophie's pulse is thready, a delicate wing beating inside the skin of her wrist. Near, then far, then near again. Her fingers hold their shape around my own, but the pressure is light. She's ebbing away.

It's a slow retreat. I watch, keeping myself as still as possible. Believing, perhaps, that sudden movement might awaken her as if from sleep, awaken her again to the pain and imprisonment of her body, to the torturous cadence of days anticipating only an end. Wanting to believe, perhaps, that I still hold some power to change the present yet choose not to exercise it.

I wait beside her. Because that's what she wants me to do. Because it's what she'd asked of me. It's dark and I'm cold, my clothes clammy now, the mist rising from the grass. I hold her hand.

I don't know when it happens. When her heart stops beating. I can't say with confidence. I'd become accustomed to the pulse rising and falling with lessening pressure. I'd become accustomed to the missed beat, or two, then the return. I'm watching her drift away like a leaf on the mirror of a stream. But I can't say I know the moment she's fully gone.

I clasp her hand tighter when I notice. It's automatic, the way I might throw my arms out in a dream of falling. I clasp her hand but she isn't there. It's only then I can look at her, though I still keep my movements light and contained, though I remain quiet, holding even my breathing shallow. I can hear the inhalation in my ears, feel my own pulse where my fingers touch my palm.

Sophie's head has slipped to the side, toward me, chin on her shoulder, mouth slack. The blanket has fallen away from her shoulder. I lean over, righting it gently with my free hand before settling back into my chair, staring across the yard at the grey trees rising from the grey earth, the moonlight tepid in the mist. I hold to her hand.

When I let go, I'll have to stand up. I'll have to carry her into the house. The night will have completed itself and I'll take the first step toward meeting myself where I am, a thin thread of emptiness always present, an ache. I'll already be moving away from her and some barbed acceptance will have to begin. When I let go of her hand I'll have to deal with the vast space boiling up between us.

When I let go, she will fall away from me, all at once, the assurance of her presence becoming vague and insubstantial. When I let go, there'll be only me.

I clutch her hand so tightly my fingers ache, the tension knotting my arm into my shoulder. I notice the pain for a long time, an angry red throb pulsing into the base of my neck. I try to relax my fingers but find it difficult to distinguish them in the gnarl of flesh curled on the arm of the chair between us. I don't look down at my hand; I keep my vision on the darkened lawns. I will my hand to take its own shape; I will the fingers to loosen and, as they do, Sophie's hand uncurls within my own, her fingers resting, abandoned in my palm.

That's when I look. At the cold ivory of her hand inside mine, the cuff of her blouse, the forearm disappearing beneath the blanket. The tilt of her head against the back of the chair, chin resting at the border of the blanket.

I move very slowly. Or I think I do. I turn her hand and smooth it, palm down, on the armrest. I drop my palms to my armrest and inhale, pushing myself upward until I'm standing. I tuck the blanket around her more tightly and step away, a few steps away but no more, to stand at the tree-line.

I know there are rows of houses behind me, a few windows lit, and beyond that the road, a car passing with a low hiss, the sound declining into the distance. There's the bowl of dark sky above my head and the litter of stars, the scent of grass and the coolness on my skin. I put my hands in my pockets so I don't have to think of them; I stare into the grey bars of trees.

I want to believe in something. I want to conjure a picture of Sophie drifting to another world. I want something to hold to, something other than absence. My mind is a panicked rhythm of images and thoughts. A catalogue of answers, from bands of angels and choral music, to pyres and thick drumming.

I want to believe. In reasons. And plans. And an abiding fate drawing us all into its embrace. In a movement toward unity and love and the understanding that every life happens in exactly the right way and ends at exactly the right time. I want to believe. In answers.

I know I struggle every day to understand the people around me, every day to find a way to begin to love. I know my desire to believe can overcome my sense of truth and I can willfully enter into lies. I know I return, again and again, to simply trying to know I am alive, in a single moment.

I know every way I failed Sophie, and myself. I know every instant I turned away from her pain or her joy, her smiles or her tears, her touch. I know every instant I could not be for her.

I number my confessions, staring into the trees.

My body is a shell, my clothes heavy against the skin. Feet apart, hands in pockets. I'm swaying in the moonlight. I stumble into the ringing hollow of my body. I'm dropping, tumbling, unable to open my arms, unable to break the fall, backward into the dark earth beneath me, held in place at the edge of the lawn by my clothes.

The earth beneath me opens up and I continue to fall, a sharp wheel turning in the pit of my stomach, a hard fist at my throat, dizzy with vertigo. My eyes are closed. I know the tree-line before me, the houses at my back. I know the damp grass at my feet.

Though I cannot find a way to trust some larger plan that might place and hold Sophie and I, I do know one thing: that two people, alone in a room or on a lawn, comforting each other, is the bleakest and most beautiful moment we can have.

I come back to Sophie. The first night of our reunion. Leaning back against me on the sofa, her body warm and light along my own, my arms folded over her stomach, her hands clasped with mine. She rises and turns, I take off my t-shirt, then she settles into me again. My face is in her hair, my arms around her. She rises again, unbuttoning her blouse and leaning back, her bare skin against my own.

She has left me. Her body waits. And though the emptiness yawns wide and full, I feel myself rise. Knowing her body is at my side, head askance in the chair, palm motionless on the armrest. I will not believe in anything that makes her absence easier.

I open my eyes. It's dark, the moon further away or behind clouds. Sophie is a pale shadow in the raft of her chair.

I approach from the open side. The blanket blots her body, only the pale of her face is visible, turned away from me now. The arc of her bandana, the tip of her ear protruding, the rising ridge of her cheekbone.

In a moment I'll slide my arms beneath her, lifting her to my chest. I'll carry her into the house and lower her to the bed, the bedside table littered with the empty bottles of the pills she'd taken and the note she'd written this morning.

I kneel beside her chair, my knees wet in the clumped grass. I press my forehead against her empty armrest. It's hard, relentless.

In my version, we learn to kiss as innocently as small children. The press of lips or an awkward, wet lick. Our affection rattles in our arms. Eyes closed, we reach out, fingers open, lips pursed.

Our first kisses are soundless, wordless, and when they're complete we're left clumsy and ecstatic, our bodies too frail for feeling. Each kiss is the slow capture of vocabulary, then the mostly accidental arrangement of one word beside another until a sentence forms that we pass back and forth.

She kisses me and says, "You're a mess."

I know I'm a mess, and it's alright. I touch her. "Hold still, just for a minute," and she's motionless, tremulous in my fingers. One of us pauses, before or after speaking, and the other falls into the pause, a silence enveloping us.

Something in me is constantly afraid of missing the moment or catching up to it too late; something in me struggles just to accept being in the room with her. Then, all of that falls away or is gloriously forgotten in a simple gesture or a smile or the way I might watch her tenderly pick up a brush.

I tell my versions to Maggie. Matter-of-factly. As if these things happen every day. I'm pacing back and forth, something in me barely contained. Memory rising like storm water, loud and furious.

We're in the front room of her gallery. It's a small, wide entranceway separated from the actual exhibition space by a wall with a drawn curtain in its center. The walls are an orange closely resembling the color of Maggie's hair. There's a table with a guest book on one side, a table for goodies on the other.

I'd watched her before I knocked at the glass door. She was carrying supplies from the back, boxes with bottles and napkins and snacks. Her cheeks were flushed; she was breathless, and though I couldn't hear her, I could see she was singing to herself. Her lips were moving, and a certain melody translated into her step and the rhythm with which she unpacked.

She seemed surprised when I knocked, by the knock itself and by me rocking foot to foot on the other side of the door. Surprised I'd come, after all. She must have sensed my hesitation when she'd called a week earlier to invite me. It had been our first conversation in months and we hadn't been sure of what to say to each other, now that all practical concerns had fallen away. We hadn't known what there was left to talk about.

At the door, she grinned broadly, swinging it wide to let me in then throwing her arms around me in a momentary embrace. She locked the door behind us, turned to talk to me in earnest, but I was too jumpy from some kind of phantom charge in the air, so she returned to her work.

I talk. Preemptively filling the room with words and a certain tenor of the past. I pace, rattling on. The air around me is sparking, as she sets the table with a bright orange tablecloth, then plastic cups. Wine bottles follow, a cheese tray wrapped in film, a large bowl of animal crackers. She's methodical, hands flashing, eyes occasionally rising to meet mine with a nod or a smile. She wants me to know she's listening.

The closed street on the other side of the gallery window begins to fill as dusk approaches; couples arrive to stroll the arts district, buskers with a guitar or a violin, families piling out of mini-vans. The neighborhood has changed; I wonder where the starving artists live now.

"You'll have thirty minutes or so before I open the doors," she'd told me on the phone. "You'll have the place to yourself."

In my version, I notice her long before she notices me: almost weekly in the grocery store, in random passings on the street, once at a concert. I know things about her before we meet: the light in her hands, moving and at rest, the way she curls her hair behind her ears when she's thinking, the resolve in her walk. I know something about her before she pins me speechless in the produce section, locked by proximity before the squash.

My version is less a story than hers. There is no narrative, simply a catalogue of scenes. Moments, rising and falling, crashing awkwardly together, drifting apart. My version won't settle into the frame; it's always pushing past the edges, spilling over.

My version won't become a story. A story is too close and too wrong. My version chooses to remain in motion, as unpredictable as cloud. It's a thing I guard by leaving unattended.

I see her standing before the draped easel, uncertain whether to reveal her new piece. Fingers playing in the folds of the stained sheet, palm flattening along the top as she decides against it, puts it off for another moment or another day, saying: "The painting isn't complete until someone sees it."

Maggie glances up with a smile. She's resting far inside herself, confident and close. Her eyes search some interior space as her hands come to rest on the table. I can't tell who her smile is for.

"I remember," her voice hangs close to her. "I remember what Jim said to her. He had this twinkle in his eye whenever they talked. Those two were as close as bread and butter. Like old friends that never had to say a word."

Maggie notices me again, her voice settling back between us. "Jim said: 'Seeing isn't easy, you know. The thing has to reveal itself the same moment you're watching.' Jim says things like that all the time. I just nod, I'm used to it.

"But Sophie smiled, this easy, knowing smile. Like they'd stumbled onto something together, she and Jim, a cave or a new species of bird."

I can't stop moving, back and forth, the length of the entranceway. Maggie returns to action, nestling bottles into bowls of ice and fanning red napkins beside the clear stacked cups. As I pace, she fidgets with the table, adjusting the angle of the napkins, the height of the cups.

"He'll be here later, if you want to stay," Maggie tells me after a moment, as if she's remembered again I'm in the room, or simply needs something to say. "He likes openings. He likes to watch the people."

She's lost in some private past and I don't want to disturb her. I keep to myself swinging wide by the window, sliding my finger along the cool glass, pretending my nervousness is some form of confidence or appreciation.

We hold our separate worlds, Maggie and I. She's abandoned to a certain joy, a light juddering her limbs, while I'm dispersed again, far and long. Thoughts bounce against the glass beside me in ripples, interfering with each other into chaos.

In my version, memory is an embrace and a blow. It happens without warning.

In the preceding months, my life has taken on an outline again. Its features slowly gather into something like a shape. In the beginning, I'd felt like the victim of some brutal execution, my dismembered limbs buried in separate, shallow graves, my body spread and strewn, in an attempt to arrest my soul.

The writing had come first, like the thread of a road in deep mist: the ritual, the quiet, the shadow of an idea or an image slowly revealing itself. The waiting, the constant waiting. As I wrote the hands came into view, then the arms, then the rest of my body around them. I became something like a human again.

The writing came as another way of being. A different room where the souvenirs of the past didn't have the same weight. They were still there, either ghostly or slowly becoming something else. The grief, the loss, was still there but I wasn't quite as naked before it.

It took time and quiet, broken by rage and tears. It took time, cold, empty, raw time, crawling over my limbs, threatening never to end. It took time, and the patience not to hate her for vanishing.

Slowly I become a person again, or something like a person, the beginnings of a person, the elements not yet completely assembled. I drift clear of her wake. I find calm water. It's like not moving at all, exhilarating and disorienting until the moment I accept the new current.

Then every version of our history churns again in the anticipation of tonight and Maggie's desire that I stand before the paintings, the show she's arranged as a kind of final act. The current of the past grew stronger as the date approached, ebbing in and out, sometimes ghostly, sometimes catching hold.

Maggie is listing the others I know who will be coming tonight but I have no need to see them. One has married again and is very happy. Another has a great new job. Old friends are changing, becoming new people. I am not.

"And look at you," Maggie says, turning to face me. "A new book contract. An author." Her eyes are twinkling in contentment, so I can't be too angry.

"I'm narcissistic and neurotic," I reply, unsure of my own tone, trying to find a sense of humor. "I can't balance my own checkbook, forget to pay bills. I'd forget to feed the cat if it weren't so noisy. I'm not as hysterical or angry as I was before…"

"Art has a way of changing…"

I interrupt her. "Writing hasn't made me a better person. I make things. They don't change me but I make them. Now and then, I think…"

Maggie's listening intently; she's listening past my words.

"Hell, I don't know what I think."

"Sophie never needed you to be a better person," she tells me quietly.

In my version, years after the break-up, I drive to D.C. to see her paintings in a gallery, not expecting her to be there a week after the opening. I sit in a coffee shop across the street, watching her pass in and out of the sunlit shadows of the gallery, the glare against the glass cutting the planes of the windows into angles that reveal, now and then, fragments of her work and the slope of her shoulders or the tilt of her head.

I could cross the street and open the door. I could enter the gallery, surprise her, and she might smile a wide welcoming smile that would shift to the crooked one, curled to one side as if she were whispering my name, and we could walk the gallery slowly as she tells me about each painting, her arm slipping into mine.

But I don't cross that street. Instead, I drink cup after cup of coffee, spending most of the afternoon with my eyes trained to the windows for a glimpse of her form broken by the sunlight and the angle of the glass and the distance; I fall backward as if into trusting arms, back into a place that is us, a place to embrace us, contain us, and the once we were.

I know the space won't last, the way every film fades to a blank screen, every play ends with an empty stage. The way every book must eventually be closed.

"Here," Maggie says. "It's time."

She's standing in my path; I stop before her. There's an instant when neither of us know what to do, as if the moment itself has trapped us. She closes her hands gently around my forearms. Her fingers are cold from the ice and wine bottles.

"There's a painting," she tells me. She's flushed, her eyes searching my face for something. She holds to my arms, squeezing them, tilting gently right to left. I've never seen Maggie embarrassed before.

"I'm sure it's new. It smells new. It was in her studio, against the wall. She'd wrapped it in paper. Put your name on it.

I've had it in the back. I've been holding on to it. I think I was afraid if I gave it to you before, you wouldn't come tonight. And I needed you to come tonight."

"It's sitting by the back door," she gestures beyond the curtain and into the gallery. "You can take it with you when you go."

Maggie releases me, eyes skirting my face. She plants her feet and smooths her sweater, reflexively, until she notices the gesture and stops herself. Her eyes come up; they're bright, blue, holding mine.

"I'm sorry, I'm acting like a little girl. Don't know why I'm embarrassing myself. It's just important somehow, that's all."

I put my arms around her; her head falls to my chest, bumps against my ribcage, her hands to my waist. I hold her close. It feels good. She sinks into me and we remain there for a moment until she draws herself upright. Something is ending for her tonight.

She's warm, soft; her breathing is slow and even. I can feel her struggle to a place of stillness, a certain rest and pause. In a moment her arms drop to her sides and we stand apart as the past closes up behind us.

"Go on in," she says. "I'll be out here, preparing for the restless hordes."

She holds the curtain back and I duck beneath it. Her hand slides from my shoulder, down my spine to the small of my back. She gives me a gentle push just before she drops the curtain to the floor with a soft thud.

The room is filled with light, its walls a fresh white. It's large and deep, the polished wood floor as clean as raked sand. It has a stillness, a sense of newness, that stops my breath, bringing me up short the way a shout might.

She's used the paintings from the clothesline. She hasn't framed any of them, choosing instead to hang them by wooden clothespins from wire line parallel to the floor. There must be twenty or more, most of them large, four by six feet or more. The backs of some canvases are juxtaposed with the fronts of others. They hang in nested rectangles opening to a center aisle, resembling a maze pulled apart at the middle.

Wire has been fastened to the bottom corners then to bricks resting on the floor to keep the edges taut. The pathways and turns between them are just wide enough for passage. Down the center aisle, across from the doorway, is the only canvas hung on a wall. It's completely blank. I know it's the last one she'd prepared. By the door along the back wall is a package wrapped in brown paper.

I imagine I cannot step further into the room, that I might stand here just inside the threshold like a lost child on a street corner until

Maggie returns to collect me. I might be waiting for invitation or rescue. In the end, I manage a tentative step toward the center of the room, then another. The paintings rise and drift toward me.

Some have curled at the edges in the weather, some have been torn, frayed by the wind, ribboning just above the floor. A weathered clothespin, the wood speckled and grey. The taut steel wire. Threads of canvas trailing like strands of hair.

Reds in deep sensuous bursts. A flash of emerald, a swathe of rich loamy brown. Sections of the paintings have bubbled or peeled away in the elements, leaving only shadows of what was intended. Then, in the strangest places, a section bright and nearly untouched. A bug, a twig, clinging steadfastly to the canvas exactly where she had placed it.

At the back of one canvas, along the bottom, a border of mud splashed in a forgotten thunderstorm. At the edge of another, a wasp's nest no larger than a teacup. From the top of another, a long thin line of rust running nearly to the bottom from the rusted spring of the clothespin above. Here a dimming shadow of sun has bleached a triangular section nearly to white.

The smell of earth, of rain, and something else I'd rather not define.

In the center of the room, I stop, unable to will myself further.

A spreading green specked with blue, shuddering, its borders indistinct. A slope of umber, a ridge of grey. A wide valley dappled in yellow and gold. A branch of rust, a thin trickle in silver.

The canvases pitch around me, knitting and falling away, their landscape never resting, vibrant in a dance of light. This light has its own will; it rests around the paintings, visits them, but isn't contained by them. Something not comprised of pigment and oil, knife and stroke. Something impossible.

The walls disappear, giving way to new landmarks. Familiar, alien. I don't know where I am.

I'm filling, a long and slow breath. The walls fall away yet I know they are there. There's the press of each room against the other. The cool of the glass, the heat of the street on the other side. The dull murmur of voices at the door, on the sidewalk. A man tunes his guitar a block away. The sounds of breathing, whispers, a cough. A shout, a wave, the slip of one hand into another.

Something tearing. An emptiness taking shape, finding voice. Glorious in its abundance. A deep inviting darkness. I'm rocketing into some unknown space, the canvases smearing to banners of colors, whistling past.

I know where I am. I'm turning. At first, I'd thought the room was moving.

Arms raised, head back. Turning the way Sophie turned when she first visited the studio after the robbery, the way we both turned, in the parking lot before the first gallery. The stars thin to arcs circling our heads, blurring into strokes or scratches carved into the empty blue-black sky.

We spin in the parking lot, arms held out, staring up, concentrating so as not to trip over our own feet, arms held out, passing over or under the other's most times then striking, glancing off, the contact bumping us slightly from our orbits. Turning, because the only way to be truly still is to turn.

Stumbling into each other, we continue to stare up, giggling low and throaty, keeping it going as long as we can, spinning with the night blurring around us, spinning with the loose sensation of the earth beneath our feet but only the etched sky in our vision. We keep it going until we fall into each other, clutching at shoulders and arms to keep from falling, the earth tilting beneath us, stumbling sideways, legs a tangle but not falling, catching ourselves and each other and not falling, managing somehow to stay afoot until we come to a stop gasping, one and the other, hunched over, hands on our knees staring at our shoes in the grey fading light, our shoes which, when they finally settle into place beneath us, seem very far away.

Acknowledgements

Thanks to the North Carolina Arts Council, the Arts Council of Winston-Salem, and Creative Capital for supporting this project.

Special thanks to a wonderful group of people who also supported in their own ways: Jim and Stacey Carson, Brian Lampkin, Mickey Norman, Carol Roan, John McGrath, Fred Chappell, Mike Gaspeny,

And Deonna

OTHER C&R PRESS TITLES

NONFICTION

Women in the Literary Landscape by Doris Weatherford et al

FICTION

Made by Mary by Laura Catherine Brown
Ivy vs. Dogg by Brian Leung
While You Were Gone by Sybil Baker
Cloud Diary by Steve Mitchell
Spectrum by Martin Ott
That Man in Our Lives by Xu Xi

SHORT FICTION

Notes From the Mother Tongue by An Tran
The Protester Has Been Released by Janet Sarbanes

ESSAY AND CREATIVE NONFICTION

Immigration Essays by Sybil Baker
Je suis l'autre: Essays and Interrogations
by Kristina Marie Darling
Death of Art by Chris Campanioni

POETRY

Dark Horse by Kristina Marie Darling
Lessons in Camouflage by Martin Ott
All My Heroes are Broke by Ariel Francisco
Holdfast by Christian Anton Gerard
Ex Domestica by E.G. Cunningham
Like Lesser Gods by Bruce McEver
Notes from the Negro Side of the Moon by Earl Braggs
Imagine Not Drowning by Kelli Allen
Notes to the Beloved by Michelle Bitting
Free Boat: Collected Lies and Love Poems by John Reed
Les Fauves by Barbara Crooker
Tall as You are Tall Between Them by Annie Christain
The Couple Who Fell to Earth by Michelle Bitting

CHAPBOOKS

Atypical Cells of Undetermined Significance by Brenna Womer
On Innacuracy by Joe Manning
Heredity and Other Inventions by Sharona Muir
Love Undefind by Jonathan Katz
Cunstruck by Kate Northrop
Ugly Love (Notes from the Negro Side Moon) by Earl Braggs
A Hunger Called Music: A Verse History in Black Music by Meredith Nnoka

CPSIA information can be obtained
at www.ICGtesting.com
Printed in the USA
FFHW021028031218
49720594-54137FF